MURDER OF A BEER BUDDY

Honey Lovejoy

DEDICATION

This book is dedicated to the writers in The Villages, Florida who make writing in retirement such a joy.

The authors of *Murder of a Beer Buddy* wish to express their gratitude to The World of Beer for the use of their name in this book. The merriment experienced by The Beer Buddies of Brownwood in their Tuesday afternoon meetings was, in part, the inspiration for this book. So far as we know, none of the patrons have murdered any of their friends.

ACKNOWLEDGMENTS

The Beer Buddy writers wish to acknowledge the editorial work of Dick Walsh, Clay Gish, and especially Mark Newhouse. Their tireless efforts made this book possible.

We also wish to thank Clay Gish for the cover design and Mark Pryor for his fine production of the cover.

Murder of a Beer Buddy

Murder Most Fowl

Darkness fell quickly under a cloudy, moonless sky. There would be rain later. The humid Florida evening was pregnant with the possibility of evil. This was the kind of oppressively sweaty evening when violent men beat their wives, and fear-filled women took knives from the kitchen.

The biker entered the thickest part of the glade and made his way down the dark lane. He did not wear a helmet.

A golf cart approached from somewhere behind him.

'Share the path,' a sign read.

The cart's engine grew louder as it neared. The small gas motor sounded like a lawnmower.

The biker slowed and pulled slightly to the side, waving the cart by. *Why is it staying on my ass? Damn annoying.* "Share the road," the biker shouted. "Asshole," he muttered. As he turned his head, the lights of the cart blinded him.

The cart revved up. It passed. Close. Unnecessarily close. The cart swerved, and then stopped suddenly.

The biker braked hard, pulled the bike off the path, just missing a birdhouse. A disturbed bird squawked and flew off into the trees.

Jumping off his expensive two-wheeler, the biker shouted, "What the hell are you doing? You could cause an accident. Share the road. You, dumb sonofabitch."

The cart did not move. The headlights went off.

The biker looked for the reckless carter. He found it difficult to see in the fading light. He stormed ahead, and then broke into a smile. "Oh, shit. It's you. What are you doing here? You have a problem with your cart?"

The end came swiftly.

The biker was too surprised to scream. He raised his arms to protect his face. Too late. The heavy weapon slashed through the darkness and smashed into the side of his skull. He did not die with the first blow, nor with the second. By the time the tenth blow struck, blood flowed from the victim's nose, mouth, and ears. The stream of blows obliterated his face. His heart slowed, and then stopped beating.

With the victim in a fetal position on the path, blood pooling around the body, the murderer grabbed a can of *Bud Light* from the cart, pulled the tab, and poured the foamy beer over the dead man's face and chest. Wiping the can with a handkerchief before crushing it, the killer placed the smashed empty on the corpse's forehead.

The murderer returned to the golf cart and putt-putted into the darkness.

And that was the end of Danny Barfright. His last thought, *Damn, I should have worn a helmet.*

THE

SUSPECTS

Murder of a Beer Buddy

Chapter 1

The Beer Buddies Gather

The bar was known as World of Beer. It was almost empty. The Beer Buddies had not yet shown up.

Bud Schweitzer arrived first. He took his usual seat across from the door of the bar, looking for someone else to enter. He sat less than five minutes when Margarita Gose and the barmaid, Honey Lovejoy, arrived at the same time.

"Hey, ain't this sweet? Two babes, and only one dude. A man can't have too much of a good thing. That's what I say," he gave both ladies a toothy smile.

Margarita, looking great in leather pants and a form-fitting green sweater, said, "Hi Bud. I guess we're the first ones here tonight."

"We'll need to have a *ménage-a-trois,*" Bud leered.

"You think you're man enough?" Margarita teased, leaning over, exposing a bit of cleavage.

"Try me," Bud smirked, not quite patting Margarita's taut butt.

The Beer Buddies considered Bud to be their ladies' man. He had been a professional athlete and football coach before retiring to Florida. No longer relying on steroids, he compensated by averaging three hours a day in the weight room. He wasn't shy about showing off his 'bod.' He wore tight pants, and whenever possible, too-tight tee-shirts.

"Do you guys know what you want?" Honey, the barmaid asked.

"I'll have a light ale, maybe *Stella*," Margarita said.

"I'll have one of those too." Bud slapped his rock-hard abs with a resounding smack. "Gotta keep things tight, ya know."

The drinks came just as Danny Barfright entered the bar. He took a chair beside Bud and across from Margarita

"How was your golf match?" asked Margarita.

Danny broke into a mischievous grin, displaying his hallmark gold tooth. "You mean with the guys? I've done worse."

"I'll bet you have," Margarita retorted. Then, looking at Bud, she added, "This guy's a shark. When he says, 'I've done worse,' that means he's won a bundle."

Bud sipped thoughtfully at his beer.

Minutes later, Sam Adams and Tony Bellome ambled in within seconds of each other. They took chairs on either side of the table.

"I heard you were big losers on the nines," Bud said to the newcomers.

Tony pulled his chair up and waved Honey over to take his order. He smiled at Bud and said, "Is that what Barfright here said? Three strokes! Three damn strokes, and he acts like he's running the table at Vegas or something. Besides, I don't even like golf. I just took it up a couple of weeks ago to pass the time. I only go out to count the alligators in the ponds."

Danny grinned, eying Honey.

"Danny didn't say anything," Bud replied. "Margarita said you got your asses kicked."

Honey interrupted, "What can I get you guys?"

While Tony ordered, Sam complained, "You know I think this SOB . . . I mean, excuse my French, ladies, this 'gentleman,' is a shark. He three-putted every hole. Then we get to the eighth. He wants to bet me he can make this down-hill twenty-footer, so I bet him twenty bucks. And he sinks the sucker."

"Just luck, my friend," Danny chuckled. "Say, Bud, why don't you come out with us some time? You're always bragging about being such a macho athlete. You'd be a natural."

"Not my kind of game. I'm into physical sports. You know what I mean."

"So, you're saying real men don't play golf?" Danny asked.

Bud knew better than to say that. Some of these 'old farts' had hair-trigger tempers. "Okay, yeah, golf is a sport. But I like sports where strength, endurance, agility, and speed are involved. Golf is too cerebral. If you know what I mean?" What he meant was, 'real men don't play golf.'

Just then, Amber Bock walked in and took a chair. With Amber here, it would be a while before the conversation turned again to sports. Amber, the youngest woman in the bar, was a knockout. She looked especially sexy today, in tight white jeans and a short black top that exposed her firm belly. With killer curves and red hair cascading below her shoulders, the guys joked that she looked like a Playboy bunny. Behind her back, of course. Some questioned why such a young woman chose to live in a retirement community, no matter how 'active' the owners advertised its fifty-five plus residents. All the men had eyes for Amber, but she seemed especially interested in Danny Barfright.

A chorus of welcomes from the assembled Beer Buddies greeted Nathan Lambic and Pillsbusch Frapp — known to his friends as Busch — as they came into the bar. The two men briefly acknowledged the welcome, but continued discussing the relative merits of the Toyota Land Cruiser and the Range Rover as they made their way to the table.

Busch, partially retired, was a part-time auto mechanic, as well as a deputy sheriff. "I've worked on both. You take your everyday Land Cruiser, change the sheet metal, and up the price seventy-five-thousand, and you have a Range Rover," Busch insisted.

"Hardly," Nathan snorted. "There's no comparison with British engineering for an off-road, luxury experience. I don't care if most safari outfits use a converted Toyota diesel truck. They're just out to pack people in."

The argument had gone on for some time, with no agreement in sight. So, the two friends set the discussion aside and joined into conversation with the rest of the group.

The Beer Buddies drank beer and made locker-room talk as usual when Danny looked at Bud. "Bud, you need to go out golfing with us. It would do you good."

"It's like I said, golf isn't my thing."

Danny sneered, "Yeah. I know. You like 'contact' sports." He burst into laughter.

Sam jumped in. The 'old man' of the Buddies, Sam spoke with a Jewish accent. "You've never been to Bud's house. I tell you, it's like a museum of athletics. He's got a whole room what could be from a sports memorabilia hall of fame."

Danny looked impressed. "Is that right? But no golf ball signed by Arnie Palmer?"

"He's got about everything else. Tell him about that bat you got, Bud," Sam urged.

Bud was in the spotlight, and he ate it up. "Yeah, well, I got this bat signed by Stan Musial. He was already an old guy when he gave it to me, himself. He had a nephew playing for me when I coached Division II football. He said he didn't have any use for it anymore, and he wanted someone should have it who would appreciate it. He signed it right in front of me. It says, 'to Big Bud Schweitzer.' He signed it, 'Stan' with a big old slash under the S."

"No shit," Danny said.

Bud, though not a big Danny fan, smiled at the attention. "Stan said it was the bat he used to hit a homer in the bottom third in the 1946 World Series. The game was tied zero-zero, and Miller Schmitz pitched him low and inside." Bud's eyes glazed over as he reveled in his Stan Musial story. He was in his world, 'the star' again.

"That's not all Bud got," Sam Adams interjected.

Sam was usually full of bad jokes, so Bud expected him to say something like, "Bud's got the clap." He braced himself, wondering why some guys wanted to be the center of attention in the middle of 'his' story.

Sam did not hit out with a bad joke this time. Instead, he said with some reverence, "Bud, tell them about Joe Namath's helmet. You should go to his place, Danny. I've been there. It's worth seeing."

Danny nodded, "Okay. I'll get over there this afternoon. I gotta see this joint. Where do you live? I gotta get my bike ride in. It'll give me an excuse to see your shit."

Bud gave Danny the address. "I'd give ya' directions, but I don't know where you live."

Sam piped up again, "If you are going by bike, the easiest way to get there from your place is to go to the Parkway gate. Then take that cart path by the pond and marsh." He tapped at his hearing aid, a mannerism that made him appear even older. "Nobody goes that way. It's a nice ride. You'll come out at the Glenmore gate. Bud's place is near." He replaced the aid behind his ear.

"Got it," Danny said. "I'll be there this afternoon." He rose from the table. "I just hope your shit is worth the trip."

Come on, Margarita, let's find some action."

Margarita stood. "Isn't he a sweetheart," she said and followed Danny into the pool hall.

Yes, he is, someone at the table thought, wondering how Danny Barfright had lived this long.

Chapter 2

Bumphrey Pillsbusch Frapp, II

June 29, 1976, 11:55 p.m. (Forty-two years earlier)

Busch stared at the TV, the only light in the room, through glassy and bloodshot eyes. He found nothing funny in Johnny Carson's jokes or Ed McMahon's predictable guffaws. Clad only in his favorite pair of cut-off Levi's, the twenty-two-year-old was comfortable. With a bottle of beer in his left hand, the fingers of his other toyed with his left nipple as he studied the small assortment of tattoos that graced — yes, he believed they graced — his pecs. He vowed *never* to regret getting the tattoos, no matter his age, and no matter how much his pecs might start to look like sagging boobs if he ever made it to old age. He would always choose to stay fit. He zoned out as he gaped at the small but bright screen when he heard a familiar jingle that broke his trance. He shook his head as if to clear away cobwebs. *Yeah, right! I'm glad I use it, and I wish everybody did!*

Busch was in a dismal mood tonight after another unproductive 'time-waster' of a day looking for work. He turned to beer at dinnertime and had not stopped drinking. Uncertain about the future since his Navy discharge, he felt lost and unwelcome in his hometown. In only six or seven weeks, it had been driven home to him that being a Vietnam vet was nothing special in the minds of many. Indeed, it was no badge of honor. He drained the last of his

Rolling Rock and shoved the empty green pony bottle onto the coffee table along with the others.

Family matters had also consumed his day and added to his depressed mood. He hated feeling sorry for himself and longed for the camaraderie of his Navy buddies. He even doubted his decision to forego a nice re-upping bonus and stay for another four years.

Busch's eyes drifted to an envelope he had tossed on the coffee table yesterday. When it arrived, he ripped it open, yanking out its contents as if his life depended on what was inside. Now, he picked it up again, unfolded the pages, and reread the letter from his shipmate.

Busch sniffled as he finished reading and used his forearm to wipe tears from his cheeks. Memories transported him back three years to the explosion that nearly cost him his life. If it were not for Machinist Mate Second Class Jeremy Chance's quick thinking, Busch would have been fatally scalded that day in the *USS Decatur* engine room.

The beer made this day a bit more palatable, and Busch decided this was as good a time as any to answer Chance's letter. He chuckled at the image of himself, a drunk trying to appear sober. He knew that it was not the first, and probably not the last, time he would try to drown his troubles, but the letter awaited him.

Busch pushed himself up from the couch, turned off the television, and walked into the kitchen. Once there, he grabbed two more bottles of *Rolling Rock* from the fridge. Opening the first and tossing the cap into the sink, Busch set both bottles on the kitchen table. He found a Bic and a writing tablet in a drawer near the silverware.

After hitting the wall switch, he pulled out a chair and sat. Through the open kitchen window, he could hear a radio interrupted by occasional car noises on the street as he began to write.

> Hey Slim,
>   You made my day yesterday with your letter and news from Nebraska. You sound so happy to be back home. I'm envious. My guess is you didn't think you'd hear back from me so

soon. Do you believe we've been out almost two months already? Are you sleeping-in any? Me neither. I guess old habits die hard.

I knew before we detached that you couldn't wait to see Anne. Your letter made it clear that your reunion was all you hoped it would be. Though the perv in me was disappointed, I admit, you were right to spare me the details. Anne is a gorgeous lady. And to think she waited almost four years for you. DAMN! Just kidding. She's lucky to have you. I know you will have a beautiful life together. When you two set a date, be sure to let me know.

Things aren't very good back here in PA. My old man is still the happy drunk he's always been. I was hoping he would take life more seriously and maybe straighten up after my Mom and my sister died, but he hasn't. He is never sober, so it's tough even to talk to him, let alone have a conversation with him.

Today, I met with a lawyer about Mom's and my sister's estates. I didn't think Dad did anything after they died, and I wanted to make sure everything was OK according to the law. It turns out there isn't anything that needs to be done. At least now I feel better that I checked into it. The lawyer says I can clean out their stuff and give any usable clothing to Good Will. I'll take some time to work through that. To be honest, I'm not looking forward to it.

Even before I got your letter, I planned on writing to tell you of my plans to move away from here. My hometown is depressed, and there are no jobs. There's nothing left for me here, no reason to stay. So, I'm going. I need to fix-up some stuff on my GTO (water pump, thermostat) and tackle a few other repairs before the long drive (oil, filter, plugs, belts). As soon as she's roadworthy, I'm out of PA. Hopefully, within the month. I don't plan to return. I'll drive south until I find a place I like and get a job. If lady luck is on my side, that'll be in Florida. I'd love to work in a repair shop or even a dealership, but we'll see how that goes. Like I told you when we were shipmates, my dream is to own a repair shop. I know that will take time — and bucks. When I find a place and decide to settle and put down roots, I'll write to let you know where I am.

Busch put down the pen, pushed back from the table, stretched out, and folded his arms across his bare chest. For a few quiet moments, he appeared pensive, as if gathering thoughts. Then picking up the second green pony bottle, the Navy vet twisted off the cap and pitched it into the sink. Choking up, he reached for a Kleenex on the counter and blew his nose. After another swig from the bottle, he picked up the pen and continued writing:

There is a second reason I'm writing now.

My heart is speaking now, buddy. Slim, I don't think I ever told you how much you mean to me. <u>You are the best friend I ever had</u>. You were my rock the whole time we served.

You hauled my sorry ass home when I drank, and you always, <u>always,</u> had my back. We both know you saved my life, a fact the Captain acknowledged when you got your commendation. There are so many times I still believe I was supposed to die that day. But I am alive, thanks to you. Slim, I may be leaving PA, but there is <u>no way</u> — NO WAY I want to lose contact with you. To be honest, buddy, I feel like you're all I have right now, and I swear to God, I'll make it up to you someday for all you did for me.

Please give Anne a big hug for me. I can't wait to meet her one day. I know you two will have tons of fun making Jeremy, Jr.

Always your friend,
Busch

P.S. Since I'm not sure who might get to read this, I figured it was best just to sign it 'Busch!'

A few minutes before noon the next day, Busch addressed an envelope to Jeremy Chance, RR #9, Kearney, NE 68846. He affixed a fifteen-cent stamp in the corner and ran a beer-dipped finger along the glue to seal it. At least one person on Earth would know he was still alive.

Busch quietly resolved that if he wanted to live a decent life — and not end up like his father — he had just downed his last beer. *Could life in Florida be good without booze?*

Chapter 3

Peroni Azzurro

Peroni Azzurro parked his lime-green Caddy in the lot behind the Empire Video Rental and Donut on Yonkers Avenue. Empire Video Rental and Donut was, among other things, a brewpub. At two o'clock on a Wednesday afternoon, Peroni had no idea what he would find inside. He had only been there once earlier at the invitation of a representative of the Ugandan Christian Liberation Army. The Ugandan ate a chocolate cake donut with sprinkles while Peroni drank an *East River Porter*. In addition to the donuts, the Ugandan purchased two-hundred cases of Kalashnikov rifles.

This time, Peroni was in Yonkers at the invitation of the brother of Sara Nevada, an ex-girlfriend, mother of his forty-two-year-old daughter, whom he had never seen.

Stepping from the Caddy, Peroni checked the sky, searching for any sign of rain. Finding nothing but a cloudless blue canopy overhead, he left the convertible top down. He made his way to the front entrance, checking the other cars in the lot and along the street. Inside, he saw nothing more unusual than a glass display case of donuts sandwiched between the brewpub bar and a rack of DVDs and CDs. Few customers were in the restaurant at mid-day. The only activity in the place centered on a large round table on one side of the entrance. Nine men, Peroni's age, retired, he presumed, were holding a spirited gabfest.

Peroni took a chair at a table on the other side of the room. From his vantage point, he had a good view of the door, the outside lot, the restaurant's few patrons, and the rear exit.

"Can I help you, Sir?" asked a portly, middle-aged man, who, from his olive skin, black hair, and thick mustache, looked like he might be of Mediterranean descent. He held an order pad at the ready.

Peroni, having previously sampled both the donuts and the Porter, knew he did not like either enough for an encore. "You can bring me coffee. I'm waiting for someone."

The server started to leave.

Peroni stopped him. "I'm curious, why is a brewpub called Donut and Video?"

The man lowered his order pad. "When I es-start in business, I am a shoe-repair man, but nobody gets shoes repaired in You-Ess-of-Ay, so I start video rental place. When nobody rents videos, I start donut store. That business not so good too, so I start brewpub. But too expensive for sign that say, 'Empire Video, Donut and Brew Pub,' so I no change name." The man shrugged and went back to the bar for the coffee.

Peroni considered the name and the lack of change thereof. He concluded the name change was not worth the expense, especially considering the *East River Porter* tasted about like one would expect a beer called *East River Porter* to taste. A name change of the brewpub would not turn an *East River Porter* into a *Samuel Smith's Taddy Porter*.

Minutes later, as the proprietor set the coffee in front of him, Peroni noticed someone approach the restaurant's front door. His hand dropped to his pocket.

The stranger wore a Jets baseball cap pulled down over his long, greasy hair. Wild strands hung out from under its rim. With a pinched face and pointy nose, he looked like a mouse. He must have weighed about one-hundred-twenty pounds counting his heavy black leather bomber jacket.

Peroni thought the man acted as mousy as he appeared, head twitching side-to-side and back toward the parking lot. As the man came closer, he recognized the 'mouse' as his long-lost girlfriend's brother. He moved his hand away from his coat pocket, but remained ready to grab his gun at the slightest wrong move.

"No cats here?" The Mouse asked, eyes still darting around.

Peroni nodded.

Satisfied Empire Video Rental and Donut was devoid of cats, the small man settled into the chair across from Peroni.

Peroni knew Warren Nevada, aka Mouse, from high school. Warren had been a freshman when he and Sara were seniors. That was forty-some years ago. He aimed curious eyes at his visitor. "What do you want, Warren?"

"You sure there ain't no cats?" Warren sniffed.

Peroni thought Nevada had changed surprisingly little in those years. If anything, his nose and Adam's apple were more prominent than when he was a teenager. He was the same mousy little person he knew only as Sara's brother when he and Sara graduated.

"What's up?" Peroni asked. "What's all the noise about?"

Eyes darting to the front window, Warren hissed, "You gotta get out of town."

Peroni had never spent much time with Nevada back in the day, but it was enough to know the man's nature. Warren Nevada had always been a skittish person, but now he looked apoplectic. "Take it easy, Warren. Take a deep breath and tell me what this is all about."

The Mouse sniffed the air again. "I've been running numbers in East New York all my life. Ever since you and Sara got together back in high school."

"Yeah. That's old news."

"Well, a guy in my line of work . . . he hears things. I mean, what I'm saying is . . . people tell me stuff. I hear a lot of stuff." Warren's eyes darted left and right. "I talk to a lot of guys. I don't say much, you know, but I listen. You know what I mean?"

"Yeah, okay. You listen. What did you hear?" Peroni was losing patience.

"Well," Warren bent forward and whispered, "you gotta get out of town." He looked again over his shoulder toward the group of older men, then to the back door. "Gaspo wants you iced."

Peroni was surprised, but not totally. He had expected something like this most of his adult life. "Are you sure it's me you heard about? I haven't been with the Gaspo family for twenty years. I made him a lot of money. He knows that…."

"Well, the word is, the Don got himself a new bookkeeper. Real smart guy. MBA from Princeton or NYU, one of them colleges that don't have a basketball team. Real smart guy. Word is, the guy digs back into the books and figures you skimmed from the drug deals. They say the dope came from Columbia to St. Lucia, then to St. Pete, or Jacksonville. Only some of it don't make it all-the-way to New York." He leans closer. "And you were the guy keeping the books handling the transit. So, Gaspo figures you done it." A sly smile spreads on the Mouse's face. "And he's sending someone to hit you."

Peroni's neck felt moist. After twenty years out of the mob, he thought he was home free. *Damn the NYU MBA.* He lowered his voice, "Warren, thank you. But I ask, why you would want to save my ass? If Gaspo finds out you tipped me, you'll be as dead as me." He leaned closer. "You might even pick up some extra dough by turning me in." He searched the entrance of the bar.

Warren Nevada let out a deep breath.

Peroni smelled cheese.

Warren smiled sheepishly, "The truth is, you was some kind of hero of mine back in high school. You didn't take shit from nobody." He leaned closer. "Maybe 'cause you liked my sister, but you always treated me decent."

Peroni was surprised by that. He never treated anyone decent. If that got out, it would ruin his reputation.

Warren continued, "I knew you got in with the Gaspo mob right out of high school. You was smart and had the guts. I saw you had the good clothes and a fast car. But you never flashed it around. You know what I mean? And when Sara got pregnant, you coulda walked out on her. Most guys would. She said you told her you woulda married her."

Peroni nodded. "I would have."

Warren sighed. "My sister is stubborn. She didn't want no kid growing up in a gangster family."

Peroni nodded again.

"I keep in touch with my sis out in California. She told me you sent a check every month to take care of your daughter, even after she married." He made a fist with his small hand. "What a loser that guy was. I always thought you was a stand-up guy with Sara."

"I tried."

"So, this is a payoff for all them years taking care of my sister and her kid."

Peroni focused on Warren's eyes. "Your sister was a good girl. She deserved better than me. I was hoping life would be good for her when she got married. I was sorry when I heard he died." He sighed. "But my biggest regret is I couldn't see my daughter grow up. I think about her all the time."

"Sara says her daughter is a wonderful kid. She doesn't know anything about her past, and she's making a life for herself. Sara makes sure of that."

"I'm glad I did one thing right," Peroni said.

"You did." Warren looked eager to leave. "But now about you, Peroni, what are you gonna do?"

Peroni sighed. "It's probably better if you don't know. Damned if I know myself, but I'm outta here. New York isn't big enough to hide me." He smiled sadly. "Anyway, I'm an old man now. I'm ready to retire. This 'hit' shit is as good an excuse as I'm gonna get. I guess I'll go somewhere where it doesn't snow. Yeah. I'll sit under a palm tree, wear shorts, drink beer, and watch the sunset over the ocean. Get as lost as I can." He stood up.

Warren rose from his chair, eyes shooting toward the door again.

Peroni took a fat roll of bills from his pocket. He peeled off two one-hundred-dollar bills and handed them to Nevada.

Warren grabbed the bills. "You don't owe me nothing."

"I owe you my life. This here is just a small way to say thanks." Peroni looked down at the Mouse. "Don't say anything to Sara about this. We lost track of each other after our daughter graduated from college. It's not healthy for them to know anything about me. Fortunately, her daughter took Bock's name. That will give her some protection." He held out his hand. "You know, I'll kill anyone who'd want to hurt her . . . either of them."

Warren stared uneasily at Peroni's hand, and then shook it. "Yeah. I know."

"Do you know where she is? My daughter," Peroni held the Mouse's paw.

Warren tried to pull his hand loose. "Sara will kill me."

"Hey, I may just drop by and see she's okay. That's all."

"She's in Florida. She works in some retirement place down there."

Peroni slipped his hand around the gun handle. *I'll find her,* he promised himself, *and make sure she stays safe. That girl is the only decent thing I've ever done in my life. I'm not going to let anyone fuck her up.*

After Warren left, Peroni sat back down at the table to ponder his situation. He was safe for the moment, but he was a marked man. If he went to any of his hangouts, he was at risk of leaving on a stretcher. His friends, Marty, Vinny, Lucille, all the others, were poison. His gun-running business was over. There was a price on his head, and Gaspo would keep the pressure on until Peroni died.

As he thought, he listened to the old men chatting and laughing over their donuts and beer. How did his life bring him to this place so different from the joyful lives of these guys? He had used the half-million embezzled from the drug trade to stake himself. Why should he set up the deals, deliver the goods, and turn over all the profit to Gaspo? But he couldn't stay in drug smuggling without running afoul of the Gaspo mob, a recipe for a short trip to the cemetery. So, he took a brief detour into the blood diamond trade. He made a lot of money quickly smuggling diamonds, but the value of diamonds packed into a small package made every two-bit thug a potential assassin. After a near-miss, he got out before the hammer fell. Diamonds were, after all, only a means of paying for arms. With knowledge of the African smuggling trade, he switched his focus to arms dealing. He soon had a thriving business trading arms from the U.S. and Albania, Ukraine, Malaysia, Vietnam, and elsewhere. It was a dirty business, but it was the business he knew, and he was good at it.

That was over now. Gaspo would make sure of that. He had enough money to live comfortably, and he had thought of retiring. But to what? He could never have what many men have — a wife to come home to, the joy of starting a family, seeing children grow. He looked at the men again. He envied what they had, friendship and relaxed conversation.

Peroni left a two-dollar tip at the table and went to the counter to pay his tab. While waiting for the waiter to ring up his bill, he heard one of the old men say, "I'll never forget the day in nineteen fifty-five when the owners voted to let the Dodgers leave New York."

Peroni turned to the table and said, "Nineteen fifty-seven."

"What? No, it was Nineteen fifty-five," the man shot back.

Another man, powdered sugar from a donut on his lips, said, "No, Fuzzy, it was fifty-seven. I remember my dad got a new Chevy Nomad wagon that year. I wanted a two-door, but he had to have a Nomad to take the family to Disneyland."

"Hell, Frank, you've been eating too many donuts," Fuzzy replied.

"The guy's right. It was nineteen fifty-seven" a third man said, looking at his cell phone.

"Maybe you're right," Fuzzy said to Peroni. "Come on over and join us. Have a beer or a donut. Any fan of the REAL Dodgers is welcome at our table."

Peroni pulled out a chair. "Unfortunately, I'm right. It broke my heart. I was a Dodger fan. I still haven't forgiven them for leaving."

They all yacked about old cars and old times. When they were talked out, ready to leave, about a half-hour later, Fuzzy turned to Peroni and said, "Hey guy, what's your name and where you from?"

Peroni thought quickly and answered, "I'm not from here. I'm just visiting from Florida."

"Well, you lucky SOB. I've got a brother-in-law retired down there. He loves it. He brags that he spends his time shooting pool, swimming, and fishing. He lives in a place called The Villages." Fuzzy laughed. "The SOB spends more time in his golf cart than in his car."

Peroni nodded and replied, "The Villages. I never heard of it. Sounds like a place where a man could get lost."

Fuzzy shrugged his shoulders. "He keeps bugging me to come down. My wife wants to visit her sister. Maybe I will, someday. By the way, what did you say your name was?"

Peroni thought for a minute, then said, "Danny Barfright."

Chapter 4

Bud Schweitzer

Bud Schweitzer had been edgy all morning. This Friday was the last day for Abita College to exercise their option to extend his coaching contract for an additional year. He expected a call from the office of Athletic Director Stubby Stein with the offer. It should be a sure thing. For the last six years, he had built Abita into a Division III powerhouse. Last year, the Schooners made it to the division playoffs before being defeated by the Erdinger Lone Stars. A field goal by the Lone Stars' all-American kicker in overtime was all that prevented the Schooners from coming home with a championship trophy. Next year, he was confident that with eight returning seniors on defense, four others on offense, including the all-conference quarterback, his lifetime of hard work would be rewarded. The Golden Pitcher championship trophy for Division III college football would come to Anderson Valley for the first time.

Then the call came.

"Good morning Bud, this is Stubby."

"Hey, man. I've been expecting your call."

"Can you be at President Brownale's office at two p.m.?"

"Sure. Can you tell me what this is all about?"

"No. I don't think so. President Brownale will tell you."

When Stubby hung up the phone, Bud got an ominous feeling in his gut.

On the walk across campus to the admin building, Bud tried to imagine why President Brownale wanted to talk to him. It might be a personal congratulations for bringing glory to the college, but he knew Brownale was not a sports fan. He resented every dollar of tuition money that went into the athletic budget and, especially, into Bud's salary, which was higher than that of the Dean of Engineering. Bud sensed Brownale's antipathy ran deeper than financial priorities alone.

Brownale was a petite man. He was always well-groomed with a square of a handkerchief in his jacket pocket, the pattern matching whatever tie he wore on any given day, setting off his crisp suits. A neat fringe of hair framed his shiny bald head. He carried a gold-headed cane, not because he needed it, but as a fashion statement. It was also his symbol of authority.

Bud was Brownale's direct opposite. He spent more time in the weight room than most members of his team combined. He had a barrel chest and a deep baritone voice. More often than not, chili stains marked his team polo shirt. He could have been mistaken for a pro linebacker if there were any sixty-six-year-old linebackers in the NFL.

When Bud arrived at the administrative suite, Stubby Stein stood waiting outside the president's office. He knocked on the polished wooden door. Without waiting for a reply, he led the coach inside.

Brownale was seated at his desk. The college president gestured toward a chair.

Bud preferred standing because he towered over the president, but decided this was not an appropriate time to refuse. He sat down on the shiny red leather chair and felt as if he was in his elementary school principal's office again.

President Brownale tapped the eraser end of a yellow pencil on his desk as he addressed Bud. "Coach Schweitzer, I know you are a man of action, so I'll come right to the point. We have elected not to exercise our right to retain you as coach next year." He paused, waiting for Bud's reaction. When there was none, he went on, "My institution is extremely grateful for all the work you have done with our boys during your six-year tenure. Bringing the team to its current position of prominence is nothing short of remarkable."

"Then why aren't you picking up my contract?"

Brownale tapped the pencil faster and looked toward Stein, who was still standing.

Stubby said, "You know Bud, the news got out. A couple of people came to my office. I checked around a bit..."

"I think what Mister Stein is trying to say is," Brownale interjected, "the players on the team are young men. They are youngsters whose parents support their boys, the team, and are donors to the college. As a coach, you are a visible symbol of the vitality and virility of the Abita man and..."

"What the hell am I accused of?" Bud asked. But he knew the answer. And he knew they knew. He had no defense.

Stein said, "We don't need to argue here, Bud. There is no need for accusations or recriminations. We're just not going to pick up your option. That's all anyone has to know." He glanced at Brownale and continued, "Bud, I know you've already bought that little retirement place in Florida. Think about it. Golf every day. Drinking a beer on your lanai. You told me how much you were looking forward to retirement. It was this year or next." He looked for an approving nod from the president. "We're thinking we'll just make a public announcement that you are retiring after an outstanding college athletic career." He looked at Bud. "Nothing has to get into the media about any aspects of your personal life."

"In fact," President Brownale interrupted, "we would like you to accept this fifty-thousand-dollar bonus as an expression of the esteem in which a grateful college holds you." He waved the check. "The bonus is, of course, contingent on your signing a non-disclosure agreement. The agreement precludes any discussion of the details of your separation."

Bud deflated like a balloon out of air.

The president slid the non-disclosure agreement across the desk along with a check for fifty-thousand dollars. "You may take the agreement with you. Perhaps go over it with a lawyer if you feel it's necessary."

Bud took a pen from the holder on the president's desk, signed the agreement unread, picked up the check, and left.

Once outside, he stuffed the check in his pocket, a murderous look on his face.

Chapter 5

Amber Bock

"Amber, they're all alike. These bastards take what they want and don't care how much they hurt you." Sara Bock paced the floor while her daughter, Amber, sat on the hospital gurney listening with a deep weariness.

"Mom, you've said all this before. Miller's having trouble finding work. That's all. He's frustrated…"

"You can do better, Amber. Lots better. You're a beautiful young lady. You don't have to live with that guy."

"I'm not a young lady anymore, Mom. I'm a 42-year-old woman with a lousy paying secretarial job. I'm doing the best I can."

"It doesn't have to be this way. I'll tell you, my neighbor, Beth, you know her — she's a snowbird — bought herself a little place down in Florida. Some swanky place filled with rich old guys. She says these guys lavish her with presents, and she's out to dinner with a different one every night."

Amber shook her head.

"Ms. Bock, I've got your x-rays." The ER doctor walked into the cubicle and snapped the images into a lightbox. "You've sustained two broken ribs this time. I can tape them up, but you'll need to take it easy for a few weeks. No heavy lifting. No workouts."

"Thank you, Dr. Dunkel. I'll be cautious," Amber said.

Dr. Dunkel peered at Amber through his glasses. "Do you plan to press charges? I can photograph the bruises and make you a copy of the x-ray."

"No. No. No. I told you I fell down a flight of steps."

Sara looked her daughter in the eye. "Amber, stop lying. That no-good bastard did this to you. You don't even have stairs in your apartment. You live on the first floor."

Dr. Dunkel sighed. "Ms. Bock. This is your third visit to Torrance Memorial ER this year. With different contusions and broken bones. Your injuries are not consistent with a fall. If you do not press charges, I'll be obliged to report it."

Amber looked into the doctor's eyes. "Please don't. I'll handle it. I promise."

Sara shook her head. "Amber, honey, this is getting really bad. He hasn't hit that beautiful face of yours yet, but he will."

Dr. Dunkel turned to Amber. "Actually, abusers often choose to hit their victims where the bruises can't be seen. Still, Ms. Bock, these situations only get worse. It's your life I'm concerned about."

Amber looked surprised. "What do you mean 'choose,' doctor? Are you saying he thought about where to hit me before he did it?"

"I'm sorry to say, yes, I am. Please, Ms. Bock, go to the police," Dr. Dunkel said again. "I can take photos and give you this x-ray. Just say the word."

Amber had never considered that Miller struck her deliberately, premeditated. She always believed his abuse was a spontaneous outburst of anger. *He thinks about where to hit me, so it won't show and raise suspicions? That bastard. I've blamed his rages on his frustration about work. I've even blamed myself.*

When Amber was released, her mother tried to persuade her not to go home. Against her mother's wishes, Amber wanted to return to her apartment.

"Please, stay with me a few days, at least," Sara pleaded again. "Let him cool down."

Amber took her mother's hand. "No. Mom, I need some time to think. Don't worry. I'm going to make some decisions — about my life, about Miller."

"Just be careful," Sara said.

--- 🍺 🍺 🍺 ---

When Amber arrived back at the apartment, she found an enormous bouquet of roses in a vase on the kitchen table. A note on the vase read, "Please forgive me, babe. You're the best." It was signed, "Miller." She stared at the flowers, deep in thought. *He's always sorry after he hurts me. I always forgive him. Eight years of forgiving him. It's only gotten worse.* She heard a key in the door.

"Hey, sweetheart, you're home. You like the flowers?" Miller beamed that wide, dimpled, smile that had at first reeled her in.

Amber smiled back. "They're beautiful." She leaned over to smell the colorful bouquet. "Just lovely. Thank you."

"Hey, no problem. Anything for my girl. I wanted you to know how sorry I am." He held his hand over his heart.

A thought occurred to Amber. "How did you pay for them?" Miller had not worked in five weeks.

Miller continued smiling. "Well, your purse was here. I used your credit card. I mean, it's ours, right? We live together."

Amber looked at him, trying not to show her disbelief. *Of course. He not only expects me to pay the bills, but he thinks I should pay for my own gift.*

Miller read his card, and then looked up. "Listen, Babe. Some of the guys are getting together down at the bar. One says he's got a lead on a job for me. He says, it's a good union job." He turned his cutest puppy-dog eyes toward her.

"Sure. Sure. Go on. I wouldn't want you to miss out on an opportunity."

"You're the best," Miller kissed her cheek and hightailed it out door.

As soon he left, Amber checked her wallet for her credit card. Nothing. She picked up the phone and called Chase. "I'd like to report a stolen credit card," she told the automatic voice system.

The system patched her through to an agent.

Amber repeated, "I want to report a stolen credit card."

The agent said, "So, your card has been stolen? I'll cancel it immediately and mail you a card with a new number at your listed address. I just need a bit of information to confirm your identity."

Amber replied, "Please don't send a new card. I want to cancel the account for now. I'm in the middle of a move, and I don't want it to get lost in the shuffle."

"No problem. I've canceled the card. Please tell me your last purchase so I can give you credit on any fraudulent charges."

"My last charge was lunch yesterday at the Seaside Palace on Sepulveda Boulevard." Amber smiled to herself. No roses. No drinks tonight for the 'boys.'

The agent said. "Alright, Ms. Bock. It's all taken care of."

"Thank you so much." Amber replaced the phone and hurried into the bedroom. She pulled her suitcase from under the bed and packed quickly. By the time Miller was ready to pay his tab later tonight, she would be long gone.

After she packed, Amber pulled out her nightstand drawer. In the back of the drawer, she had taped a bank card for an account Miller knew nothing about. She opened it a year ago because she feared his spending sprees would put them in the poorhouse. Her 'just-in-case' cache had only a few thousand dollars in it, but it was enough to get her out of the city.

Taking a last look at her apartment, she was about to leave but had one more thing to do. She tossed the flowers into the trash can on top of Miller's empties.

Three doors from her apartment, Amber knocked on the super's door.

Paul Rainier was surprised to see her, "Amber, what can I do for you? Is that radiator acting up again?" He spotted her suitcase. "Are you going on a vacation?"

"Mr. Rainier, I'm moving out of the apartment. I'm sorry to give you such short notice. Please keep the security check."

Rainier sighed. "Oh. I'm sorry you're leaving. You've been a great tenant." He noticed that she was alone. "Is Miller going with you?"

Amber hesitated. "No. I'm going on my own."

Rainier smiled. "Listen, Amber. I'm happy to hear that. Come the first of the month, and I'll happily throw that bastard out on his ass. You deserve better."

"Thank you, Mr. Rainier. I'm trying to make myself believe that."

On the street, Amber easily hailed a yellow cab. The young driver pulled up and popped the trunk for her suitcase. As she settled in the back seat, she told the driver, "LAX."

While they sped north along the San Diego Freeway to the airport, Amber pulled out her cell phone and dialed her mother. "Mom, where did you say your friend Beth moved to in Florida?"

"The Villages, north of Orlando. Why?"

"I've left Miller. I'm moving to The Villages."

Sara could barely hold back her tears. "Oh, thank God, Amber. I was afraid someday he was going to kill you."

"Or I might kill him?"

"You're not capable of murder. Are you?"

"Under the right circumstances," Amber replied and laughed.

Chapter 6

Sam Adams

He stared out at the arid sky over the golden Dome of the Rock. He had changed over the years. His face, once clean-shaven with striking eagle eyes, Paul Newman blue and frightening in their intensity, had aged. The eyes had lost some of their sparkle. The cheeks and chin were now leathered by the Middle East sun. Losing a wife can age you. He wasn't sure he was up for another mission. Still, Captain Manny Shevitz, commander of the counter-terrorism squad, had called for him, so he would find the reserve of will. The worst that could happen? Somebody might kill him.

"It has been a long time," Captain Shevitz said. "Please, sit down, my friend."

"I'll stand."

Shevitz sighed. "We're all sorry about Hannah."

"Don't mention her name."

"It's because of her, I asked for you."

"You know who killed her?"

Shevitz bit his lip.

"Then what the hell do you want?"

Shevitz slid a folder across his desk. "We know who sold the sniper rifles Hamas used to kill her." He paused to measure the effect on the veteran agent. "He is the largest weapons smuggler for Hamas and Hezbollah, and it was his sniper rifle…"

"I want him," said the blue-eyed man.

Shevitz leaned forward and flipped open the folder. He slid it across the desk.

"Is this him? He's a damn American?"

"He is."

"You want me to kill an American?"

"I never said 'kill' anyone," Shevitz said, glancing at the door. "Let us just say we want more intel on him."

"I'm not interested in spying on this guy. If he sold that murder weapon…"

"You need to keep this in perspective, my friend."

"Fuck perspective. I want Hannah's killer."

"You're an agent of Mossad first. Do you understand? Listen, Shmuel, I want Hannah's killer too, but it is more important for us to stop this supplier of terrorists. He has Israeli blood on his hands and his money. We have information that this man is about to smuggle thousands of military-grade drones into the occupied territory. These drones could carry bombs, grenades, even biological or radioactive payloads into Israel. We have a mole in his organization ready to take over and divert the shipment, but first, we have to assure that it is this man."

The agent studied the photos. "Why me?"

Shevitz laughed. "The sonofabitch lives in Florida when he's not running around selling his shit in the Middle East…"

"Florida?"

"You've never been there?"

"Once."

Shevitz sighed. "I remember. I couldn't imagine you shlepping around with a bunch of cartoon characters in a goddamn amusement park."

"That was Hannah's dream."

Shevitz nodded. "Yes, there was that side of her. But she could kill a man with her bare hands or legs." He looked into the agent's eyes. "So could you."

"Are you asking if I can still do that?"

"No. I know you can. I'm asking if you can control that?" Shevitz leaned forward. "We need to learn how this man operates." He smiled sadly. "Once we have that, you will, if we approve it, be allowed to 'neutralize' him. Shmuel, it may take some time."

"I'm in no hurry."

"Our intelligence says the drones will ship in seventeen months. We can have you in Florida in two days."

"I'm ready."

Shevitz hesitated. "There is another reason I picked you. This Barfright lives in a retirement community…"

"What did you say?"

"I was shocked, too. It is a perfect way to appear inconspicuous. When he's in America, he pretends to be an old fart in a senior community. It's an ingenious disguise. Who would suspect such a man?"

"So, you picked me because I look like an old man?"

Shevitz smiled, "It takes an old fart to catch an old fart."

"I can still gut a man with my hand."

"I know. But nobody else will suspect you." Shevitz reached for a gray envelope. "Your air tickets are in here. Since Shmuel translates to Sam in English, we've given you the name — Sam Adams."

"My last name is Adamowitz. My family died in the Holocaust because of that name. I won't change it."

"Not even to kill the man responsible for Hannah's murder?"

Sam sat down in the chair. He saw Hannah standing next to him, holding binoculars against her eyes. He heard the almost undetectable sound of the bullet slamming into her face as she jumped in front of him. He felt her body fall into his arms, her weight pulling him away from the second bullet, her blood making the sniper think that he was killed as well. He heard a voice cry out in agony. It was his voice. "What else?" he asked.

"We've given you the usual undercover gear — a pen with a homing device. Press the pen four times, and an extraction team will find you. Concealed in the watch is a master key that will fit most American handcuffs. If the Americans catch you, we will not attempt to rescue you."

"Of course not. Why would you?"

Shevitz shrugged. "Here is your cover story: I understand your uncle owned a bra factory in New York?"

Sam eyed Shevitz. "A bra factory interests you suddenly?"

"That will be your story. You manufactured bras."

"I made bras?"

"Why not? Who would suspect a shmuck whose bra company went bust of being one of Mossad's deadliest agents?"

"I think you've gone *meshuga*. First, you name me after an American beer, and now you want me to pretend I made bras?"

Shevitz smiled. "It will give you a great deal to talk about with your new American friends. Who knows, maybe one day you'll retire to Florida and find a nice old woman with big knockers to warm your old body."

Sam shook his head vehemently. "There was only one woman for me."

"We'll see, my friend. Now get that sonofabitch. Use your natural charm and wit." Shevitz stood. "Good hunting. God bless you."

"God bless Barfright," Sam said and rose from his chair. "Thank you, Manny, for this opportunity to avenge my Hannah."

Shevitz grabbed Sam's arm. "Shmuel, this is not for revenge. This mission is to end the daily terror this man has rained down on our state. Remember, Sam Adams, bra manufacturer. Your first responsibility is always to our beleaguered nation." He released his hold on Sam's arm, still taut despite the agent's supposed retirement. "You are not 007. You are an agent of Mossad."

Shmuel aimed his eyes at Shevitz. "May I go now?"

Shevitz watched his friend, someone he hardly recognized anymore, leave the armor-clad office. He returned to his desk and closed the Danny Barfright folder. If anyone could end the reign of terror this demonic fugitive had unleashed with his illicit weapons, it was Shmuel, but not if hate blurred his vision.

Shevitz placed the folder in the wall safe hidden behind the Israeli flag painting. Then he walked over to the refrigerator and pulled out a bottle of wine. He laughed. *Manischewitz.* He poured himself a glass and peered out the window at the Dome of the Rock. "Here's to Manny Shevitz," he said, and followed it with,

31

"God bless Sam Adams. May he survive the wilds and wilder widows of Florida!" He threw back the cup of wine and sat back in his chair. He felt as if he'd launched a missile at the terrorists, but couldn't help wondering what collateral damage it might cause.

Chapter 7

Honey Lovejoy

It snowed all night, stopping just in time for Gloria St. Pauli's car to be plowed in. Fortunately, being Boston, nothing stopped the school buses, and the boys were off to school on time. She would have canceled her ten-thirty appointment, but with her only book generating modest royalties, she could not afford to miss the meeting with her publisher. With her student loan debt payments and two children to support, she barely made ends meet. She needed an advance to help her while she worked on her second book. She donned her most "authorly" outfit — gray slacks and lilac knit turtleneck sweater — and was ready to do battle with a literary giant. As important as the meeting was, she skipped the heels and put on flats that fit inside her snow boots. While not appropriate for a meeting with an editor, the waterproof boots were what a well-dressed snow shoveler wore on a November day in Boston.

Her publisher, Hefeweizen Global Media (HGM), was located in a suitably modern office complex one block off the Charles River. The building was close enough to Harvard and MIT to sport an academic cachet. HGM was a newer firm, still hunting for A-list authors. Gloria St. Pauli was determined to join the A-list.

Gloria arrived at the Hefeweizen office thirty minutes early for her appointment. She and the receptionist were the sole occupants of the second-floor waiting area. Severely appointed in chrome and glass, the office would have appeared sterile, but for the plush red carpet and gold wallpaper behind expensively framed abstract art. The black leather waiting room chairs were surprisingly comfortable. The receptionist offered, and Gloria accepted, a service of black espresso.

The doors of the three editors' offices were glass. Black lettering on the one behind the receptionist showed it belonged to her editor, Stella R. Troy.

Gloria had barely finished her drink when the office door opened, and Stella escorted out a delicious-looking man over six feet tall. He looked as if he just stepped off the cover of GQ's Rio edition. The man nodded and smiled with straight white teeth at Gloria on his way out.

Without a further goodbye to the departing stallion, Stella strode over to Gloria and greeted her with a smile. "Dear girl, I've been so looking forward to our meeting. Please come in." Stella turned to the receptionist, "Hold my calls except for the Saigon office." She turned back to Gloria, "I hope you won't mind, dear girl, but we are having a devil of a time with the supply chain to our printing plant in Vietnam."

"Of course not," said Gloria, impressed.

Stella, tall, slender, perfectly coiffed, settled into a chair beside a small glass table and motioned Gloria to join her. Cocking her eye toward the door, she said with a conspiratorial air, "So, what's your opinion of Señor Ricardo Modelo?" Without waiting for Gloria to answer, she added, "Unfortunately, he sambas to a different beat."

Gloria laughed.

Stella continued, "It is partly because of you that Ricardo brought his book to us."

Gloria looked questioningly at Stella.

Stella tittered, "Our Latin friend has struggled against male domination in his world, and he appreciated your depictions in *The Power of Pink*, which — by the way — has been doing well. It is especially gaining ground here in the northeast."

Gloria did not know how to react to the compliment.

Stella leaned forward. "Which is why you are here today. Unless I am very mistaken, darling girl, you want to write another book and be in our stable? Tell me what you have in mind."

Gloria smiled. "I was thinking, something along the same lines as *The Power of Pink*."

"Fabulous! The depiction of male abuse of power in the manufacturing workplace perfectly caught the mood of resentment among men and women. That is why it's so promising. Tell me where you are going with your next book."

Gloria crossed her legs. "I want to write about male chauvinism in the service economy. I've tentatively titled it, *Pink in the Bar Room*."

"Interesting."

That's it, Gloria thought. "I recently visited an aunt in her retirement community in central Florida. She is about to go on a year-long, around-the-world cruise and asked me to stay in her house while she is gone."

"Interesting."

"While I was there, I dropped into a bar and talked to the owner. He agreed to offer me a job."

"I presume no one there knows your background?"

"No. If anyone knew my identity, I'm sure they would not treat me the same as any other minimum-wage barmaid."

"So, you're using a fake name? Interesting."

"Yes. I applied for the job under the name Honey Lovejoy."

Stella Troy uncrossed her legs and leaned back, eyeing Gloria. "I love the name. Most apropos. But are you sure you can do this? I know you have a mountain of student debt from your MFA and two kids to care for."

"I'm sure," said Gloria. "My mother has agreed to take care of my twins while I head to Florida."

"Won't it be tough to be without your boys for that long?"

"It will, sure. But they're ten, they'll understand, and they love living with grandma. Besides, they'll have something to look forward to — coming down to Florida during school breaks. As for finances, I'll have no rent to pay, my royalties should partially cover my student loan, and I'll have my salary as a barmaid." She hesitated. "I was hoping you'll give me an advance on my new book. You did say it sounded promising."

"Of course, dear girl, I'd love to give you an advance. You know, I am sure, that advances are not what they were a few years ago. I could offer you something substantial if you had several strong selling books in print." Stella laughed. "But if you had several strong selling books in print, you wouldn't really need an advance, would you?"

"So, no advance?" St. Pauli's shoulders dropped.

Stella hesitated a moment, peered at St. Pauli, and steeled her jaw. "Without a bestseller, dear girl, the best I can do is ten-thousand dollars. I know it's not much, but it's something. We'll have a check here for you tomorrow. Consider it an incentive. I look forward to seeing your manuscript. It does sound interesting."

Gloria sat upright. "Thank you. I promise I will not disappoint." She noted that unlike her escorting of the Latin Stallion, Stella remained at her desk while she left the office wondering if she would ever be one of the 'thoroughbreds' in the stable.

On the ride home, the soon-to-be Honey Lovejoy began plotting *Pink in the Barroom* in her head. She had visited too many bars and heard the catcalls, the double entendre, and the rude behavior toward female staff members. She had smacked away the unwelcome hand on her buttocks. But there was another reason why she wanted to write this book. She was still haunted by the memory of lying in bed at night and listening to the sounds when her father brought women home. Most of his playmates were softened-up with alcohol from bars. She resented that he seduced them and had his 'fun' with them in her mother's bed. What made it worse, her dear mother lay in a memory care hospital dying from Alzheimer's disease. God, she hated him. She couldn't get revenge on her faithless father, but as Honey Lovejoy, she could shine a light on the world of male dominance that would reveal to the world what sneaky snakes men were and make her book a best seller.

Gloria thought again of what she would have to endure. She knew what she would find working in a bar and hated the thought of it. She despised men that took advantage of women. She had felt their contempt and put up with their snide remarks. She even faced danger from them. She would expose their evil for the world to see. And if anyone posed a threat to her, she would take good care of him. Her self-defense classes had made her feel confident that if any bastard got too rough with her, he'd pay a hefty price.

Chapter 8

Tony Bellome

Tony Bellome stood nervously in the foyer of Don Gaspo's Mansion in Bensonhurst, Brooklyn. He was uneasy at being here. He had not seen the Boss for a couple of years, not since he retired with the Don's blessing. *Why does the Don want to see me now? I'm retired.*

Louie Guacamole, the Don's ever-present Capo, approached. "Two-Ton Tony, so good to see you. How ya' been?"

Tony had held Louie's position as Capo for nearly twenty years. He understood the Don's 'fix-it man' takes care of any things that need 'fixing.' Although Tony didn't like the handle 'Two-Ton,' he couldn't shake it, not since the Don used it years ago. Louie seemed friendly enough, so he replied, "I'm okay. Couldn't be better."

"You like retirement?" Louis asked.

"Sure beats working. You know what I mean?"

"The Don will see you now," Louie said, opening the door to the private study.

Tony entered cautiously. He had only been in this private room of the mansion twice: when the Don first made him 'family,' and when Tony told Don Gaspo he wanted to retire. His knees still knocked, thinking of that experience.

"Tony," the Don said with all the enthusiasm his open arms could muster. "How are you and Sophie and the kids?"

"Fine, fine. Except Sophie died a few years ago." Tony realized he was more anxious than he thought he would be.

"What? Sophie died? Nobody told me?" The Don looked stormy.

"It was sudden. A small funeral. You were in Italy." Tony thought quickly. "We know your thoughts were with us."

Don Gaspo was still frowning. "And the kids?"

"Both doing well. Thanks for asking."

The Don looked at Tony. "If I can do anything, only ask." He leaned forward. "But I need you now, Tony. I need some fixing and only Two-Ton can do it. Right, Louie? That's what they all say. Only Two-Ton can fix this one."

Tony's hands gripped the chair armrests. "Sure, Don, anything you need."

"Remember Peroni Azzurro, my former Capo."

"Yeah. He worked for you about twenty years ago. He made you a lot of money…"

"And stole from me, the piece of shit. Reissdorf Kölsch, my new accountant, found holes in the books when he started looking. First little ones; then big ones. That rat stole over five-hundred grand from me over the years. That cheating bastard made himself rich by skimming off the top."

"I thought he was a nice guy…"

"Nice? Stealing from me?" Gaspo had steam coming out of his eyes.

Tony recognized the signs. "He's a sonofabitch," he shot quickly.

The Don hit his fist on the desk. "I put a contract on the rat, but somebody must have clued him. He lamed out of New York a couple of years ago. I only got a lead on him because Big Eddy Schwarzbier launders money out of a used car lot in central Florida. Peroni's lime-green Cadillac showed up on the lot. That bastard must be living in Florida in some retirement village under a different name. On my money!"

"That's not good."

"You're damn right, Tony. And he ain't gonna' live too much longer on my money. I want him rubbed out."

Tony gripped the armrests harder. "Don Gaspo, with all due respect, how about your other Capos? I'm retired. I'm an old man."

Gaspo stood, took Tony by the arm, and led him across the room. "I want you for three reasons," he said almost in a whisper.

"First, you would fit into a retirement village. The others I got are too young. Second, you are smart. The others are too dumb. And third, I want him done the way only Two-Ton Tony does them."

Tony wished he hadn't been that good at his old job.

"Listen, Two-Ton, this hit is personal. I'd do it myself if I could. To be sure the job gets done, I'm sending a kid along to help. The squirt is a Puerto Rican named Juanito. He'll report to me, cover you, and finish the job if anything goes wrong."

Tony gulped.

"Now listen good, Two-Ton. You watch what you say around Juanito. He's a crazy son-of-a-bitch. He'd as soon slit your throat as shake your hand. I'm sending him down to work with the Orlando mob that handles the trucking operation, but he'll be around to lend a hand if you need it." Gaspo smiled. "And, as a way to ease you into retirement, there is two-hundred grand in this for you, only after I hear Azzurro is history."

Tony thought he could use the dough. But a rub-out at his age?

"Louie," Gaspo called his bodyguard. "Send Juanito in."

Louie opened the door, stepped out, and soon returned with a dark-skinned Hispanic at his heels.

Tony quickly sized him up. Juanito was about five feet six, sharply dressed in tight black pants, white sport-coat, black shirt, shiny purple tie. His long black hair fell out of a pork-pie hat down to his narrow shoulders. Although 'the kid' was small, his eyes, which looked sleepy, and his neatly trimmed goatee, gave Juanito a satanic look that commanded fear.

Juanito seemed to measure Tony with his eyes, and then shrugged.

Tony could imagine a stiletto in the boy's hand. He'd have to watch out for this one.

Gaspo dropped his hand on Tony's shoulder. "Two-Ton, I don't expect my money back. I want that piece of shit dead beyond recognition. I want his balls on a silver platter on my dining room table. You got that?"

"Capisce," Tony replied, wishing there was another choice. "Where is he in Florida?"

Gaspo looked annoyed. "In some damn village. Juanito knows the place."

"What does the mark look like? How old is he? Is he married?"

"You writing a book?" The Don barked. He took an old, folded, prom snapshot out of his inside coat pocket and handed it to Tony. "Here's an old picture. The bastard never married. Always liked his broads and beer."

Tony studied the photo. "This looks like a prom picture," he said.

"The smart SOB hated cameras," Gaspo barked.

Tony wondered how he'd recognize the mark from an old prom photo. He looked closer. Azzurro was in a tux, standing with his arm around a beautiful young woman in a gown. At first, he wondered what the bastard's hand was doing behind her ass. He glanced up at her face.

"You find that bastard and do what you do," Gaspo said.

Tony hardly heard him. He stared hard at the young woman in the photograph. It couldn't be. He had not seen her since she graduated from high school. She was someone he would never forget. Someone he regretted losing years earlier.

"You seen a ghost?" Gaspo asked.

Tony pocketed the photo. He prayed she would not be there when he dealt with Azzurro.

Chapter 9

Margarita Gose

Margarita Gose was the recent widow of Doctor Clint Gose. She looked around the study where she and her husband of six short years had spent hours talking, planning, and securing their future. Elegant volumes, bric-a-brac, and statuary lined the walls. The magnificent room, one of many in the gold coast mansion on the shore of Lake Michigan, would never be the same for her. She turned toward the bay windows. The waters of the lake looked gray. The life she had envisioned after the honeymoon had soon turned sour. A husband who was self-absorbed and cold. No children. Now, even he was gone. Her charade for the other wives, all thinking they were better than her, of the joys of life with a man of medicine, gone. All gone. She viewed Clint's death as one more cruel trick life played on her. There had been many. Now it was time to make her mark and get even. She knew just who to call.

"Hi Max, it's Mags. I'm ready to make a move to Florida and run the southeast operations for the consortium." She waited several uncertain seconds for the reply.

The voice on the other end said, "Call me when you get down there."

"I will." Margarita hung up. Her next call was to her personal assistant, Hoppy Palm. She let him know that she was putting the Chicago house on the market, preparing to move to the Gose residence in the wilds of Central Florida. "I expect you to make everything run smoothly," she said and cut him off before he could ask questions.

Margarita smiled. The joke was on Clint. She had never revealed to him how she funded her extravagant lifestyle before their marriage. *He must have been blind,* she thought. *Thoroughbred horses, fashions from famous designers, country club memberships, all on the salary of a pharmaceutical representative? Those alone should have raised questions.* When he asked once, she lied that the money came from a trust fund her uncle set up at her birth. "Uncle Stavros, my godfather, always promised to look after me. He was a saint."

Clint Gose never questioned his wife's bullshit story. The egotistical bastard thought only of himself and liked the endless flow of money. How she got it, her past, it didn't matter.

Margarita had fallen in with a drug cartel connected to a former boyfriend in her early years as a pharma rep. Young and ambitious, she had pushed her way up the ladder, but wanted an easier life. The criminal enterprise, the consortium, tried to keep Margarita on board after her marriage, but she declined. Her ex-boyfriend, Max, now a regional manager, told her to keep her options open. "Life can change at the most inopportune times." With the death of Clint, it had changed. The bastard had screwed her again. He had left her with unpaid tax bills and staggering debt.

After she hung up on Hoppy, Margarita made another call.

"Hi, Slinky," Margarita said when Stewart Growler replied.

"You know I hate that name. What's up, Mags?" Growler asked and quickly added, "Oh yeah, sorry to hear about the old man. Heart attack, eh?"

"Yep. Old Dr. Clint is gone now. Good riddance. I'm looking to get back in the business."

There was no response.

"You still have enough connections to get me a steady supply?"

Still no response.

"I'm heading up the consortium's Southeast operations. I need quality, consistency, and someone I can trust. You in?"

Growler held his tongue for a long, uncomfortable pause.

"I asked if you're in," Margarita glared at the phone.

"Let me check around a bit, Mags. You've been out of touch for over six years. You sure you want back in?"

"The consortium gave me the okay. That should be enough for you. Are you gonna back me or not?"

"Cool your pipes, Mags. I'll back you. I just wanna make sure you don't burn me. You were always square in the past and never got nailed. I just need to make sure this goes the right way…"

"I'm gonna say this one more time. The consortium gave me its approval. They would not do that if they were not satisfied with my abilities — past, present, and future." She let that sink in. "Now, what do you say?"

"Okay, you're in. When do we start operations?"

"I'm moving down to my place south of Ocala in a couple of weeks. Let me get my feet on the ground, and I'll be in touch. If something comes up that calls for us to move quicker, I'll be on the horn pronto."

"You're moving the whole kit? Everything? Nothing left for you up here? You even gonna take your pool stick?" Growler asked.

"You know me, Slinky. I head to where there is money to be made and cold beer. And I go nowhere without the Pink Panther. That cue is my good luck charm and my only source of relaxation."

"You're good with that stick for sure," Growler said.

"Damn right. I hear they got some high stakes games down that way. Lots of old retiree money."

Growler laughed. "Good luck, Mags. Call me when you land. I'll be waiting."

Margarita fished a small vial of coke out of her purse and snorted a spoon up each nostril. *Ahh. Back in the game. God help anyone who gets in my way.*

Chapter 10

Nathan Lambic

Nathan Lambic glanced at his watch. Duncan was ten minutes late for their breakfast at the Lion Coffee Shop in the town of Kadoma. The place was still popular with the old white farmers in this region of Zimbabwe. That was the primary reason Nathan decided to meet Duncan there.

He and Duncan Hawthorne went way back. When Nathan first came to what was then Rhodesia, during the Bush War in the mid-1970s, Duncan coordinated his training in the Rhodesia Light Infantry or the R.L.I. Although Lambic was a U.S. Army veteran with two tours in Vietnam as an infantryman, he soon learned the R.L.I. had its 'special' way of doing things. Thankfully, Duncan was in the same Stick, or combat squad, and guided him through their first encounter with the Russian-backed insurgents crossing from the Zambian border.

Nathan transferred with Duncan to the Rhodesian Army special forces outfit, the Selous Scouts. They went through hell together and survived. Theirs was a special bond, forged while protecting each other in fire-fight after fire-fight. Even after the Bush War was over, they fought together in Mozambique and Angola. There had been too many wars in Africa, with all sides willing to pay handsomely for military experience.

A server arrived with a tray holding a pot of coffee and two mugs.

Nathan moved his newspaper to make room on the table. "*Maita-basa*, thank you."

"*Ta-tenda,*" the server responded respectfully in the local Shona language and left with a delivery for another table.

Nathan filled a mug with coffee. As he returned the coffee pot to the table, he caught sight of Duncan. "Morning."

Duncan slid into the opposite chair. "I'm running a bit late today, chum. My old Jag wouldn't start. It must be the damn starter again. Had to drive the Land Rover."

"No problem," Nathan smiled. "Thanks for coming at such short notice."

"Fiona's miffed. She wanted to see you too."

"Yeah, sorry." Nathan shrugged. "This is one of those 'just between the two of us' breakfasts. Hope your wife understands."

"Ah," Duncan nodded, "I thought that might be the case. Fiona said if she couldn't come with me, you need to join us for lunch today. She's doing a *braai* and has some lovely kudu fillets to put on the charcoal."

"That's nice of her. I already ordered you the full English breakfast, by the way."

"Perfect." Duncan leaned back in his chair and folded his arms. "So, what's up?"

Nathan pointed to the pot on the table. "Coffee?"

"Not yet, thanks. I'll wait for the food." He looked into Nathan's eyes. "What's this sudden *tete-a-tete* about?"

"I think it's time to make a move."

Duncan gave him a puzzled look. "What do you mean?"

"It's time for me to go home."

"You are home."

"No, I mean back to the States."

"After thirty years? To America? Why go back across the 'pond?' You've made a life here. You're one of us now."

"I'm not a Rhodie, Duncan."

"Might as well be." Duncan stared across the table at his friend. "I know times here are bad. Hell, some ZANU-PF bastard just took the farm down the road from us. Another agricultural venture stolen without compensation."

"I heard." Nathan took a sip of coffee.

"The party big-wigs know they're untouchable," Duncan waved an arm in the air. "The rule of law doesn't apply to these shits. State-sanctioned theft is another of the benefits of bloody independence — if you have the right connection to President Mugabe."

"It isn't that." Nathan put his mug back on the table. "Besides, I don't have any land for them to steal."

"Right. And you wisely took my advice about putting your earnings into secure, offshore bank accounts. You, my friend, are protected from all the asset-stealing shenanigans around here."

"Pretty much. Thanks to you."

"So, why leave?"

"Somebody is watching the place, Duncan." Nathan lowered his voice. "I've seen the same car stopped down the road from the driveway gate. It parks at different spots, but it's the same car."

"Internal Security Office?"

"Maybe."

"I still have a couple of contacts on the inside. One of them can be bought to turn-off whatever pressure is being applied to you. Want me to check it out?"

"No." Nathan shook his head. "I'm tired. I don't have the energy anymore. I'm tired of all the brownouts, the endless excuses from ZESA of why we can't have an uninterrupted supply of electricity. I'm tired of the potholes in the roads never getting fixed. Tired of having to pay through the nose for consumer goods, which are a quarter of the price in countries next door. Frankly, I'm worn out."

"Oh, come on. After we finish with breakfast, ride back to my place. We'll sit on the veranda and open a bottle of nice scotch. You can help me annoy Fiona by keeping me from my promise to help her with the *braai* before the other guests arrive. We'll make a plan together to solve all your problems."

"I'm happy to drink your whiskey, Duncan." Nathan watched the server returning with their breakfast on a tray. "But I've made up my mind."

They stopped talking until the breakfast order was on the table. After the server departed, Duncan said, "Nothing I can do to change your decision?"

"No, my friend. Afraid not." Nathan picked up a fork. "After cancer took my Jenny last year, it's not the same. I rattle around in that house." The memory of his wife's battle with the disease cut into his gut. It often did. He saw Jenny as she first looked when they met in the border town of Umtali. It was after he participated in an operation to ambush insurgents infiltrating Rhodesia from Mozambique. He was not looking for love. But following a whirlwind romance, they were married. He was surprised that she wanted children right away. Though he had doubts, he gave in, but they accepted she would be childless after years of trying. Now, there was no Jenny. No children. Nothing to hold him here.

Nathan used a knife to cut the banger on his plate into neat cross-sections. "My sister keeps telling me I should join her in a big retirement community in central Florida. She and her husband love it."

Duncan laughed. "You in a retirement settlement? You'll be bored stiff."

"There are tons of things to do there. Sis sent me links to the floor plans of several houses for sale."

Duncan shook his head. "You can't go Tiger fishing there. We've had great times on the Zambezi and Limpopo rivers."

"Fishing will still be an option, and hippo-free." Nathan took a bite of the baked beans on his plate.

"No hippos? That's no fun." Duncan reached for the marmalade jar on the table and twisted off the top. "Without hippos, what are you going to look at while waiting for the fish to bite?"

Nathan smiled. "I'll just have to soldier-on without hippos."

"Uh-huh." Duncan spread marmalade on a piece of toast. "And no game parks."

"True, but I won't have to beware of mislaid land mines either."

Duncan wagged his knife. "Africa isn't for sissies."

"True. I think I've more than proven I'm not one."

"No doubt, my buddy." Duncan chuckled, "I still think you might find retirement a bit boring."

"Maybe. Still, I'm ready to give it a try."

"We'll miss you, old man." Duncan extended his hand across the table.

Nathan shook it.

Duncan teased, "We'll keep the guest room ready for when you come back."

Nathan sighed. "My friend, my killing days are over. All I want is peace and quiet."

Duncan laughed. "Once a soldier, always a soldier. You can't escape what you are."

Nathan replied, "I can try."

BEFORE

THE

KILLING

Chapter 11

Tony and Juanito shared the last row of seats in first-class on JetBlue 478, en route to Orlando International Airport. The 1:00 p.m. flight left on time.

Tony sat back, drinking a scotch on the rocks and eyeing the flight attendant.

Juanito nodded, "She's got a nice ass."

Tony drank to that. He had not expected first-class accommodations, nor the ride to the airport by Don Gaspo's chauffer and lunch in the JetBlue lounge. The luxury treatment almost made him forget why the Don was sending him to Florida. Almost.

Juanito was a talkative kid. Tony didn't mind — as long as Juanito kept his voice down and watched what he said. So far, so good.

They had been in the air for about an hour when Juanito leaned over to Tony. "You know this dude?" he asked.

"I knew him a little."

Juanito smiled. "Tell me about him."

Tony felt uneasy, but replied. "Back in the day, his name was Peroni Azzurro. Don Gaspo says he changed it since then. He was a couple of years behind me in high school."

"So, you do know him." Juanito's eyes were like daggers.

"Not really. Azzurro was already doing some work for Gaspo before he got out of school. I kind of envied him. He had money, wore nice clothes, had a car." Tony saw the hungry look on Juanito's face. When he was young, he wanted what Juanito seemed to want now. "But unlike some of the other big-shots, Azzurro didn't flash it around. I probably wouldn't have paid any attention to him, but I was in love with his girl." *Why the hell am I telling this to him?*

"In love? With the mark's girl?"

Tony sipped his drink. "Yeah, kid. Big time. There was something about this girl. Sara Nevada was her name. I thought she was the most wonderful girl in the world. I wasn't in her league. She only had eyes for Azzurro, and he was in the mob. I coulda been killed if I made a move."

"Must be some dame," Juanito's eyes glowed.

"I guess. Some dame. Back then, nobody else measured up. Anyway, a little while after graduation, she disappeared out of sight. I never knew what happened to her. Somebody said she moved to L.A."

"Amigo, that's one sad story," Juanito said.

Tony was surprised that this kid, a punk working for the Don, could show such sympathy. Maybe he wasn't such a hood after all. Or perhaps it was the booze in first class making him loose-lipped. "Yeah. I always wanted to find her."

Juanito smiled, "And now, you get to do her boyfriend. Revenge is yours at last."

"That's not why I'm doing this," Tony hissed.

Juanito laughed. "Bullshit man. You know you want to *do* this dude. You and old man Gaspo are just alike. You want the dude wasted, but you want some noble motive. If you get cold feet, I'll slice the dude and forget about it before his blood dries on the carpet."

---  ---

When they landed in Orlando, Juanito went to the rental counter to pick up a car.

Tony pulled out the picture the Don had given him. Peroni Azzurro. The more he looked at the picture, the more the long-buried memories of Peroni Azzurro came back. He wondered how much Azzurro had aged. What he looked like now. He took out his phone and snapped a picture of the old photo. He got on the App Store and purchased an 'aging app' that advanced a person's appearance. He played with the app. It showed some changes. He added a hair color change to gray, a mustache, beard, laugh lines. He had several versions of the man he had to wipe out on his camera by the time Juanito pulled up to the curb in a new Caddy convertible.

Hey, this is class, Tony thought.

"We're going to a village," said Juanito. "I got the address. We should be there in about an hour and twenty minutes. Relax and enjoy the ride. This is Florida. What's not to like?"

Tony sat back in the plush leather seat and watched the palm trees fly by his window. The sky was blue and bright, the lawns green, and the lakes clear. "Hey, what village are we going to?"

"We are going to a place called The Villages," Juanito replied.

"No, no. I'm going to a village." He thought, dumb guy, doesn't know English. "You know a village — with a church, a piazza, some shops, a ristorante."

"Yes. This place has three squares, a thousand churches, and more restaurants than you can find in all of Brooklyn. It's what you said."

"What are you talking about? I'm supposed to get to a village. How am I gonna find this guy if you can't even find the place in the first place?"

"Mr. B, these are the instructions I got from Don Gaspo himself. Relax. It's all under control." Juanito nodded to reinforce his control of the situation.

With the mention of Don Gaspo's name, Tony could do nothing but relax. *Some guys just don't understand English,* he thought again and settled back to watch the palm trees turn into pines; the superhighways merge into four-lane roads, and the city morphs into green fields populated by contented cows. *We're in the sticks!* He shook his head, positive Juanito had gotten it wrong. *Gaspo will fix him good. Poor kid.*

Within an hour, Tony spotted the first billboard. In big, bold letters, it read, "To The Villages." He scratched his head. *There really is a place called The Villages.*

As they passed through a little town called 'Wildwood,' Tony heard Juanito say on his cell phone, "We'll be there in fifteen minutes."

"Who ya callin'?" Tony asked, suspicious of the driver with the satanic face.

"The real estate agent. Don Gaspo has a villa rented for you for your stay. The agent, a Miss Blanche De Bruxelle, wanted to be notified fifteen minutes before we arrived. She wants to have the place ready for you."

"Is she good looking?"

"I don't know. I never met the dame. But she'll get you settled in." Juanito glanced at Tony and just shook his head.

The kid thinks I'm an idiot and a prick. He said aloud, "That's good. The Don thinks of everything." Tony looked out the window to see if there were more cattle grazing in the fields. He liked that sight. There was a loud, rumbling noise.

A train, a long train, rolled into view.

Juanito said, "That sonofabitch train had 270 cars. Can you imagine? We have to wait for some pissant train?"

"You counted?" Tony laughed at the foolishness of counting train cars. He looked out the window and found himself counting little strip malls, churches, and trailer parks. He closed his eyes and was soon asleep.

"We're here, Mr. B," Juanito said a short time later.

Tony opened his eyes. He was surprised to see house after house lined up and down the street. They were all much the same, with some small variations in trees and shrubs. They were all cream-colored with light fixtures affixed to the wall next to the garage. They all had name posts with signs declaring their owners. He shook his head. Why would anyone want people to know where they live? He wondered if Azzurro would make things that easy for him.

Juanito pulled up to one of the houses.

Tony saw a black SUV waiting. He never liked seeing cars waiting like that, especially black ones.

"Welcome to Hacienda Villas, Mr. Bellome. You're going to love The Villages." A shapely young blond in high heels and a tight blue dress strode over to Tony with her arms outstretched, a clipboard in one hand. She hugged him almost before he got out of the car. "I'm Blanche. Let me show you around," she gushed as she grabbed his arm and led him into the house.

Tony liked her legs and motioned to Juanito to bring the bags.

Juanito grunted, but fetched the bags.

The blond led Tony into the kitchen-dining room-living room. "This is the great room," she said, spreading her arms.

Tony, accustomed to small, cluttered apartments, gawked in disbelief. This place did look like a 'great' room.' "Nice," he said.

Blanche nodded. "The bedroom is over there."

Tony wondered if she was hinting.

Blanche continued, "You have your en suite bath."

"Nice," Tony said, not understanding what she meant.

Blanche pulled open vertical blinds. "And this is the lanai."

"It's like a patio. Nice," Tony said, staring at the sun glaring overhead.

Blanche pulled open the glass doors. "This is your private garden. Mr. Gaspo wanted you near the town square because that's where the music, dancing, and restaurants are."

"Is this a garden?"

"Yes. Isn't it beautiful?"

"Where are the tomatoes?"

Blanche looked puzzled. "Tomatoes?"

"Every garden has to have tomatoes."

"Oh, tomatoes. Yes, tomatoes. They're coming tomorrow." Blanche looked at Juanito, who shrugged his shoulders.

"Anything else, Mr. Bellome?"

"Yes, where do I go for food, a ristorante, wine?"

"Yes, just down to the square."

"How do I get to the square?"

"Oh, just down Flores and left on Del Mar, and you're there."

"Do I walk?"

"Oh, no, no, no. This is The Villages, Florida's Friendliest Hometown. Let me show you." With that, Blanche took his arm and dragged him into the garage. "You take the complimentary golf cart."

"What's this?" Tony said, looking down at the unfamiliar vehicle. "I don't play golf. Show me what I do with this."

"I, I can't. I have another appointment. Juanito will show you. Ta ta," Blanche called as she ran out the open garage door.

Tony followed the sashaying figure as the realtor left. *I wouldn't mind going to town with her. But in this?* He looked at the golf cart. "What the hell kind of vehicle is this for a guy like me to drive?" He almost kicked the damn thing out of the garage.

Juanito laughed. "Don't worry, Mr. B. I'll show you how to drive it."

Tony shot the kid a chilling look. "That's what I'm worried about."

For the next hour, Juanito showed Tony how to operate the cart. He took the mobster up and down their street a dozen times.

"This ain't bad," Tony said. "Let's go someplace with this thing."

Juanito was about to get into the driver's side when Tony stopped him. "I'm driving."

"Yes, sir, Mr. B." Juanito kissed his St. Christopher medal and made the sign of the cross.

"You ready?" Tony asked.

"Ready as I'll ever be," Juanito muttered.

"What'd ya say?" Tony looked ready to knock the punk out of the cart.

"I said you're a great driver," Juanito replied and clutched the grab bar on the roof of the golf cart.

"Thanks." Tony gunned the cart to its 24-miles-per-hour top speed. "This little shit is faster than I thought." Tony sped down the cart path with Juanito directing him into the town square. "How do I lock this thing? It ain't got no doors?"

57

Juanito sighed. "Nobody's gonna steal it from here. You ain't in New York no more."

Tony looked around at the pueblo-style architecture in the square and grunted, "I hope they got more than tacos."

As they walked around the town square, Tony studied all the people parading along the sidewalks. "These guys all look alike. They all got white hair and wear shorts." He shook his head. "I ain't never gonna wear dem sissy pants."

"That's the style."

"Shit on the style. No grown man would be caught dead in dem things."

"You'll see," Juanito said, laughing. "You'll look great stuffed into a pair of shorts with knee-high black socks and leather shoes."

They kept walking. Finally, Tony grabbed Juanito by the arm and rasped, "How am I supposed to find this guy? All I got is a fifty-year-old prom picture in a town with a hundred-thousand people. And they all look alike."

"Beats me," said Juanito. "The town ain't got a hundred-thousand saloons, though. If I was you, I'd take that golf cart of yours and snoop around the local bars. I'd be surprised if you don't find the mark in one of them."

Tony gave Juanito a hard slap on the back. "Damn, boy, that's the first good idea I got from you. Beer to a punk like that is like bait to dem fishes. You can take the punk out of New York, but you can't keep him from his beer."

"Glad to help," Juanito said, with a malevolent look at the aging Mafioso.

"Come on, Juanito. I'll buy you a beer," Tony said, starting to think this kid wasn't that bad after all.

Chapter 12

Amber Bock easily talked her way into a job at the cosmetics counter at Belk's department store in The Villages. She really enjoyed the job. She took pride in helping her older female customers hold back — or conceal — the ebbs of time. Besides, her flexible work schedule gave her time off on Tuesday afternoons so she could meet up with the Beer Buddies.

Amber started attending meetings of the Beer Buddies soon after she arrived in The Villages six months ago. She had not expected to become a regular, but enjoyed the gatherings down at the bar. She thought the Buddies were sweet old guys who loved to flirt with her and whoop it up. She doubted their exaggerated claims of 'daring-do' pasts, but enjoyed listening. She figured they needed someone to talk to, and Amber needed the attention.

But then there was Danny Barfright.

When Amber first met Danny at the bar, his air of confidence drew her to him. Not bad looking and freewheeling with his dough, Danny Barfright seemed the perfect Sugar Daddy after Miller. Amber was disgusted with bastards slapping her around. She was furious at men who took what they wanted, and then left her high and dry without even a thank you. She had spent too much hard-earned money on those creeps. They swore they loved her, and then, like Miller, sponged off her. No more. She now set her sights on guys with white on the rooftop and green in their pockets.

The first afternoon when she met Danny, she dressed deliberately. Full-out bait meant to lure someone to her hook: tight, black leather skirt, low-cut leopard-print blouse, and three-inch high heels. *My hunting outfit.* She smiled at her reflection in the bar window and waited for her prey. When she saw Danny, she swooped in and sat down at the bar seat next to him. "So, soldier, buy a girl a drink?"

Danny smiled. His voice, soft and reassuring. "Absolutely. Honey, please serve some up for the lady. I'll take a *Bold City Dukes Cold Nose.*" He turned to the new arrival. "And who are you, sweetheart?"

"I'm new in town. Amber. Nice to meet a local." She offered him her hand.

Danny looked at her face closely for a second, and then held her hand in both of his. "Well, Amber, the first thing I'll teach you is that nobody's a local here. We're all transplants. Most from up north. But, welcome." He smiled. "By the way, I'm Danny. Danny Barfright, originally from Bensonhurst, Brooklyn."

Amber answered brightly. "My mom grew up in Bay Ridge, but moved to California about the time I was born."

"Oh yeah. Nice area, Bay Ridge. I like that long park out by the water. Like I said, nobody's from here."

Touching Danny's arm, Amber said, "I'm hoping for a little guidance about the ins-and-outs of this town." She gave him her most 'helpless' smile. "A woman all alone might get taken advantage of. You know, by realtors, contractors, and such."

"I can see that," Danny said.

Amber was dismayed that he did not take the bait and offer to help her out.

Danny leaned back and waved. "Hey, here's some of my pals. Guys, this here is Amber."

Bud, Nathan, and Busch said hello. Big Tony gave her his customary "Yo." Sam shook Amber's hand, "Join us at our table, Sweetie. We can always use another woman."

The group of men eagerly surrounded Amber at the table.

When Margarita Gose walked in a few minutes later, Danny called her over and said, "Mags, meet Amber. She's new in town."

Margarita gave Amber the once-over. "Nice to meet ya, kiddo." She turned to Danny, "We need to talk."

"Excuse me, Amber," Danny said and followed Margarita outside.

Amber waited. She saw Margarita and Danny talking for a few minutes. Neither looked happy.

When they returned to their seats, it was as if nothing had happened.

As the afternoon turned to evening, Amber did her best to hook Danny with her charms. She could not believe he hadn't taken the bait. The way he looked at Margarita, she suspected they had something going on. *Who could blame him? Margarita's body is fantastic. Even nearing 60, she's rocking it.* But maybe that won't last, she thought, knowing how men like Danny became when 'younger stuff' was around.

Still hoping to land Danny, Amber began meeting up with the Beer Buddies every week. The other guys treated her sweetly — even Tony in his bull-dog way. Because Danny had introduced her, the other men seemed to think she was with him and did not try anything. That was fine by her. None of them attracted her the way Danny did. She worked on him for months, not used to men turning her down.

Finally, frustrated, Amber decided it was time to try someone else. *Bud will be all over me in a minute if I let him. Not bad looking. Hunky guy.*

Amber decided to chat Bud up one afternoon. She began by praising his physique and intelligence. "I hear you were a football coach," she cooed. "What was that like?"

Bud was an attractive man for his age. He had the chest and arms of a man half his age, but he was a little too interested in sports to be her ideal man.

Besides, Bud, being a member of the Beer Buddies, seemed more a friend or brother than a potential mate. She looked around the bar, but became frustrated that all she saw were a stream of old, mostly overweight men, many wearing wedding rings. *Maybe a retirement community wasn't the best idea I ever had.* Depression crept in. While she was starting to feel at home in The Villages, she did not see where life was taking her. All of her efforts to land a rich husband had failed. *Is it time to move on to greener pastures?*

Amber began to drink. Usually, she sipped wine or beer. Today, Amber knocked back several tequilas. Always able to hold her liquor with the best of them, this afternoon she could not handle the drinks and her emotions.

Bud slid over. "Hey, Amber, how about a dance? I love this song. Da Boss!"

Amber wanted to refuse, but replied, "Sure, Bud. Why not?"

Once on the dance floor, Bud slobbered all over her.

Amber pushed him back, but Bud was a bull with hands like an octopus. He trapped her in an unwelcome embrace, and then grabbed her ass. Just as she was ready to scream, she heard someone's voice.

It was Danny. "Hey, Bud, give Amber a little air." He took Amber's hand.

Danny said, "Let's get you home, young lady."

"I'll take her, Danny," Bud said, barely able to stand.

"What are you trying to prove, you old fart? Back off, Toots," Danny replied.

Bud raised his fist into Danny's face but backed away, an angry scowl aimed at his rival. "I'll fix you, you snotty sonofabitch," he slurred, dropping into his chair.

"Come on, Amber." Danny grabbed her purse and jacket and led her out the door to his car.

Amber did not argue. Was Danny finally paying attention to her? Was he her knight in shining armor?

Danny drove in silence to Amber's house. He parked outside by the curb.

"How do you know where I live?" Amber asked.

"You must have told me."

Amber did not remember telling Danny her address, but what did it matter? He was here and watching her every move. She fumbled for her keys.

Danny took them from her. "Listen, Amber, some fatherly advice. You can do better than those old guys in the bar. You're young and beautiful. You should find a good guy, someone your age."

Amber felt insulted. "Ha! Those kinds of guys treat me like shit. I'm done with them. Sure, the guys here are older. But they're sweet to me. They treat me good." She gazed into Danny's eyes. *Come on, make your move.*

"Sweetheart, I think you need to look someplace besides a bar if you want a better class of guy." Danny turned the key in the door lock. "Take a class. Join a group. Go to church. Just get out of the bar scene. Nothing good is ever gonna happen there." He bent toward her.

Amber anticipated his lips on her mouth. She closed her eyes.

Danny kissed her on the cheek.

With the alcohol swirling through her brain, Amber nearly stumbled through the door.

Danny watched until Amber got safely inside, then walked back to his car. He stood by the door for a few seconds.

Amber flipped on the light switch. Instead of being grateful that Danny took her safely home, anger simmered inside. *The sonofabitch never made a move on me.* She thought again of his smug face. *I spent all this time trying to catch his attention, and he kisses me on the cheek like I'm a kid. Damn him! Who does Danny think he is, anyway? Too good for me? I'm sick of these sonofabitches. I'm sick of Danny Barfright!*

Chapter 13

Honey Lovejoy's shift at the bar began in an hour. Time enough for her to morph from Gloria St. Pauli, struggling author, to Honey Lovejoy, barmaid, unmarried mother of two, but she had to hurry. On the counter by the sink stood vials of perfume, makeup, brushes, lipstick, rouge, false eyelashes — all the subterfuge of a modern woman. She hated this charade, but it had to be done. If you want to know about pigs, you had to get down in the mud with them.

Was all of this worth it? Was she beautiful, pretty, plain? Some people think a woman never really knew herself except by the compliments of men. She knew men used compliments as a weapon. A weapon that too many women hand to them.

At World of Beer, she was Honey Lovejoy, a twenty-nine-year-old single mother, working hard to support ten-year-old twins. She was pert. She was sweet. She was accepting and naïve. She had to be everything the Beer Buddies wanted her to be.

At the bar, it was all about tips. The lipstick, the mascara, the short skirt — all about tips. After work, in her aunt's lakefront house, it was different. There she was Gloria St. Pauli, thirty-six-year-old ambitious author of *Power of Pink: How Women Fight Dirty*. And now, she was halfway through her next expose, *Pink in the Barroom: Power of Women at the Tap*. The book was not going well, but that was about to change.

Honey had worked at World of Beer for four months. The pay was poor and the work hard. She came home after long hours with sore feet and throbbing headaches. It would have been nice to drop into a soapy tub and let the aches and smells of the bar soak away. But every evening like clockwork, she called Boston to speak with her mom and her twins. She asked about their day and about school, made sure they were doing their homework, and confirmed with her mom that they were behaving themselves. She missed the twins dearly and treasured her time with them on the phone, but it cut severely into her writing time. Every evening, she hoped to record the day's events and to write another thousand words in her book, but it was a continuing struggle.

At the bar, in the center of the retirement community, Honey met some drunks and some jerks. They were good material for her book, but there were not enough of them. Most patrons were older men, retired from work, soaking up a few beers, watching sports on TV, and chatting with anyone who came near. There were also some couples and a few people on late-life dates. There were some no tippers, average tippers, and even some good tippers, but she wasn't getting the meat for the type of exposé that she had counted on for her book to become a runaway best-seller. "I need more action." She realized she might have to find a way to help it along.

Honey decided to focus on a group that met at World of Beer every Tuesday afternoon, the Beer Buddies. Like most of the regulars, they were mainly older, retired men. They often acted politically incorrect, sexist, but in a harmless, good-natured way. Their behavior gave her some material she could work into the book, but not what she sought. She decided to focus on the one she labeled the alpha male of the group, Danny Barfright. He would be the star of the salacious exposé of male dominance over women in the bar scene. She realized there were risks if he found out, but she made up her mind that they were worth it.

It wasn't that Gloria hated all men, but men like Danny reminded her of her past. When Gloria was eight years old, her mother began suffering from Alzheimer's disease. When Gloria turned twelve, her father committed her mother to a memory care facility where she spent the last eight years of her life.

Gloria's father tried to take care of his young daughter, but being both father and mother was beyond him. He began to drink heavily. He often left her at home alone at night to go out to bars. Soon, he brought women into their house. A handsome charmer, he succeeded often with women; she lost count of his one-night stands. She stayed in her room trying to study, afraid to see the whores he brought to her mother's bed. But no matter how she tried to muffle the noise, she would hear her father and his latest pick-up in the bedroom next door.

Honey might have hated the women who so easily surrendered to her father, but was it their fault? No. He was the one who brought them to their house while her mother wasted away all alone. It was her father she hated. And as the years passed, she hated him more. After her mother's death, she left for college, but her anger remained with her. It poisoned her relationships and eventually destroyed her marriage.

After her marriage failed, Honey started to write. Her goal, not entirely unconscious, was to get revenge on the men that exploited women, and especially the bastards who abused the trust of faithful women who loved them.

Danny Barfright exemplified the worst of the species. Gloria hated remaining silent while he heaped insults on everyone around him, including her. The more she saw him in action, the more she wanted revenge. He would be the man who would pay for all the others. In the silence of her room, exhausted from trying to capture her feelings on paper, she believed that if it were not against the law, she would kill him. She really would.

Chapter 14

The Beer Buddies had already started to gather when Honey first got to their table.

Sam Adams, the eldest of the men, was telling one of his cornier jokes to Tony Bellome. Honey thought Adams was a friendly old gentleman who never seemed to tire of telling jokes, though his efforts resulted more in groans than laughter.

Bellome, whose northeasterner's accent marked him as New York or New Jersey, was an appreciative audience unless Honey was around to distract him. "Honey, how you been?" Bellome asked.

Before Honey could answer, Sam said, "Hey, Honey, I was telling Tony this joke I heard about a man from Nantucket."

Tony said, "I think she's heard that one. Ain't you, Honey."

"Yeah, I heard it. What do you 'gentlemen' want?"

"Let me have a *Foster's*," Tony said.

"Make that a pair," Sam chimed in and gave Honey a naughty wink. "I used to own a factory for those things."

Honey pretended to be amused. "Sam, you're impossible. But I like your accent."

Sam frowned. "It's pure New York."

Honey shook her head. "There's something else there..."

"Stop flirting with the girl," Tony interrupted. "I want my beer."

Sam shrugged his shoulders, "At my age, flirting is all I can do."

Honey smiled. "For an old dude, you're pretty fit."

Sam shrank down in his chair.

"May I please have my *Foster's*?" Tony said. "I've got things to do."

Sam laughed. "I see two things I'd like to do."

Honey shook her head again and turned to get the beers.

Tony turned to Sam. "Hey, snowbird, you gotta be more careful. You never heard of sexual harassment?"

Sam shrugged his shoulders. "Foist, I'm a chickenboid..."

"What the hell is a chickenboid?"

Sam leaned closer, "It's a New Yorker who's too chicken to stay up there in the goddamn snow and cold all winter."

Tony burst into laughter. "Well, just don't try and get warm with our Honey over there."

Sam gave him a leering look. "So, it wouldn't hurt."

"She'd probably kill you."

"It's a good way to die."

Tony nodded.

Sam glanced at his watch.

As Honey returned with the *Fosters*, Nathan and Busch walked up to the table.

"Hi, guys," said Busch, "Anybody seen Danny?"

"Not here yet," Sam said, glancing at his watch again.

Tony said, "That's a fancy watch, you got, Sam. It looks like somethin' out of them spy movies."

Sam held it up for Tony to admire. "I used to be a spy."

Tony laughed. "So that's a watch like double-oh-seven wears, right? Got a laser in it and a secret decoder?"

"Damn straight. The deadliest watch on the planet." Sam moved his wrist under the table before Tony got too good a look.

Tony burst into laughter again. "You're such a bullshit artist. You told us you owned a factory in the garment center."

"That too. I made bras. Who wants to say that they spent their lives making 'stop 'em from floppins'?"

Tony grunted. "I wouldn't have minded working with boobs all my life." He cast a glance at Honey.

Sam sighed. "It was fine until the broads stopped wearing bras."

"They stopped wearing them?"

"My business deflated. I went bust." Sam gave Tony a wink, and then burst into laughter.

"Oh, I get it," Tony laughed. "Bust . . . deflated. Damn, Sam, I wish you weren't a snowbird..."

"Chickenbird."

"Whatever. You crack me up."

"My mission in life," Sam said and sat back in his chair. He reached his hand down to his ankle and came up just as Honey was about to put a tray on the table.

"Hey, what the hell ya doin'?" Tony barked. "Ya almost knocked my beer over."

Sam looked sheepish. "My ankle itches. Where I wore my gun."

Tony burst into laughter. "You're one crazy sonofabitch."

Honey laughed too.

Sam smiled at Honey, his blue eyes and white teeth, making him look younger than the eighty-three years he claimed to be. "I'm an old cocker," he said when anyone asked him. With his neatly cropped gray hair and round wire-frame glasses, and, of course, striped shorts, Sam looked the part. Unlike some of the old farts, though, he never wore knee-high black support hose.

Honey said, "Maybe you could catch the serial killer."

"What serial killer?" Sam asked.

"Some guy going up and down the coast killing people," said Honey. "Right, Deputy Busch?"

Busch said, "Yeah, we got a bulletin on this weirdo over at the Sheriff's office yesterday. The guy kills his victim, dumps the body in an alley or a ditch somewhere, then pours beer all over the dead body. He leaves the beer can on the dead guy's head."

"He don't even collect the deposit?" Sam asked and chuckled at his joke.

Busch took a chair. He was the nearest any of the Beer Buddies came to being a real Floridian. He said, "Honey, please bring me a *Cigar City IPA.*"

"*Less is More*, Buschie?" Honey gave him a quick wink the others couldn't see.

"Yep," Busch nodded.

Tony said, "If he kills me, I hope he lets me drink the beer first."

Sam said, "We better get busy and drink World of Beer dry. If the guy can't find a beer, he won't be able to kill anyone else."

Everyone chuckled.

Busch laughed too, but he appeared to be deep in thought. He was one of the Beer Buddies' older members, coming to World of Beer since it opened. Tall and lean, everyone knew Buschie, as they called him, was a Vietnam vet. He didn't talk much about that, but most vets didn't. Instead, after he drained a couple, he would grumble that he struggled, unhappy at several jobs after Nam until deciding to try Florida. He harbored a keen interest in internal combustion engines. He still did auto repairs in a well-outfitted garage he occupied off U.S. 301 when he had spare time from his job as a deputy in the local Sheriff's department, the most boring job in the world. "Nothing bad ever happens in Florida's Friendliest Hometown."

Although one of the Beer Buddies, Honey regarded Nathan Lambic as a man of mystery. He, too, survived the Vietnam War. There was a rumor that he worked later as a soldier of fortune in Africa. He did have a slight accent that could have been from Africa, but he talked little about any of his experiences, least of all military exploits. Most people in the bar knew from experience that the men who spoke least about their life in the military often had the most harrowing adventures locked inside. So, most of the bar chums did not ask too many questions, not of Nathan Lambic.

"I'll take a *Foster's*," Nathan said, "Make it two."

"A pair," Sam said and gave Tony that jokester look.

Tony burst into laughter.

"What's so funny, you two?" Nathan asked.

Tony leaned closer to Nathan. "Pair. Get it?"

Nathan sighed, but kept his thoughts to himself.

Honey went off to fill the orders as the Beer Buddies began their raucous Tuesday get-together. She wasn't offended by the flirtatious, even off-color comments of men like Adams. Barfright was another story. Working with these elderly guys, she learned to hide her distaste and to feign good-natured playfulness at their jokes. More than her tips depended on these men accepting her as one of their crowd. They could not find out that she was collecting material for the book she wrote at night.

Honey returned to the table just as Danny Barfright and Margarita Gose took seats.

"Get me a beer," Barfright demanded.

Honey's smile dropped.

Sam grinned at Honey, "Our friend, Daniel, got up on the wrong side of his bed."

Honey glanced at Margarita. "Some guys get up on the wrong side every day," she replied.

Barfright glared at Honey.

Sam laughed. "Our Honey got you there, my friend."

The others joined in the laughter.

Barfright placed his arm around Margarita's shoulder, his hand landing on her breast, and shot back, "The problem with our Honey is she ain't got me."

Honey gritted her teeth and rushed off to get Danny's beer. Like everyone else, she was sure that Danny was banging Margarita. She thought Margarita was beautiful and could do better for herself, but sensed she had a hard edge and knew what she was doing. If Mags, as everyone called her, wanted to waste what remained of her youth on someone like Danny Barfright, that was her business. Gloria didn't feel sorry for her.

Just then, Amber Bock came into World of Beer wearing white cutoffs and a striped top, tied high enough to display her belly button. She waved to the group and sauntered over.

Bud waved back. "Amber, baby, you're looking hot."

Honey recoiled at Bud's sexist remark.

Amber laughed, and so did the other 'Beer Buddies," as Honey called the regulars.

Honey felt sorry for Amber. Only in her forties, Amber was too young for these old leches. She had no business at this table and their weekly Tuesday afternoon drinking sessions. Worse, Honey resented that Amber, like she, was used and abused by guys like Barfright. Every time she thought of that guy, she felt rage build inside her.

Barfright was a handsome man with wavy, steel-gray hair. His strong square chin and dark eyes made him attractive to most women. Compared to the other bar regulars, he appeared virile and a playboy. He had a winning smile, but it seemed deceptive, like a barracuda or a shark. With his over-confident moves and cocky demeanor, he exploited women and then threw them away.

Honey knew too many men like Danny. He was exactly like her father. A man who would screw anything in a skirt. In her quiet moments at night, she wrote her thoughts in her notebook. It was the awful memories of her father that kept her going and fueled her anger. She remembered many nights when she dreamed of bashing his handsome head in with one of his baseball bats. She laughed at the vision of his blood splattering in slow motion into the air like hundreds of red stars.

"Are you deaf or something?" Danny glared at her. "Where my goddamn beer?"

Honey smiled, "Coming, Sweetie." God, she hated Barfright.

Chapter 15

Nathan's trip to the barber took less time than he estimated. The few patrons wanting a haircut meant he didn't have to wait. He glanced at his watch, and then headed for the bar.

While walking toward the entrance, Nathan ran his hand across the back of his neck. It was the third time he had checked to see if his hair was short enough. He still wanted the familiar military-standard cut. Some old habits carried on in his retirement.

A glance at his watch again confirmed he was twenty minutes early to the regular Tuesday-afternoon gathering. Nathan chose not to drive home first. What was the point? If he did, after ten minutes, he would have to leave again to make it to the bar on time. *Oh hell, just have a beer before the guys get here.*

At the bar's door, Nathan ignored the "Please wait to be seated" sign and side-stepped the empty reception stand to go straight to their regular table. He stopped in mid-stride. The table already had an occupant.

Danny Barfright sat alone. Two beer bottles and a half-empty beer glass sitting on the table announced Danny had been there a while.

Nathan thought of leaving. Something about Danny wasn't right.

Danny waved Nathan to over. "Hey, Nathan, I was wondering how long I'd have to wait before someone else got here."

Nathan pulled out the chair across the table from Danny and sat. "I'm at least a quarter-hour early. How long have you been here?"

Danny smiled, revealing a prominent gold incisor in his top row of teeth. "I don't know. Forever. I didn't bring a watch." He leaned forward and rasped, "I needed to get out of the house."

"Okay," Nathan said, but wondered what Danny meant.

"Let me buy you a beer? I'm way ahead of you." Danny visibly weaved as he twisted in the chair to face the bar. He raised his glass, pointed to it, and then extended two fingers into the air.

Honey smiled at Danny, but as soon as he turned his back, she returned his salute with a one-finger gesture.

Nathan pulled his chair slightly away. *This guy has had more than the two drinks on the table.*

Danny brought the glass down too quickly. Beer sloshed onto the table. "Shit, sorry." He laughed. "Hell! There's more where that came from."

Nathan was glad he backed away. "You're supposed to drink it, not wear it."

"Right. Absolutely fucking right." Danny leaned across the table and slapped Nathan's shoulder hard. "You know, Nathan, I like you. I do. You're not a big talker. Some guys are. They brag about what they did before they retired. They tell bullshit stories about things they say they done." He burst into rude laughter. "Some of these old farts even brag about the adjustments they made to make their golf carts faster. Can you imagine? Racing golf carts?" He tapped his finger on Nathan's chest. "You know who I mean. But not you. I've seen how you just sit in your chair and listen." He held two fingers unsteadily across his lips. "You're the quiet type. I watch you. You always gotta watch out for the quiet fuck…"

"Suds up," Honey interrupted, arriving with the two *Dogfish Head 60 Minute IPA's* and a pair of chilled glasses. She shot a disparaging look at Danny. "Hi, Nathan. I'm glad Danny finally has someone else to talk to besides me."

Danny raised his eyes and focused on Honey's chest.

"Nice to see you, Honey." Nathan watched as she poured beer into the glasses. "Is this a standard shift today?"

"Yep, I'm off at six." Honey shot another look at Danny, turned, and walked away.

Danny twisted in his chair to look in Honey's direction. He shook his head and exhaled with a soft whistle, "Nice ass." He faced Nathan again. "You said you was overseas for quite a while before you came back to the States to retire." He aimed his eyes at Nathan. "So, what did you do all those years abroad . . . in Africa, wasn't it?"

"Among other places," Nathan said, wondering where Danny was heading with this.

"How long were you in Africa," Danny said, eyes fixed on Nathan.

"Around thirty years."

"Jesus, that's a long time."

Nathan shifted in his chair. "I came back to the States from time to time. To visit my folks and family."

Danny shook his head. "I couldn't do that. You know, live in some other country. What did the President call them? I can't remember." He looked at his beer, and then shot his eyes back at Nathan. "You were gone a long, damn time." He paused. "So, what line of work were you in?"

It was the question Nathan heard too often. He had a standard answer — practiced and delivered hundreds of times. "I was in the military. Later, I worked in a private security firm and had a few private ventures. That sort of thing." What did Danny know? Was he as drunk as he appeared?

Danny looked bleary-eyed. "All in Africa?"

"Various places." Nathan did not want to be too specific. "Southeast Asia, the Middle East; but, mostly in Africa."

"You know, Nathan, old chap, I've had some experience with international business dealings myself. Been around. Seen things." Danny brought the half-empty beer glass to his mouth and took a long, full drink. "Ahh, that's good. Yeah, sometimes I did business in Africa, too. There are some real shit-hole places there. Yep. I always was glad to get back on the plane and get the hell out of that continent."

Nathan felt anger rising inside him. His fist tightened. The ignorance many Americans displayed about other parts of the world, particularly Africa, irritated him. He witnessed first-hand the high cost in human lives such ignorance could produce. "Yes, some spots are not nice. But Africa has wonderful places too. Some are spectacular."

Danny smiled a shark smile. "There've been a bunch of little wars in Africa, too." He placed his hand around the full glass Honey left him. He looked at Nathan and took a swig. "Those wars offered excellent business opportunities, but . . . shit, that place is fucked up."

Nathan's eyes narrowed. He could barely contain his anger, but knew he had to try. "Africa has problems, for sure." He did not need this drunken guy to tell him about the history of conflicts in Africa. He fought in three of them — made and lost good friends in them. *What does this asshole know about it?*

Danny looked thoughtful. "I can't believe you chose to live there. You know, in Africa, for God's sake." He used his left forearm to wipe his lips, then belched. "Hey, so what? It takes all kinds in this world." He looked hard at Nathan's face. "I know about your kind." Suddenly he laughed. "Yeah, it takes all kinds."

"You got that right." Nathan scrutinized the drunken man slumped in a chair across from him. An old habit — sizing-up an enemy in his gunsight. "Yes, it takes all kinds."

Chapter 16

Sam sipped at the beer Honey sat before him. It had a too-sweet taste, American beer. It was a bit like their women, he thought, grown soft and mediocre in flavor, except maybe for Honey. Something mysterious about that one. She did not belong in a bar in some Florida retirement community. She was too attentive, always listening in on their conversations, often aiming her eyes at Barfright. She would have made a great spy, like Hannah. He bit back his anger, but his eyes darted to Barfright. The sonofabitch.

Barfright spotted Sam's hostile glance. He looked puzzled.

Sam caught his slip and quickly gave Danny a friendly smile and an 'old man' shrug. The slight hunching of his shoulders was a small mannerism he practiced before a mirror. It, and the fake business with the hearing aid he didn't need, was one of those quirks that convinced the others he was one of them. *I'm just another harmless old man waiting to croak in a retirement community.* Like American beer, nothing spectacular, but mellowing into old age. It was a masterful disguise, but there were dangers — more than just being discovered as a Mossad agent, a peril he had not anticipated.

If he wasn't vigilant, he'd become one of them — the men whose highlight of the day entailed meeting in a bar and flirting with female servers and heavily made-up widows. He was becoming good at faking that and at all the dumb jokes. He fooled them all. Being discovered wasn't the danger. Even Barfright was not a threat. Honey was. Could he reveal his true self to her if she showed any sign of losing her interest in the loathsome gunrunner?

As much as he had loved Hannah, always would, he sensed Honey could be someone that might end his loneliness. It was why he delayed the completion of his mission. In the haven of the retirement community, where no one suspected his true identity, he was falling into a trap he had successfully avoided since Barfright's rifle killed Hannah. If he gave Danny more days to live, Sam might learn Honey's secret. He might fall in love again.

"You made bras," Tony asked, bringing Sam back to the present. "I'd love working with all them boobs."

"It was good until the market deflated, and my company went bust," Sam repeated his tired joke, but it was partly the truth. His Uncle Max started an undergarment factory in the garment center of New York after he left Poland in 1947. When Sam asked why a bra company, Max replied that his wife often complained that wearing a clean bra was something she missed in the Holocaust. So, Max started making bras in her honor. Sam worked there while in high school, so it was a good cover. He used to joke with his station chief that Max's bras were great 'support.'

"Just be careful they don't let you down," Manny warned.

"Sam, how did you measure the cups? I always wanted to know that?" Tony asked.

"Oh, for goodness' sake," Honey said and moved away from the table. "You men are impossible."

Sam wished Honey didn't include him in that generalization. He had a simple way of deflecting questions about his bra company. If anyone got too curious, he'd say, "I don't like talking about it. I had to let my hands off the bras when foreigners got their mitts on them." After the laughter subsided, he'd angrily add, "How could we let all our manufacturing go to foreign countries? Can you imagine all our tits are in foreign hands?" Of course, everyone at the table jumped in with their raucous puns and various views of America's takeover by insidious foreign forces. The discussions got quite heated, and he could relax, his false bra business cover as strong as the underwires of his supposed products.

One person sat silent during the discussion. He was never in danger of losing his business. It did not matter where his products came from as long as they were deadly.

Sam called Barfright, the middleman, the *gonif*, the thief. He was someone who made nothing except money, lots of money, from other people's misery. The gunrunner had no sense of loyalty, no sense of patriotism. He sold to anyone willing to pay. He sold the sniper rifle that killed Hannah, and the bullets her body stopped from slamming into him. Why is he staring at me? Does he suspect? "My friends," Sam said, putting on that idiotic smile he loathed, "you are getting all heated up over my bra business. It went bust. It is old news." He turned toward Barfright, "So, Danny, tell us how you made your money, my friend."

Barfright shot Sam a wary glance. "I've got to leave. I got a date waiting for me." He rose from the table, his eyes still on Sam. "Adams? I never thought about it before. That's a funny name for a Jew. Ain't it?"

Sam shivered. Was the bastard suspicious? "My father's name was Adamowitz. Nobody could pronounce it when they came to Ellis Island. So, they named him after the beer."

"That's a good one," Tony exclaimed, hoisting his beer glass. "Here's to Sam Adams."

Barfright nodded his head slowly. "In school, they taught us that Sam Adams was an American patriot in the damn Revolution." He leaned over to Sam. "Every American school kid knows that."

Sam smiled, "You mean the Declaration of Independence wasn't made in China like everything else?"

Tony burst into laughter. "Damn, Sam, you crack me up."

Barfright didn't laugh. "What was the name of your company again?"

Sam stopped laughing. "Big Girl Bra Company. Why do you ask?" He tried to keep smiling. Why was the bastard so inquisitive today?

"I like to know who my friends are," Barfright said and grinned. "I'll see you girls later." He headed toward the bar.

Sam glared at Danny's retreating back and nervously twisted the wedding band on his finger. *My Hannah, soon, I promise. That devil will get his due.*

The others were still absorbed, discussing how America was losing the manufacturing war.

Sam pretended to listen. Out of the corner of his eye, he saw Barfright at the bar speaking into his phone. Trained in reading lips, he saw Danny repeat his name. He let out a low moan.

"Are you okay, Sam?" Nathan asked. "Is your heart okay?"

Sam nodded, but knew his time was running out. Damn Danny Barfright. He was getting too suspicious.

Chapter 17

Margarita walked out of World of Beer around ten p.m. She had no intention of calling it a night. There were four pints of *Guinness* and a shot of Patrón Tequila in her belly. The liquid fire instilled the sense of calm confidence she adored when drinking her beverages of choice. Two tiny spoons of coke put her in what she called 'the place.' Now she was ready to play.

Margarita pushed max-speed out of her vintage Sunbeam Tiger. The little car's Ford V-8 engine, modified by a pro, was a beast. Mags liked the power and, more often than not, she could 'talk' her way out of any difficulties her driving habits produced.

It was league night, so The Eight Ball was humming.

Margarita walked through the swinging Dutch doors and plowed her way to the back tables, reserved for the money players. Her tight white leggings and midnight-blue cover-up set off her platinum blonde hair like candles in the dim light.

Duke Bruski, the owner of the pool hall, gave Margarita a short wave and a smile. He knew when Margarita came to play, the serious players would stay around, and the gawkers would buy drinks just to make sure they missed nothing. When she leaned over the felt, they came alive, staring at her taut buttocks and dreaming of her hair splayed across their bed. Margarita was good for business.

Danny Barfright leaned over, ready to knock the eight ball into the side pocket. He paused, catching a whiff of Mags' unmistakable perfume. "Shit!" He missed the easy shot, turned to see that his nose had been spot on, and smiled. "Hey, Mags. Looking good."

"Thanks Danny." Margarita returned the smile. "I'm in 'the place,' and I'm looking for a game. Your stick available?"

"For you? Always."

Margarita signaled to Duke Bruski, watching her from behind the bar.

Bruski reached for the bottle of Patrón.

The black leather case under Margarita's arm came down. She opened it as a man pulls down the zipper of his bride's white gown, slowly, teasingly, knowing eyes were watching. She fit together the two pieces of her infamous flamingo-pink pool cue in a series of silky-smooth twists. A cube of custom black chalk came out of her case, and she worked the tip of the long pink stick. It was sensuous, whetting their appetites. "Ready boys?" she asked.

They were more than ready.

Duke plunked down a jigger of tequila on the high-top table next to Margarita.

Margarita threw the jigger down her throat. "I'm all worked up. The night is young. Who's taking me on first?"

"I'll always take you on," Barfright said.

"You'd like to break my balls," Margarita taunted.

Danny didn't answer. He was too busy staring at Margarita's ass as she leaned over and smashed the crap out of the gathered balls on the table.

At 1:30 a.m., with the match tied, Danny wanted a break. They met outside, in the back of The Eight Ball, and shared a joint Margarita pulled from her bra.

"You haven't lost your touch," Danny said. "You know just how to handle the stick."

Margarita replied, "And the balls, Mr. Barfright."

"Are we still on for the shipment?" Danny asked abruptly.

"All is good from down south. Are your connections in Cleveland set?"

"As good as ever." Danny looked Margarita over. "You still got game, Mags. Do you ever lose?"

"Not too often playing eight ball. Don't even think about taking me on in straight pool." She dropped her smile. "But forget the games for now. When the drop goes down tomorrow night, I need to make sure you don't fuck it up. Who's got you covered?"

If anyone else had asked this, Danny would have slugged him. He replied, "Duke in there, behind the bar. Don't worry—he's got this."

Margarita trusted Duke, but had doubts about Danny. She had her contacts up the distribution line check into Danny Barfright, and she did not like what they found. He had a history of smuggling arms and blood diamonds, but he had been out of the fire for several years. Her sources reported some of his supply lines had collapsed, taking down several of his associates. Some suspected he had fingered them to the Feds. While she doubted that he had the balls to turn in his own people, the big money wanted her assurance that he would produce and not rat out the operation. She had impulsively vouched for Danny one hundred percent, placing the operation and her life on the line.

Barfright passed the joint to Margarita and moved closer. His fingers landed on her ass.

Margarita faced Danny. "Don't even think about it. I'm not in this for a romp with you."

Barfright put on his bedroom eyes. "Aw, come on, Mags, we could be good together."

Margarita crushed the smoldering joint into the back of Danny's hand. "Fuck-off. We are just in business tonight. That's it." She aimed her eyes into his. "Make sure things go smooth tomorrow, or you'll get more than a burn mark on your slimy skin."

Danny rubbed his hand. "You're a bitch. Do you know that?"

Margarita smiled. "Don't you forget it." She walked to her Tiger and roared off into the black moonless night. *If he fucks up, I'm going to kill him*, she promised.

Chapter 18

In his house, curtains drawn tight, Sam fought against becoming like the others with the old age spread. An hour or two each morning, he performed the exercises he'd learned as a recruit in the Israeli military. Unlike in America, the Israeli government requires all citizens to fulfill military service. That hardens us, he thought, as he recalled how firm Hannah's muscles had been. Even Honey, with her youthful curves, was soft compared to Hannah. Honey couldn't kill a man as his Hannah did, with her bare hands. He remembered how he often puzzled at how the hands that felt so tender as they caressed his body could, in an instant, kill an enemy with one vicious blow. Could Honey do that? What was her secret? Every instinct he'd honed in years of intelligence work told him that she was hiding something.

Thinking of Honey made Sam push himself harder. One hundred push-ups, a hundred sit-ups, ten minutes of planking, squat jumps, and more, to lose the memories of Hannah in a sweat of physical exertion, none of the others could attempt. It was an obsession to harden the abs he concealed so well in his Beer Buddy knit shirts and over-sized golf shorts.

Sam hit the weights next. Repetitive motion the other Beer Buddies, with the possible exceptions of Bud and Nathan, couldn't even imagine, let alone emulate.

Once complete, he slid the weights and mat under his bed. Nobody can see them, he thought and checked as he did daily, the almost invisible seam under the queen-size mattress. He had cut out a square in the bottom of the mattress and concealed his Beretta, bullets, several passports from different countries under various names, and a bayonet in the hollow. If Barfright, or anyone else, came too close, one pull of the seam and the deadly arsenal would be available.

In the shower, Sam thought of Honey again. *Was she sincerely interested in that sonofabitch?* He wished he could reveal to her who he was. He imagined her eyes wide, surprised by his physique. He recalled how she had remarked at how fit he appeared. Was she suspicious? He replied by shooting her one of his jokes or a flirting comment that verged on sexual harassment. He hated doing that, but it made him fit in with the others. Even Tony, a character from a Mafia movie, laughed every time Sam jokingly, but with a straight face, boasted he was a spy. "Honesty is the best policy for hiding the truth," he said as he brushed a dab of gray dye into his hair. "The old cocker is back," he mused and eyed his slouch, his rounded shoulders, all part of the act.

Almost ready for the next scene, Sam strapped on his watch, black, and conspicuously out of place with his old man façade. He tested the clasp hiding a cyanide pill and the hand-cuff key. He might have to use them if he got caught. *Like these old farts could ever get wise to me. They can't even catch their drool.* Then he saw Barfright's face, his eyes studying him. He had asked a few questions. *Did he have some new information?* He had read the rat's lips. A chill shot through him. Barfright had mouthed his name to someone on the other end of the phone. He twisted the watch face.

Sam unwound a thin wire around the rigid rubber rim of the watch. The barely visible metal strand could slice through anyone's neck. He snapped it back. While the wire would be effective, even a dumb cop like Busch would know this was an expert assassination. It had to look like an accident. There could be no suspicion that an agent of a foreign power had neutralized an American on American soil. A tug of the watch face and a miniature lockpick appeared.

I need to think this over. He still doesn't know who I am. I read his lips when he spoke on the phone. He said, 'Bra factory.' It will take time before he figures it out.

Sam pounded his chest. *Hard as a rock.* He then slipped on his underwear. Made in Israel, it was the only brand he insisted on wearing even though his Mossad boss warned him against it on all of his previous missions. "Your underwear will give you away one day," Manny argued just before Sam left the service.

Sam, no longer caring about his boss's admonition, argued back, "Israeli drawers are stronger and more durable than brands made in China, Vietnam, and all the other places that now surround American men's jewels." He had a funny thought. *If I cut off Danny's jewels and shove them in his mouth, the Americans will think the Mafia did it.*

Chapter 19

Bud was excited. It was like being back in high school. There was always some guy to whom everyone looked up. In his case, it was Henry Weinhard. Henry wasn't the best athlete, the best student, nor was he the most handsome, but girls were all over him, and he was easily elected President of the class. Bud had wanted to win.

To Bud, Danny Barfright was the Henry Weinhard of the Beer Buddies.

Bud took down the Stan Musial bat from its wall mount with supreme reverence. He placed it on the table of his trophy room. *What else would impress Danny?* He looked lovingly at Joe Namath's helmet. *Yes. That will do it.* He set it on the table, assuring it wouldn't roll off the highly polished surface.

He had already placed four bottles of *Herren Hauser Premium Lager*, specially imported from Germany, in the patio's drink cooler. Everything was ready. Would Danny show up?

At just after 5 p.m., Bud heard the doorbell ring. He surveyed the room as an interior decorator might.

The doorbell rang again.

Bud straightened his tee-shirt and strode to the glass entryway. "Hey, Danny, come on in," he said. "Nice bike. How was the ride over?"

Danny stretched his arms. "Good. That's a nice ride along that lane with all those trees. I never knew that path was there. I'm surprised, but there wasn't a soul on the trail."

"Yeah, it's pretty quiet away from the town square."

"So, what do you got to show me?" Danny asked, removing his biking gloves.

Bud led Danny into the house. "Well, make yourself at home. The second bedroom is my trophy room. It ain't all that much."

Danny's eyes ran around the walls and shelves crowded with sports memorabilia. Pictures of Bud posing with athletes, many young, some more famous than others, hung in frames on the walls. On the shelves were scores of Bud's championship trophies, more photos, and signed baseballs. Athletes signed all the images. There were several dressers with more championship trophies on them. "Damn! Sam was right. You got a museum here."

Bud led Danny around the room, explaining the history behind each piece. Then he went to the table on which he had posed Musial's bat and Namath's helmet. "These two are my crown jewels," he announced. "I'd say they're the most important items in my collection."

Danny leaned over the table.

"Say, can I get you a beer?" Bud asked, observing Danny looking at the memorabilia.

Danny straightened up. "I don't know. I've got to get back before it gets too dark. I'm going to drop into that Dunkin Donuts at the end of the path on the way home."

"Oh, it won't take a minute. I'll pop out on the patio and get us a couple of brews." He rushed off before Danny could object.

Bud took two crystal beer glasses from the cupboard on the patio and opened two of the German lagers. He poured the beers making sure the head was right before going back into the trophy room. "Here you..." He stopped in mid-sentence.

Danny stood there, holding a sheer silk teddy in one hand and a pair of yellow lace panties in the other. He wore a leering grin on his face.

Bud saw one of his dresser drawers was open, revealing lacy women's underthings. His closet was ajar. He stared at lingerie and evening gowns neatly hung on hangers. With two beers in his hands, he couldn't move.

Danny laughed. "Well, Bud, my he-man, it looks like you have interests other than football. I LOVE your collection."

Bud's face grew ashen. He could think of nothing to say, no lie that could conceal the truth of his hidden wardrobe. He put the glasses on the table. "What the fuck are you doing in my stuff? Get out of my things."

Danny waved the panties in Bud's face. "I always suspected you were hiding something behind that macho bullshit you throw. Wait until the others hear about your special collection," he said, that grin still spread across his face.

Bud tore the garments from Danny's hands. "Get out! Get out of my house! How dare you go through my things?"

Danny laughed. He laughed on his way to the door. "Man, the guys are going to get a kick out of this."

"You tell anyone, and I'll kill you," Bud yelled after him.

Danny shook his head and picked up his bicycle. "Like you're man enough to do shit," he said and walked the bike down the lawn.

Bud rushed back into his trophy room and grabbed the first thing he saw. It was the Stan Musial bat. He slammed the meaty end repeatedly into his left palm. It was too late to lie. Maybe he could talk some sense into Danny. He could explain how important it was not to be exposed, to be made a fool of in front of the Beer Buddies. As he weighed his options, he slammed the bat into his hand. Whap! Whap! Whap! At last, a little calmer, he hurried to his garage and his golf cart. He drove to Dunkin Donuts.

---  ---

Bud waited in his golf cart, his eyes glued to the store window. He saw too many people inside. This busy shop was not the place to confront Danny. Maybe the sneaky bastard would be more amenable after he cooled down, back at Danny's house.

Bud watched with growing fury as Danny gobbled up the last of a chocolate-covered donut. He watched him suck the icing from his thumb, wipe his thumb on a napkin, and dab at his lips. Every action made him despise Danny more.

Bud grew impatient until Danny came out and got on his bike. He let Danny get a good head start down the trail. He secured the bat next to him.

After Danny disappeared, he started his cart. He knew where Danny was going.

Danny rode fast.

Bud didn't expect to catch up with Danny on the trail, but about half-way to the end of the path, he spotted Danny's bike. I'll talk to him here. Nobody's around, he thought, seizing the bat in his fist.

Chapter 20

Saturday night, Honey returned to her apartment after a long shift at World of Beer. She yearned to talk with the twins, but it was late. They were in bed already, and she was exhausted. She locked the door behind her, placed her keys on the small table near the door, and then walked into the kitchen and glanced at the mail on the table. Back in the living room, she tossed her bag on the sofa and tiptoed to the bedroom to peek at her slumbering boys. Honey studied their two innocent faces and regret welled-up. Though the boys had come to see her during their school vacation, she had spent little time with them. She closed the door quietly to not disturb their sleep.

Kicking off her shoes in the living room, she returned to the kitchen, where she poured herself an extra-large glass of Chardonnay. She took a spinach and cheddar quiche from the freezer, read the directions, and set the oven to preheat. In the bedroom, she got out of her work clothes and put on sweatpants and a pink t-shirt. She came back to the kitchen to get out a bag-salad when her phone rang.

"Hello?" she answered.

"Gloria Saint Pauli?" the caller asked.

"Who is this?" said Honey.

"I am with Hefeweizen Publications, and I need to speak to Ms. Gloria Saint Pauli."

"Speaking," said Honey.

"Hold for Ms. Stella Troy."

"Gloria. How are you, dear girl? Bearing up well?" Stella asked.

Gloria wondered what the editor wanted. "Just fine," she lied.

"So, the research is progressing?"

"Just fine," she lied again.

"And the men are the sleazeballs you anticipated?"

At last, Gloria felt she could be honest. "Oh, Stella, this has been harder than I thought. I can't wait until this book is in print. When I am out of this place, and back in Boston, I don't think I can ever face another beer."

"Interesting." Stella coughed. "But what about the book? When will I be gifted with the rest of the manuscript?"

Gloria thought she picked up impatience in the snooty editor's inflection. "The writing is going well. Very well. I'm coming to the last chapters soon."

Another dainty cough. "That's what I called to talk about, my dear. You know I love your writing, dear girl, but I thought I should call and give you a head's up. Make sure we are on the same page, sweetheart."

"Is there something wrong?"

Just then, the oven dinged.

"Just a minute," Gloria said. "I've got to put my dinner in the oven." She set the phone down and went to the kitchen. When she returned to the sofa and picked up the phone, she said, "Is there something wrong? You sound a bit concerned." She chose her words carefully.

"Wrong? No, no, no. I would not say anything is wrong, exactly. I just wanted to make sure we march to the same drummer — to use a writerly cliché. I'm editing chapter twenty-four, and you haven't shown me that the men in the bar are the monsters you promised. It is all very well to call them abusers, but darling, I haven't seen much monstrous conduct."

"I am getting there," Gloria said. "Chapter twenty-four? I thought that was the chapter where I told of the old man asking me to sit on his lap, and the other about to tell me the dirty Nantucket limerick…"

"Yes. I just read that, and it is part of the reason I called."

"I hope that wasn't too explicit."

"Explicit? Hardly, my dear. If anything, it makes the old boys sound like harmless codgers rather than lechers and abusers. For heaven's sake, they could be someone's sweet old grandpas.

No. No, my dear. I'm afraid, writing talent aside, you'll have to show a lot more than that if you want us to publish this book."

Gloria bit her lip. *What the hell does she want from me? Does she want me to get raped or beaten?* "Don't worry, Stella. I'm working on a scene now that will get everyone's attention."

"Wonderful, dear girl. I knew you could do it. I'll let you get back to your dinner. I'm so looking forward to your returning to Boston."

Me too, Gloria thought.

"On another issue, dear girl, it is imperative that you finish *Pink in the Barroom* sooner rather than later. My office has been getting calls asking about your whereabouts. Some calls inquire if you are in central Florida. It is getting increasingly difficult to fend them off."

Gloria wondered who could be hunting for her and why. "Thank you for protecting me. I'll be out of here in less than three weeks. My twins have been here with me this summer, but now I need to get them back to Boston for school. I plan to drive north with them in a couple weeks."

"Wonderful, we can do the final edit when you are back here in Boston. I'll talk to you later, dear. Tata."

"Tata, Stella." Gloria hung up the phone. She was worried. She did not have the "smoking gun" she promised Stella. None of the Beer Buddies had put a hand under her skirt or offered her money for sex. It was not nearly as easy as she had thought it would be to get these men to show their true natures. Stella was growing impatient, and money was running low. Royalties from the *Power of Pink* were never very good and the meager advance on *Pink in the Barroom* was all but eaten up. And now, someone was on her scent.

Gloria ate her quiche deep in thought. There was one hope. One man in the study group seemed to fit the bill. Like it or not, she would have to get the chief abuser, Danny Barfright, to make a move. But what if the action was even more aggressive than she feared? What if he wouldn't be satisfied just making lewd suggestions? What if he were to attack her, force himself on her, attempt to rape her?

Gloria pulled over her handbag. She had a license to carry the pearl-handled .32 police special she kept in her purse. Florida's laws made it easy to shoot someone legally if the shooter felt his or her life was in danger. She picked up the gun. Barfright was dangerous, not only to her, but to all womankind. She pointed the weapon at a photo she had taken of the Beer Buddies. Danny was in the middle, his hand behind Margarita. It would be a pleasure to take him out of the gene pool. And a sensational self-defense homicide would make *Pink in the Barroom* an instant international bestseller. "Bang! Bang! Goodbye, Danny Barfright."

Chapter 21

Amber smiled at Margarita as she sat down at the Beer Buddies' regular table. "Hey, we're the first tonight," she said.

Margarita glanced at Amber. "So, we are. The guys might still be out on the course."

"Can't say I'm much for the sport of golf. A bit too much nature for me. Besides, my kind of green is the kind that folds and buys pretty things."

"Ha! The way most of these boys play, I don't know that I'd call it a sport. But they get out of the house and do more exercise than just lifting their elbows to guzzle beer."

Since she started coming to the bar each week, Amber had grown comfortable enough with the guys that she now thought of herself as one of the Beer Buddies. Mags was a harder nut to crack. Not cold or nasty, just stand-offish. While most women resented her and tried to keep her as far away from their men as possible, Amber did not get a whiff of jealousy from Margarita. She could not put her finger on what the older woman's attitude toward her was, but she wanted to get to know Margarita better. "So, Mags, do you like living here in The Villages? You seem to have your pick of the guys."

"I could give two shits about hooking up with another man. Yeah, I like it here, enough."

Amber was not sure how she felt about living in a retirement community. She was glad to be rid of Miller's abuse, but still missed younger men. Amber studied Margarita as the older woman ordered from the tall male waiter whose eyes were not on

Margarita's eyes. *That Margarita, she's one tough cookie. She can have any guy here if she gets the urge.* She looked at her reflection in the mirror behind the table. *The old guys here are sweet to me, but it's different with her. They respect her toughness. I'm like their kid sister, except when they check out my ass and look down my shirt.*

"Well, hello, ladies. Usually, I'm the first one here." Nathan strolled over to the table.

Margarita looked up. "That old military training, huh? Always on time and ready for action?"

Nathan smiled. "Old habits." He bought them all a round of drinks.

Margarita ordered a *Bold City Duke's Cold Nose* brown ale while Amber had a *Captain Lawrence 6th Borough Pilsner.*

No sooner did Honey deliver their drinks than the rest of the gang strolled in.

"Honey, rack 'em up!" Danny waved his hand magnanimously. "Drinks for all my fuckin' friends. On Nathan, right?" He aimed a 'gotcha' grin at Nathan.

Nathan tightened his fist under the table. "Sure."

Seeing Danny in such high spirits, Amber giggled. When the drinks arrived, she held up her glass and toasted, "To whatever makes you happy. Right, Danny?"

"Absolutely." Danny looked at Amber, and then clinked his glass with hers. "Cheers, everybody!"

After two beers, Amber excused herself for a visit to the ladies' room. Inside, she touched up her makeup and combed her hair. She was about to leave when she heard voices penetrate the thin walls. *Danny and Margarita? Are they arguing?* Not wanting to walk into the middle of anything but curious, she leaned against the wall. *Shit! They sound furious.*

In the corridor outside the bathroom, Margarita hissed at Danny. "I'm warning you, Danny. Screw this up, and I'll kill you. And I don't mean I'll order it. I'll pull the goddamn trigger myself. You got that?"

"Take it easy, Mags. Don't get your panties in a pretzel. I won't screw up. This deal is not my first rodeo, you know."

"There's no room for mistakes. One wrong move, and my ass is on the line. But your ass is first. Don't forget it."

Amber heard the sharp click of high heels. She also heard Danny say, "Tough tits, you fuckin' broad."

When Amber finally heard Danny leave, she opened the bathroom door and peeked out. With the coast clear, she walked back to the Buddies' table. Margarita was gone, but Danny had upended his beer and ordered another. *I wonder what all that was about? It didn't sound like a lovers' spat. It sure soured Danny's mood.* She pulled her blouse down to reveal more cleavage. Maybe, this was her opportunity. "You okay, Danny?" she asked.

Danny turned toward her. His eyes landed on her nearly exposed boobs, and he looked away, mumbling something.

Amber heard what Danny said. She pushed off from the table and raced back into the bathroom. His words echoed in her head, "Put them away, kid. You don't belong here. Go home to your mother." At that moment, she could have killed the smug bastard.

Chapter 22

Tony sat on the veranda at Panera Bread, reading *The Villages Daily Sun* newspaper. The warm day made him drowsy. He had been in The Villages for five weeks, and he was already in love with the laid-back, easy-going lifestyle. The slow pace of life would have bothered some people. For Tony, however, the dreamy, drowsy lifestyle had surprised him. That leisurely pace was exactly what he needed. Earlier that morning, he talked to Gaspo.

"You find that bastard yet?" Gaspo rasped. "That's what I sent you down there for, not chatting up some old broads."

Tony knew his time was running out. "I found him. Whacking him should be easy."

"Well, get it done and get the hell out of there. You're turning into one of them old farts."

"I got to hang around a little longer. If I turn up one day, and Peroni shows up dead, and I leave the next, I'm suspect number one. I gotta let a little time pass."

"How much time? I want my package delivered fast."

"I'll deliver the package soon. Then I gotta hang around here for a few months until things cool down."

"You just get it done, or somethin' else will get done." Gaspo slammed down the phone.

Tony knew Gaspo wasn't a happy Don. He understood the risks of deceiving his boss, but he also knew that the Don understood that if Tony went down, blood might splash on his cape as well. He'd bought some more time to enjoy a life of coffee, donuts, and beer.

Tony had just unfolded his paper and settled into his chair when he saw Amber Bock walking in front of the Izod store across the street. She was with an older woman, a blond, quite beautiful. His eyes zeroed in on her back. Cute ass. Nice legs.

The woman turned away from the store window.

Holy shit. Sara Nevada? Tony sat up in his chair in wide-eyed amazement. Sara was the woman he had loved all his life. In high school, Sara was so far out of his league, he didn't dare to talk to her. She was also Peroni Azzurro's girlfriend. *Sara still looks beautiful. What is she doing with Amber?*

Amber and Sara walked to the next store.

Tony resisted the temptation to rush over. It would be better to take the measure of the situation before making a move. As if he could move.

The two women went into Starbucks, returned with paper cups of coffee, and took up residence at an outside table.

For the next fifteen minutes, Tony observed them, unsure of what to do. The more he saw, the clearer it became that the older woman was, indeed, Sara Nevada. But what was she doing with Amber? From the affection Amber showed her, he guessed they were related. They might have been aunt and niece, but the longer he watched, the more confident he became that Sara was Amber's mother. He had searched for her long ago and learned Sara had left New York. The word in the neighborhood was she was pregnant when she skipped out. He looked again. Sara's child would be just about Amber's age. The two looked so much alike. *Is Amber Sara's daughter?*

Amber rose from her chair and set her purse on the table.

Tony read her lips. She said she was going to the restroom and would be back in a minute.

Tony threw his paper down. He waited for a few golf carts to pass and walked across the street. "Sara?" He said, "It's me. Tony. Tony B, from PS231."

Sara gasped. "Tony B?" She smiled. "I can't believe it's you, after all these years. What are you doing here?"

Tony had to know if Sara knew. He blurted it out. "Peroni Azzurro. He's here in The Villages."

Sara's smile vanished. "Oh, no. He can't be." She looked up at Tony with sad eyes. "Peroni is the last person I want to bump into here. And absolutely not now." She looked anxiously at the bathroom door. "Tony, I can't explain right now. I'm here visiting my daughter. It's imperative that she not meet Peroni. You can't even mention him."

"I'm afraid it's too late for that. Amber and Peroni are friends." Tony saw the strained look on Sara's face. "They're just friends. We all meet with a group who call themselves the Beer Buddies, on Tuesday afternoons..."

"She knows him? She's friends with him?" Sara peered into Tony's eyes.

"She kind of knows him." Tony was not sure how much to reveal. "I think you should know Peroni is going under the name of Danny Barfright."

Sara shook her head. "Tony, I've got to talk to you about this. Not now." She shot her eyes at the bathroom door again. "Here. Take my number and call me. We need to talk." She jotted her number on a napkin and said, "Call me. Please?"

Tony took the napkin and shoved it in his pocket. "I'll only leave you if you agree to have lunch with me tomorrow."

Sara glanced at the bathroom door again. "Of course, I will. I've been waiting all my life to see you again."

Tony wondered if she meant that. She looked so frightened. Was it a ploy?

Sara grabbed his sleeve. "You have to leave now. Call me? Please call me?" She smiled at him. "And Tony, I've missed you. Now run, please. Before Amber sees you."

Tony did not want to go. He looked at Sara and decided he had no choice. As he crossed the street, he promised that if Barfright did anything to hurt Sara or Amber, he would make him pay with the most painful execution since the Middle Ages. But what if Sara still cared for the man she knew as Peroni Azzuro? Could he kill the man loved by the woman he loved?

Chapter 23

The afternoon session with the Beer Buddies lasted longer than usual. Nathan glanced at his watch as he exited the rear door of World of Beer. Seventeen-twenty . . . if he hurried, he could stop at Publix, get something from the deli section, take it home, and pop it into the microwave before it got too late.

Pulling into the Publix parking lot, he saw Sam Adams walking toward a car several spaces ahead. Nathan left his Range Rover and walked up to where Sam was fumbling with his keys beside a red Kia.

Nathan said, "I didn't know you drove a Kia."

"I don't. My car's in the shop. This lemon is a loaner. It's a bust."

Nathan ignored Sam's usual pun. "It was a good gathering today."

Sam selected one key at the end of a chain with an oversized plastic *Auto-World* fob. "Tuesday afternoons at World of Beer are all good. It's good to laugh with friends."

"True," said Nathan, "a good bunch of people."

"Some may be better than others," said Sam.

"What do you mean — some better than others?" Nathan asked.

"I don't know. I guess I just take to some more than others. What do you think about Danny Barfright?"

"I never thought much about him. But now that you mention it, he does seem a little secretive."

Sam said, "Right. He says he has been to a lot of places and done things, but he never tells much about any of it."

Nathan came closer. "You know, you're right. There's something strange. I can't figure the guy out."

"He's probably just like the rest of us. We all have our secrets," Sam said.

"What do you think he's hiding? Is he for real?"

"Why ask me? I guess he's for real." Sam turned the key to unlock the Kia.

Nathan wasn't giving up. "The other day, the two of us were at World of Beer early. Danny was a little sloshed and talked a lot. He let out he had business dealings in Africa in the past."

"So? Many people have business dealings…"

Nathan eyed Sam. "You know I spent a bunch of years in Africa. Do you think he did? Or is he bull-shitting me?"

"How should I know?" Sam said, turning away from Nathan's gaze.

Nathan wasn't buying Sam's ignorance act.

Sam had the look of a boy with a secret. "Maybe there are some things we shouldn't know about our friend Danny." He flashed Nathan a knowing smile, then opened the car door and climbed into the driver's seat.

When the door closed and the window came down, Nathan placed his hand on the car roof as though he might prevent it from leaving. "I was a soldier for a long time. I have a feeling you know a lot more."

"All I know is about bras," Sam said. "And spying. You know I was a spy."

"That's what you're always saying, but somehow you look more like a bra salesman than a spy to me."

Sam said, "A good spy is not supposed to look like a spy."

Nathan laughed, but he still harbored the feeling that Sam knew more than he was telling.

Sam attached the seat belt of the Kia. "You know, I'm getting a bit forgetful."

"You can try that on the others. I don't buy it." Nathan looked at Sam, "Listen, my friend, you can trust me."

Sam sighed. "Okay, but this is just between one old soldier and another, you understand. I happen to know that Danny once did have some business in Africa. It was a long time ago. We all did some shit when we were younger. We're maybe not so proud of now."

"What kind of business was he in?" Nathan kept his hand on the car roof.

"I am not sure I should be saying anything. This is all water under the bridge, you understand. For a while, I had a job at Israeli intelligence. I wasn't an operative or anything. I had an administrative job in procurement. We helped some of our friends in countries in Africa and the Near East procure the supplies they needed when our missions coincided. You remember Idi Amin, the Ugandan dictator?"

"Of course, what's Barfright got to do with Amin?"

"Well, Amin was a friend of Israel until things turned sour. Then, there was a group in Uganda looking to overthrow the dictator. They needed some arms and asked Israel for help. Israeli intelligence couldn't sell to the rebels, but they had a line on a shadowy company dealing arms in the region. It was my job in procurement to look into the records of these groups. In looking at one group, I found a picture of the guy who ran a major arms dealing operation. The guy's name was Peroni Azzurro."

Nathan asked, "What's Peroni Azzurro got to do with Danny Barfright."

"Same guy. I'd swear to it. He must have changed his name. Same gold tooth and tattoo of a monkey on the back of his left hand. Anyway, the outfit was shady, but they reliably delivered arms at a fairly low price."

"You're saying Danny was involved in arms trafficking."

"Nathan, you ever heard of Horizon International?"

The name sent an electric jolt down Nathan's spine. Images of that night, near the border of Mozambique, flooded his brain. He saw his men struggling to defend themselves when their assault rifles failed to fire. He heard the screams as the communist-backed rebels over-ran their position. He remembered the last breath of his wife's brother, gasping through the holes an enemy's AK-47 drilled in his chest. The bitter memories were still vivid, fanning his burning need for revenge. Nathan's fists clenched, and the muscles in his jaw tightened.

Sam said, "I am guessing you know this company?"

"Yeah. I know it." It was all Nathan could do to keep from shouting to Sam how Nathan's unit had paid Horizon International top dollar to provide quality arms and ammunition. He bit his lip, remembering that most of the ammo turned out to be defective factory rejects.

The man in the Kia morphed from Sam Adams spy provocateur to Sam Adams, former Jewish bra-maker, barely visible above the steering wheel. "So, you see," Sam said. "I was a spy. A spy in the basement of the intelligence annex in Tel Aviv. Now, please don't blow my cover to the Beer Buddies."

Nathan, still seething with his new knowledge, nodded. "Your secret's safe with me. Maybe we should keep this whole conversation between the two of us. Okay?"

"Sure," Sam agreed. "Spies and soldiers of fortune die before they talk."

Nathan watched silently as the red Kia backed out of the parking space and slowly moved away. Was Sam for real? It was a crazy story, but Nathan intuitively sensed it was true. His hands contracted into fists. "Danny, you son-of-bitch." He stomped toward Publix and a dinner that was likely to be as cold as his revenge. "This old soldier doesn't forget . . . and I don't forgive you mother-fucker!"

Chapter 24

Tony arrived at Amber's house at precisely two minutes before noon. He knew because he kept checking his watch so he wouldn't be too early or late.

Sara was waiting at the door. When she saw Tony in his jaunty yellow golf cart, she ran out and hopped in. "Are we playing golf?" she asked, a smile on her face.

"No, why?"

"Why are we in a golf cart then?"

"Everyone rides in golf carts around here. It's like having a second car."

"You ride on the street in this thing, with big trucks? No, thank you."

"No, no. We have special cart paths for these babies. We don't mix with the trucks. Now relax. Where you want to go for lunch?"

"You choose. But not with the trucks."

Tony laughed. "No trucks. I promise."

Tony drove to the town square, staying on the golf cart paths. Just once, he started to turn onto a major roadway. "No trucks," he teased.

They both laughed.

Tony pointed out the few shops he had checked out. "I ain't much of a shopper," he said.

Sara smiled. "I never took you for one."

Tony pulled into TooJay's. "This is the best they got here," he said as he helped Sara out of the cart. "But it's not Italian. It's Jewish."

"I love Jewish deli."

"I think it's as close to New York as we got in Florida." Tony looked flustered. "You prefer Italian?"

"No. Deli is okay. I've had enough Italian," Sara answered.

The hostess seated them at a quiet table in the back, as Tony requested. After they had time to look over the menu, the waiter took their orders. Tony ordered a burger, and Sara, a club sandwich.

Tony was silent, his eyes liking what he saw.

Sara smiled. "It's nice here. I can see why Amber likes it."

"I can't see why anyone wouldn't," Tony replied.

Sara leaned closer.

Tony inhaled her perfume. It reminded him of their past.

"I guess we need to talk," Sara said. "I bet you have lots of questions."

Tony frowned, not wanting to lose this opportunity. "Sara, I gotta ask, why did you run away?" He saw her eyes close to halfway. "Honestly, I thought we could be something . . . I was going to make my move if you ever broke up with Peroni."

Sara sighed. "You always did come to the point. I didn't run away from you. I had my reasons, including a great job in California. I wanted to get away from that Italian ghetto and all that pasta and wine, pasta and wine." She did not think he understood. "I needed to explore."

"Explore? Like with Peroni?"

"Let's not go there."

"We can't avoid it."

Sara tapped the menu. "I guess not." She frowned. "Peroni was a fast talker, smooth. You were a gentleman." She smiled. "I should've taken the gentleman."

Tony did not smile. "So, what happened in the almost fifty years since?" What he wanted to know was why she never called him after leaving Peroni.

Sara paused, and then said, "I don't suppose you know this. I was pregnant when I moved to California."

Tony did not react. He did not want her to know that he did know about the pregnancy.

Sara continued. "Peroni would have married me. I would have become a mob wife. I couldn't bow to the Don and his henchmen and wait for the cops to bang down our door. That wasn't me. I saw too much of it growing up." She sipped water. "So, I got a job. I did well, moved up the chain, and made a nice life for Amber and me."

"Did you ever marry?"

"My husband died in an accident, soon after we were married."

"I'm sorry. Life must have been hard for a single mother back in those days."

"It was, but I'm not complaining. Amber and I had a good life, and Peroni helped out. He sent checks every month until Amber graduated from college."

"He helped?" Tony was stunned. He had not expected that, not from Azzurro.

"With some money. Yes."

"Nothing else?"

"Like what?"

"He didn't want you back?"

"I couldn't go back to him." Sara peered into Tony's eyes. "I'm afraid. Someday, Peroni's going to get what he deserves."

Tony shuddered. *Change the subject.* "What brings you back East?"

"I'm not back. I'm on vacation. Amber has been telling me about this wonderful place, so I decided to come for a visit."

A thought struck Tony. "Does Peroni know Amber is his daughter?"

"Oh, God, I hope not. Amber doesn't know Peroni is her father either. She thinks her father died in California when she was two years old. She knows I came west from New York before she was born, but she doesn't know much about my life there, and I want it to stay that way. Please don't tell her anything. She asked me to go to World of Beer and meet the Beer Buddies. I'm glad I didn't go. I don't know what I would have done if I had run into Peroni there. If I thought there was any chance of bumping into him, I'd leave and go back to California today."

Tony didn't know what to say. He could not tell Sara that Peroni's time on Earth was almost over, and he was the appointed executioner.

"But that's enough about me," Sara said, smiling at Tony. "Tell me something about yourself. When I left, you were just out of high school. A lot of our friends got caught up with the Mafia. Were you able to avoid that trap?"

Tony lowered his voice. "You always did go for the quick. Don't worry. I'm here looking for a place to retire." He was not going to tell Sara the real reason he was here — to rub out Peroni. He hated lying to Sara, but he did not want to chase her away. She would run out on him if she knew that he was a hitman. Killing Peroni would be killing Amber's father and spoil any chance he might have with the beautiful woman across the table. Maybe he could figure out a way to not kill Danny. Was there a way out of his 'obligation' to the Don. One that didn't end up with he, himself, dead? It was a dilemma, and he had no idea how to resolve it. He made up his mind that he did not want to deal with the ugly realities of his life at this moment. He would worry about Gaspo and Peroni tomorrow. "I'm sorry. What did you ask?"

Sara said, "So, why are you in The Villages?"

"I'm retired, and I'm looking for a place to settle. What better place in the whole world to be retired? Look at all the activities, the music, the dancing." He laughed. "And the golf carts. Zoom! Zoom!"

"And not too many trucks," Sara teased.

"And yes, not too many trucks."

They laughed, and then talked the afternoon away. It seemed only minutes for their lunch to be over, and it was time to go.

When Tony looked at his watch, he was amazed to find that two hours had passed and evening was closing in. He had not enjoyed himself this much with anyone in a long time. He looked into Sara's eyes. "I can't take you home, not yet. Please, spend a little more time with me?"

"I shouldn't," Sara replied. "Amber will be worried."

Tony laughed. "How old we have become. Our children worry about us gone too long on a date?"

Sara laughed. "You're right. Okay, a little longer. Why don't we find a bench in a park? We can talk like we would have when we were just a boy and a girl in New York."

Tony found a bench in a nearby park, under a mossy oak tree. He sat, and Sara joined him. "I haven't talked to anyone like this in a long time," he said, dropping his hand uncertainly over hers. He was surprised she did not pull her hand away.

They sat together, held hands, and seemed to grow younger and younger with each passing minute.

When it was time to go, Sara said, "This has been great, Tony. I never lost the spark for you, not even after all these years." She slid closer to him.

Tony kissed Sara gently on the cheek. "I have to see you again. Let me take you to dinner tomorrow night? Next time, it'll be Italian. I'll have a surprise for you." It seemed like an hour he waited for her answer.

Sara said, "I would love that." She then aimed her eyes at his. "But promise me, you won't tell Peroni I'm here."

Tony had almost forgotten about Azzurro.

Sara continued. "You said he's your friend, but you can't tell him about Amber. It would destroy her to know that her father is a mobster."

Tony nodded.

That night, in his bed, Tony could not sleep. He kept seeing Sara's face looking down at a corpse on the ground. He could not see the dead man's face, so he didn't know if it was Peroni or him lying in the spreading puddle of blood.

Chapter 25

Margarita Gose picked up the buzzing cell phone, "Hello?"

Using a distortion device, a man said, "You have confidence in this douche bag you're working with down there?"

Margarita pushed her long blonde hair back over her forehead. "Barfright is okay, but he's involved in some other shit."

"We know. Barfright was into gun-running, but that's beside the point. We just need him to make the pickup and get the product to his contacts in Miami." The voice paused.

Margarita felt dampness under her arms. A call like this made her long for a spoonful of coke.

"And then he needs to get the money back to you, and you get it back to us. Got it?"

"Yeah, I got it. But once Barfright leaves here, I don't have any control over him."

"You better, or your past activities become visible to the DEA and the FBI." The disembodied voice continued, "After you get the cash, the dirtbag needs to vanish. We put a locker key in your mailbox. Go to the Post America office on Morse Boulevard after hours and pick up the package. It's untraceable. Make it a clean kill. When it's over, throw the evidence in Lake Okahumpka, or whatever you call that damn lake. Barfright has made enough enemies to point them local cops in a ton of different directions."

Margarita thought of arguing for Danny's life. For a second.

"Click." The phone went dead.

Margarita stared at the phone in her hand. Did she want to knock off Danny?

Margarita's next move was to get in touch with Barfright and make sure he was clear on his role and the timeline. She dialed his number.

There was no answer, not even a way to leave a message. The phone on the other end just kept ringing.

"What the hell? Where is he?" Margarita threw the phone on the living room couch. It bounced harmlessly to the floor. "Goddammit!" Thoughts of how she got into this mess flooded her brain. Where the hell was he? She had to regain her self-control to formalize the next steps. She reviewed what she already did. She had made sure Danny had the coded message on where and when to make the pick-up. She had gone over and over with him the exact timeline they needed to keep the Miami boys satisfied. "Shit!" She sat back on the couch, realizing now that Miami would never be happy until Danny was gone. Getting rid of him was the only way she could stay safe and keep her operation going. "What a damn mess."

The big mistake she made was when she brought up the scheme to Danny in the first place. A fall guy was critical to the plan. It had to be someone with a shady background. Her sources told her that Danny was connected to the New York Mafia. The rumor was he split from the Gaspo gang to freelance in blood diamonds. Later he moved on to arms smuggling, a trade even riskier than drug running. Drug cartels were ruthless, but gun buyers — most insurgents or terrorists — were much worse. Had she known he was in that racket, she never would have involved him. Her past life choices threw her into this pool of quicksand, and the more she struggled to get out, the faster she sank. She had to get ahold of Barfright to make sure this deal went through without a hitch. And then, he needed to disappear. No choice.

Margarita went to the fridge. She cracked open a can of *Wicked Weed Pernicious*, looked at the can's label, and thought, *how appropriate*. She took the ale to the sofa, put her feet on the hassock, and leaned back for some serious contemplation. Since returning to 'the business,' Margarita discovered that 'the life' was much more dangerous than it was in the old days. No one retired with a gold watch. If there was a gold watch, it was dropped into the coffin before somebody sealed the lid. A wise person in this business had an exit strategy.

Margarita took a long swig of the cold ale. In two days, Danny would hand her two duffle bags full of cash. That might be just the right time to pull the trigger on Plan B.

Chapter 26

The night was perfect for a romantic date. Rose-colored clouds in the west were darkening, and stars sparkled in the late evening sky. The air was cooling in the sunset, and the scent of orange blossoms floated on a mild breeze.

When her phone rang, Sara answered quickly. "Hi," Sara said, knowing it was Tony.

"It's me," Tony whispered. "I'm about a minute away."

"I'll be right out."

Amber, hearing her mother on the phone, asked, "Is that your date, Mom?"

"It's not a date, dear. It's just dinner with an old friend."

Amber smiled at her mother. "It doesn't look like a 'dinner with an old friend.' It looks like a date. By the way, that dress looks great on you. Quite a bit of cleavage for dinner with an old friend?"

Sara blushed and pulled up the dress bodice on her way to the door.

"Have him come in. I'd like to meet the man dating my Mom. Are his intentions honorable?"

"Bye. Don't wait up."

Tony's face conveyed his nervousness and excitement. He had on his best Villages sportswear, dressy but casual, bought for the night. When he saw Sara, in a low-cut, red, clinging dress, he stuttered. "You look . . . lovely."

Sara smiled like a teenager as she hopped into the golf cart. "Where are you taking me in your chariot?"

Tony laughed. "There's a little Italian place behind the big square. Quiet and out of the way."

"Great. I feel Italian tonight," Sara said as she settled next to Tony.

Within minutes, they were in a back booth at Mezza Luna Italian restaurant. He stared intently at the woman in front him. "Sara, I would . . ."

"Tony, before we go any further, I have to ask you something. Okay?"

"Sure. What is it?"

"Are you Mafia?"

His face fell as if he had been struck by a bullet. Sara's heart seemed to slow as she awaited his answer.

"I ran away from the mob once. I don't ever want to get near that life again," she told him quietly.

Tony gazed into Sara's eyes. "I figured we would have to talk about this sometime. I was in the gang. You know that. But that's all over now." He took a deep breath before he continued. "I'm retired from all that. I'm down here looking for a place to settle down."

"Oh, Tony, that's good to hear." Sara relaxed and felt her heart beat normally again. "Now you wanted to say something before I went off. Go ahead."

"Sara, I've been thinking this for forty years, so I just need to say it. I loved you in high school. I think I always loved you. We have so little time left. I want to spend as much of mine as I can with you."

Sara sat back.

"I would like you to go to Key West with me . . . for a few days."

Sara nearly choked on her wine. "Tony, it's too fast. I have to think about it."

"We haven't time to think. In a week, you're going back to California. At our age, we may never have time to be together again. As the poet said:

Gather ye rosebuds while ye may,
Old Time is still a-flying;
And this same flower that smiles today..."

She dropped her head and finished the poem, "Tomorrow we will be dying."

Tony smiled and took out a brochure from his pocket. He handed it to her. "This is an advertisement for Mallory Square, in Key West, the southernmost point of these United States. I've booked two rooms in an Inn off Duval Street. Come away with me for a few days?"

When she did not answer, he hurriedly added, "There is no commitment other than to be with me for just two days."

Chapter 27

Beer Buddy Tuesday was another sunny, hot day —
perfect for a few cold ones. Nathan arrived well before
the scheduled meeting time. He sat on a bench in the town square
opposite World of Beer. Using skills from his years of fighting in
the bush, he chose a position where he could observe anyone
entering or leaving through the pub's main entrance without being
easily seen.

Learning Danny was the man behind Horizon
International's dealings in Africa was fresh in his mind. He had
immediately started developing his plan for revenge. He accepted
what Sam divulged about Barfright, but had yet to formulate a plan
to take out the arms merchant without being found out by the
police.

Nathan wanted more information. He wanted a simple,
quick method, one certain to produce the desired results with the
least risk of exposure. One option was at home. He kept the trusty,
short-magazine, Lee-Enfield sniper rifle he used in Africa stored in
his bedroom closet behind his bathrobe. The gun was
manufactured before he was born, but Nathan trusted its
destructive power and accuracy. He had dispatched countless
enemies with this deadly weapon in the Veldt along the Zambezi
river. A well placed .303 round from a preserve along a little-used
golf cart path would do the trick. The problems were in knowing
where the target would be and when. The larger problem was
devising a way to extract himself without being noticed after the
gunshot. The bullet would scream assassination by a pro, a military
man.

The town square clock tolled the hour. The Beer Buddies
would be gathering.

116

Nathan caught sight of Sam Adams and Danny Barfright approaching World of Beer at the same time. As they met at the door, Nathan began his walk to the entrance.

Sam opened the door to let Danny enter World of Beer first, then followed.

Nathan considered another option as he walked. An everyday household item that could be utilized as a weapon would be better. Anyone, even an enraged woman, could become a suspect. A golf club … or a baseball bat, maybe. Something he could keep in a car without raising suspicion. Something easy to explain, needed for one of the regularly scheduled events in the retirement community. Portability also offered the advantage of ready, quick access whenever an opportunity to be alone with the target presented itself. Just go to the car, retrieve the innocuous weapon, and dispose of the double-dealing piece-of-shit.

Nathan, still deep in thought, pulled open the pub's door and entered the air-conditioned interior.

The Beer Buddies were at their regular table.

As Nathan walked in, a smile formed on his face. "Hey, guys. How's it hanging?"

Several of the buddies waved and smiled.

Nathan selected a seat next to Sam, not far from Danny. He wondered how much of an ally Sam was.

Sam chatted away as if nothing was wrong between Danny and him.

Nathan smiled but thought he had no problem killing Danny. Hell, the bastard deserved it. Still, every op needs an extraction plan. An ambush without an escape route could be devastating. He turned to Tony, "Do you want to play some golf? Danny plays every week. Right, Danny?"

Danny put his beer mug down. "Every Wednesday morning, as regular as clockwork."

"Is there anything else you like to do regularly?" Nathan asked.

Danny grinned, "Yeah, Nathan. I like to screw women."

Honey nearly dropped her tray at the remark. The look on her face conveyed disgust.

Danny burst into rude laughter. "Unlike some guys here, I still can."

Sam shot a look at Nathan, and then laughed as well.

Nathan forced himself to laugh. *I hate the crude sonofabitch*, he thought, glancing at Honey. He was surprised, spotting the look of disgust on her face. Another reason to erase this pig off the Earth. A damn good reason.

THE

INVESTIGATION

Chapter 28

Bush drove at breakneck speed to the called-in crime scene. He pulled off the blacktop and parked along the berm of County Road 466 near what looked like a fleet of emergency vehicles, their red and blue lights flashing.

Exiting his truck, he walked some fifty yards into the woods along the golfcart trail. There he ran into the crime scene investigation unit. He was surprised to see the sheriff already there. "Sheriff," he said, approaching the yellow tape marking the scene. He almost fell over when he saw the body. Bile rose in his throat.

Sheriff Marsha Tuborg looked up. "Busch, did someone tell me you know this guy?"

Busch rolled his tongue in his mouth and looked away from the battered face. "If his ID shows him to be Danny Barfright, yep, I know him."

"How do you know this man? What can you tell me about him?"

They were logical questions, fair questions. Busch told Tuborg the little he knew of his drinking friend, surprised himself that too many of his answers to Tuborg came up, "I don't know."

"We don't have many murders in Sumter County, so I'm going to need you to help," Tuborg said. "I'm overseeing this investigation myself."

Busch wasn't sure he was up to the task. Yes, he had been a detective for many years; but it had been almost two decades since he was called on for a murder investigation. He spent most of his time on the job checking out property crimes — vandalism, criminal trespass, theft, burglary, and the like. And the former Vietnam veteran doubted that his other part-time jobs — auto mechanic and ersatz beer drinker — qualified him to solve a murder. A few minutes later, when the Captain pinned him as her field investigator, he protested, but it did him no good. Tuborg carried the day, as usual. "I am the Captain," she said, ending the discussion and leaving him at the scene.

The forensic team arrived and began working. After pondering the coroner's advice that he should not venture a look, Busch looked. From that horrifying moment, it was the way he would always remember Danny. It had the makings of a nightmare.

The coroner's voice droned on. "The deceased, male, late fifties or sixties, Caucasian, was struck by multiple blows to the head. From the injuries, the blows were vicious, furious, enraged attacks. It was probably a blow to the back of his head that caused the victim's eyes to resemble two golf balls." He looked at Busch and added, "Bloody ones at that."

"Did he know his killer," Busch asked, worried he might also know the murderer.

"Can't say," the coroner replied. "If the first assault came from behind, the deceased most likely did not see his killer." He looked up from the bloody mess. "That's my preliminary judgment. The attacker came from behind."

Busch cringed at the sight of Danny's mangled face. His single gold incisor sparkled obscenely under a smashed *Bud Light* can perched on his forehead.

The coroner continued. "Not a drop of blood, nor any other discernible injury mars the victim's body south of his neck."

Busch bent lower.

"No visible injury below the subject's waist," the coroner said in a robot-like tone. "Cover him up. Get him to the lab."

Busch watched as two men in white hazmat suits sealed the corpse in a black body bag. That was someone I knew, he thought. Is the killer also someone I know?

The coroner's hand on his shoulder startled Busch. "Whoever did this wasn't after money," he muttered.

Busch wondered what kind of ghoul a man had to be to want to be a coroner as he stared down at his shadow on the black plastic bag. He cast his eyes over the crime scene, now crawling with cops. Like it or not about being put in charge, Deputy Bumphrey Pillsbusch Frapp knew where his search for suspects should begin. He prayed silently that none of his Beer Buddies turned out to be the brutal killer.

Chapter 29

The crime scene investigation unit, with Busch in charge, had nearly wrapped up the search for clues.

Sheriff Tuborg had just returned. After hearing from Busch that the team had completed their investigation of the murder site, she was about to order the removal of Danny's body and the yellow crime scene tape when four black Cadillac Escalades with dark-tinted windows pulled up. The big vehicles blocked both ends of the cart path. "Who the hell is that?" Tuborg demanded.

Busch shrugged.

The passenger door of the first vehicle opened. A tall man, impeccably dressed in a black suit with a black tie and a black fedora, stood imperiously looking up at the cart path. He wore black sunglasses with gold rims, and his face looked like it never smiled. As he made it to the crime scene, he reached inside his coat and pulled out a gold shield. He announced in a booming bass voice, "Supervising Chief Inspector Detective Oskar Blue, Federal Bureau of Investigation."

The few local cops, and Busch, froze in the officer's presence.

A woman stepped out of the driver's side of the lead Escalade. She was a slightly shorter, curvier, dark-skinned, black woman with the same imposing manner as the FBI inspector. Her black suit pants were skin-tight, and her white shirt strained at the buttons over her breasts. Black reflective sunglasses hid her eyes. Unlike the inspector, she was not wearing a fedora. Her hair, long, thick, and black, was pulled into a bun, as tight as her jaws.

Distinctive but tasteful silver stud earrings, each shaped like a pistol, accentuated each earlobe.

Supervising Chief Inspector Detective Blue boomed, "This is Assistant Supervising Chief Inspector Detective Guinness."

Guinness held out her badge for inspection. Her badge was every bit as impressive as her boss's, only smaller.

"What have we here?" asked Blue, striding through a gap in the yellow crime-scene tape.

"Well," said Sheriff Tuborg, "Somebody bludgeoned the victim, and then poured beer over his body."

"Beer?" The FBI man glanced at Guinness. "Nice work, Sheriff. My team will take it from here."

Tuborg looked angry, but stepped aside.

Blue uncovered the body and stooped down to take a closer look. Peering down at the corpse's skin, the Supervising Chief Inspector Detective put his finger in a tiny puddle of liquid, lifted it to his nose, and sniffed. He then put the finger in his mouth. "From the residual carbonation, I'd say the murder occurred between one and three a.m. last night."

A gasp of admiration arose from everyone present.

Busch whispered to Tuborg, "He tasted blood. Yuck!"

"Shhh," Tuborg hissed. "It was just beer, deputy!"

"And," Blue continued, "I can confirm this is *Bud Light*. It has a slightly fruitier taste than *Miller Lite*." He looked defiantly at the locals. "It is not imported. This crime looks like the work of the Cereal Killer!"

"Serial killer?" Tuborg asked.

"C-E-R-E-A-L," Blue spelled for her. "His murders have the signature of beer poured over the victim. Beer is, of course, a fermentation of malted cereal grain. Although . . ." He dipped his finger in the pool at the base of the victim's throat and tasted it again. "This beer is, I believe, brewed from rice."

Those assembled gasped again.

Busch poked Tuborg. "He did it again."

Blue sniffed his finger and announced, "Rice is a cereal grain, as is sorghum — which makes even worse beer than rice."

Tuborg asked, "Any chance it's a copycat murderer, Supervising Chief Inspector Detective?"

"None," said Blue. "And you needn't use my full title. I'll be working with your department. We don't stand on formality."

"Yes, Sir, detective."

"Chief Detective," Blue promptly corrected. "I will need a liaison with your department. The liaison need not be a senior member of your department, but he should be competent. Not necessarily your most competent, but an able investigator. Just don't give us some smartass that will only interfere with our work."

"Busch," barked Tuborg, "you'll work with Detect . . . I mean, Chief Detective Blue."

"Oh, shit," Busch said, nodding yes to Tuborg.

"And you better not fuck this up," Tuborg said and drew her finger across her throat.

Busch knew precisely what she meant.

Chapter 30

Busch was not rattled easily, but Danny's brutal murder shook him. After decades in the sheriff's office, he had become resigned to nothing ever happening in this paradise. Sometimes, he complained of how tedious his work as a deputy was. He never expected murder to hit this close to home. Be careful what you wish for, he thought.

It's not that he was especially close to, or even, fond of Danny Barfright. But he knew Danny. Like clockwork, Danny showed up week after week as the gang tipped back a brew or two, sharing laughs and commiserating over their lives in retirement. But Danny was a little different, often distant, secretive. Still, Busch did not peg him as a bad guy, the future victim of a bloody murder. He was more of a paradox — sometimes gregarious to a fault; other times, private and sullen, suddenly clamming up. Barfright was a puzzle. One thing was now sure: Danny was either the victim of a random act of horrific violence or the object of someone's revenge, deep hatred, uncontrolled anger. To him, that battered face suggested the latter. What could Danny have done to deserve the horrible bludgeoning?

Even worse, Busch had reason to suspect that their circle of Tuesday afternoon friends, the Beer Buddies, might include a ruthless killer. As far as he knew, they were Danny's only friends in the area. He could not recall Danny speaking of other colleagues, chums, a prior marriage, a girlfriend, kids, or even former Sunday School pals. Nope. Danny played his cards close. Even with the FBI barging into the case, Sheriff Tuborg insisted that Busch continue with his investigation into Danny's murder.

Now that the body had been positively identified, he knew he would have to look at Danny's friends — his friends — as suspects. *Was it even imaginable that one of the Beer Buddies could be Danny's killer?* Busch had been up to his eyeballs in this investigation for almost a week. He wished that he had not gotten out of bed this morning. This would be the day he would confront the Beer Buddies.

Pulling into the parking lot of World of Beer, Busch noted the familiar cars. He focused on the '66 Mustang, Amber's wreck. The mechanic in him wasn't sure how her old fugitive from a junkyard negotiated the roundabouts on Buena Vista Boulevard, even after repairing it for her countless times. He prided himself on his ability to keep the old Mustang on the road for her. He was happy to help Amber. Was she now a suspect too?

This case is bad, real bad, he thought, hesitating at the door. For once, he wasn't looking forward to being here, to seeing his old 'Buddies.'

It took a moment for Busch's eyes to adjust to the bar's subdued lighting. He headed straight for the Beer Buddies' hang-out, passing the nest of pool tables just as Margarita dropped the eight ball into a corner pocket to the cheers of her admirers. "Nice shot," he said.

Margarita nodded to Busch, taking a second glance at his police uniform. "I'll be there in a moment, deputy," she said with what sounded like a smirk. "I love a man in uniform."

There were times Margarita's snarky attitude pissed Busch off, but not today. "Make haste, Mrs. Mosconi," he shot back, a reference to her considerable skills with that long pink hardwood she was stroking.

Margarita grinned.

Busch arrived at the table. He was not looking forward to confronting the others with the news. There was only one empty chair and it had Margarita's name on it. It gave him another reason to remain standing, his preferred posture for the announcement he was about to make.

The gang was all present — except for Danny. Empties littered the table along with coasters, mugs, car keys, cell phones, and an eclectic collection of other barroom detritus.

"Hey, you're in uniform," Amber commented. "You look nice."

Sam and Bud kept yakking together. Tony wolfed down what remained of a pizza crust. He wiped his mouth with a linen napkin, something on which he always insisted.

Just as Busch was about to speak, Honey appeared tray in hand and started collecting empty glasses.

Bud said, "Hey, sweetheart, another round for everybody, and an order of mozzarella sticks."

Honey smiled. "You got it, big man. You dealing Margarita in, too?"

"Of course, pumpkin. We gotta loosen Mags up if I'm going to stop her from running the pool table in a bit."

The others laughed.

"Yeah, right," Margarita chimed in as she took her seat. "Make mine a *Mich Ultra* this time. I can see I have some work to do later, don't I, Bud?"

"Shit, Mags. I like your moves any way you make them, dear. Anyhow, if I can't take you down, Danny will." He looked over the table. "Hey, where is Danny today?"

Busch removed his hat. "Danny won't be here today. Danny won't be back at all." He paused, observing their reactions.

"Don't tell me you arrested his sorry ass," Sam asked.

Busch noted who asked the question and continued, "Danny is dead." He caught the shocked expressions on their faces. Was one faking? "That body they found last week on a cart path in the woods — we just got a positive identification on it. It was Danny. Someone murdered our Beer Buddy, folks, and it wasn't pretty."

Jaws dropped around the table. Tony spat a piece of unchewed crust from his mouth and relegated it to his linen napkin. Amber's eyes welled up so fast with tears that she could not get to her Kleenex soon enough. Nathan reached to his right and gently covered, then patted Amber's hand with his own. Bud sat back in his chair, folding his arms tightly across his substantial chest. Margarita shook her head in disbelief as her eyes sized up each of the Beer Buddies. Her also not insubstantial chest heaved. Sam fiddled with the settings on his hearing aid, but he stared straight ahead. "What did you say?" he asked, peering at Busch.

Busch said it slower and louder, "Danny is dead. He was murdered. I'm afraid I'm facing a table full of suspects."

You could have heard a pin drop but for the haunting music on the jukebox. Someone had plunked in a quarter, and a tenor voice sang "Danny Boy."

Busch wished he knew which of the friends, looking at him with such innocent and puzzled faces, had such a warped sense of humor. *Which one killed and mutilated Danny Barfright?*

Chapter 31

The remainder of the afternoon was strangely subdued. Sam Adams attempted to poke fun at Bud Schweitzer, comparing the cup in his jockstrap to the bras in his now-defunct factory. His humor produced little more than a pitiful chuckle from Tony.

Nathan tried to interest the drinkers in his exploits fishing for tiger fish on the Zambezi, but the gang's conversation did not stray far from the man who would not be at the table — Danny Barfright.

As the afternoon wore on, Busch watched the table of friends and suspects. The spirit of those present sagged more than the stock market after a housing bubble burst.

"Well, I think that's it for me. A Stouffer's Double Meat Lasagna with my name on it is calling from my freezer," Tony said. He set an empty bottle of *Funky Buddha Eternal Summer Blonde Ale* back on the table. "I'm outta here."

Busch noted that Tony was the first to leave and that he was hungry. A heartless killer might get hungry, he thought.

As Tony stood up, a chill wafted through the bar. Four men in suits entered World of Beer and spread out stealthily. Everyone in the bar stopped their conversations to pay attention.

Tony stiffened. "I smell cops."

Two of the suited men walked to an end of the bar, which ran the length of the room. They came to attention, their sunglass-covered eyes surveying their area. A third man took up a position at a table near the rear exit. The fourth stood next to the front entrance.

"What the hell is going on?" Amber asked.

Nathan said quietly, "An ambush."

When the officers were in position, a strikingly curvaceous black woman wearing sunglasses, Assistant Detective Guinness, entered. Supervising Chief Inspector Detective Oskar Blue, in a crisp black suit and fedora, followed her through the door.

Busch sighed. "Not again."

Blue grunted and strode directly to Busch. "Detective Frapp," he said, without a hint of a smile.

"Inspector Detective Blue." Busch didn't bother jumping to attention.

"Chief Detective," Blue corrected.

"Right. Chief Detective. I wasn't expecting to see you here today."

"That is the point, isn't it?" Blue commented curtly. While he said it ostensibly to Busch, as he talked, his eyes, barely visible behind the dark lenses of his glasses, darted to the individuals seated at the Beer Buddies table. "I am an expert at the element of surprise. Surprise!"

"I never thought of that," Busch replied. "What can I do for you? Do you need me for something?"

"You can introduce me to the group."

Busch, slightly flustered, said, "Guys, this is Detective . . . I mean Chief Detective Oskar Blue, FBI. Detective . . . aah, Chief Detective Blue is in charge of the investigation into Danny's murder."

There was a low murmur and some shifting in seats as Blue straightened to his full height. "Good afternoon."

Nobody replied.

Blue smiled. "I'm glad you're all here. I want to set your minds at ease. You need not worry. I can tell you now, you're not suspects."

Busch looked surprised.

There was a gasp of relief.

Blue continued. "We have ascertained that Mr. Barfright was a victim of the Cereal Killer."

There were more gasps at the table.

Blue nodded. "You have, no doubt, heard of the ghastly and horrific murders across the United States?"

Blank faces stared at the detective.

"Never heard of him," Tony said.

"I wish I never heard of Blue," Busch muttered.

Blue sighed. He raised the thumb and forefinger of his right hand to his chin and rubbed it like he was checking a plum for ripeness or searching for a whisker he missed while shaving that morning. He cleared his throat. "The Cereal Killer is a madman, a sociopath with a narcissistic complex. We believe he suffers from being weaned too early from breastfeeding. In short, he is the kind of person you might find at a Barry Manilow tribute concert."

A collective gasp escaped from the assembled bar denizens.

"I love Barry Manilow," Sam said, tapping his hearing aid on the tabletop.

Blue continued, "I have been on this nefarious killer's trail since his first murder in Milwaukee. From there, he went to the beer capitals of the country: Boston, Tumwater Washington, Golden Colorado, Kankakee, Genesee, St. Louis — everywhere men make great beer."

"Why didn't you catch him yet?" Bud asked. "He killed our friend."

Blue glared at Bud. "His completely random selection of subjects to kill rendered him un-catchable. Up to now! But like all serial killers (s-e-r-i-a-l), the Cereal Killer (C-e-r-e-a-l) has a fatal flaw." He paused, watching their reactions. "This warped individual's particular compulsion is to degrade his victims. The significant feature of his M.O.is something from his past which drives this sicko to pour beer on each of his victims."

"What a waste of good beer," Tony said.

"He must be a schmuck," Sam replied.

Blue nodded. "He marked his first kill by pouring *Angry Orchard Cider* over the dead man."

"Cider?" Tony gasped. "That's a damn insult."

"Yes, cider." Blue shook his head. "He doused his second victim in *O'Doul's* non-alcoholic beer."

"No!" Nathan said, "Can you imagine going to the grave drenched in *O'Doul's*?"

Blue nodded. "I'm afraid it's true. We believe he is trying to mock his victims' virility by dousing them in beer substitutes. His last victim, before Mr. Barfright, was covered in *Zima*."

"You gotta stop this sick guy," Bud exclaimed.

Blue replied, "We've been staking out liquor stores in the southeast that sell alcoholic seltzer, but he confounded our trap by skipping seltzer and going right to *Bud Light*." He raised his index finger in the air. "We will catch him. But he is cunning and nefarious."

"Is there anything we can do to help you apprehend Danny's killer?" Bud asked.

Blue shook his head. "I'm afraid not, sir. He has moved on." He turned to Busch. "I'm leaving Detective Busch here to wrap up the paperwork related to Mr. Barfright's murder. Please help him if he asks for your assistance. Mr. Barfright was, I believe, a random selection. Barfright happened to be in the wrong place at the wrong time. If you have any comments or concerns, voice them to Detective Busch." He turned to Busch and saluted smartly. "You are now in charge of wrapping this up. We are counting on you." Blue turned, and then walked to the bar door.

With Blue's closing remark, all of the FBI men left the bar. Only Assistant Detective Guinness lingered.

"Assistant Detective Guinness, we're leaving now," Blue called.

Near the end of Blue's speech, Margarita had gone back to the pool tables. She was bent over, stretched out, lining up a bank shot, boobs dangling over the felt.

Assistant Detective Guinness was engaged in inspecting Margarita's form, apparently interested in some undercover work herself.

"Assistant Detective!" Blue barked. "We are leaving now."

"Right, sir," Guinness replied, turning slowly from her own investigation, her silver pistol earrings sparkling in the soft light coming from the lamp above the pool table.

After the FBI left, Busch heard a collective sigh of relief. *They think they're in the clear*, he realized.

"Nobody leaves," Busch's voice echoed through the bar, interrupting the Beer Buddies' return to drinking and chatting. "You've got to all stay here until I wrap this up."

Bud jumped out of his seat. "Who died and made you God?" he bellowed.

Busch walked over to Bud and put his eyes inches from the coach's nose. "The FBI," he replied. "Until this case is closed, nobody goes nowhere, no how."

An hour later, Busch had to leave.

The others trickled out of the bar behind him. Amber asked in a trembling voice, "Do you think the Cereal Killer might still be lurking around here?"

Back at his house, a short time later, Bud was a jumble of nerves. Danny was dead. The sneaky traitor would not be telling the Beer Buddies about his fetish. The FBI said it was the work of some serial killer called, oddly enough, the Cereal Killer. Would there still be an investigation? Everyone knew Danny said he was going to Bud's house that afternoon. The police might get wind of that and decide to check it out. Hopefully, it would be Busch, his good friend.

Bud thought of what he could say. He would tell the police that Danny left his house. He said he was going to Dunkin Donuts. People had seen him there. Bud wouldn't be found to be the last person to see Danny alive. Yes, people in the store would remember Danny. There would probably be a transaction on Danny's credit card. The employees in the store would report that Danny entered and left alone.

Yes, there might be suspicion at first. Still, if Bud kept to his story that Danny left right after looking at his memorabilia, nobody would be able to prove anything different. All he had to do was stick to his account of what happened.

Confident again, Bud hid the female garments. He replaced Joe Namath's helmet on its wall bracket, admiring the souvenir of a bygone era. Now, to replace the 'Stan the Man' bat.

Where was Stan Musial's bat? Bud looked on the floor, under the couch. He checked his living room. "The cart. I must have left it there." He hurried to the garage.

The bat was not in the cart. It was not anywhere in the garage.

Bud sagged to the floor. *Where is the bat?*

Chapter 32

It was like trying to schedule a dental appointment. Even though somebody murdered his chum, Busch thought Bud was dodging an interview like a man avoiding the plague, or the 'beer drinkers' flu.' What did they call it? The Corona Virus?

Busch called several times and left messages on Schweitzer's phone. He emailed. He had the secretaries from the sheriff's office reach out without success. He had even bumped into Sam and Nathan and asked them to relay messages to their friend. But no dice. *What is Schweitzer hiding?*

Busch did not like stakeouts. Appropriating his Ford pick-up for the job, he parked just up the street from Bud's home. The truck wouldn't look out of place in this neighborhood, but a squad car would. He listened to melodies of the '60s streaming from his favorite radio station, WORM 950. A short newscast interrupted the music, and after the latest update on a flurry of presidential tweets, there was this segment:

> In other news, a spokesperson for the Sumter County Sheriff's Office confirmed today that an investigation into last week's murder is continuing. The police have identified the body as that of Danny Barfright, of The Villages, found along a forest road in Sumter County near the Village of Fenney. The cause of death has not been disclosed, and the Sheriff's

Office confirmed that there currently are no suspects. Investigators are asking for the public's cooperation. Anyone with information, contact the Sheriff's Office.

Coming up next, the weather, after this important message from the brewers of *Citra Ass Down Pale Ale.*

We made the big-time, Busch thought, prepared for a lengthy stakeout.

Suddenly, Bud appeared, leaving by a side door. He wore gray warm-up sweats and a white tank, most likely headed to the garage for a workout. *This won't be so tough after all.* Busch strolled from his truck to Bud's garage. He rapped on the door frame. Bud was looking for something on his tool bench.

Busch barked, "Hey, stranger, how you doin'?"

Bud whirled toward Busch, eyebrows raised. "Buschie, my man, you found me. I should have worked harder trying to avoid you." He chuckled. "To what do I owe the pleasure?"

"Oh, ya know, same old, same old. The boss has me working Danny's case. Just doing my due diligence. I'd rather not have this assignment. I mean, he was one of us, you know, Tuesday afternoons, and all. But somebody's gotta do it. So, I'm the poor sucker having to question my drinking buddies. It's all routine." He was easing into things.

"So, that's all you wanted? To talk to me about old Danny boy?"

"Well, Danny boy, as you like to call him, isn't going to be coming back. Is he?"

"No. I guess not. It's a shame what happened. I've been thinking about the guy day and night." Bud walked toward his workout bench, carrying a pair of fifteen-pound hand weights. "Who would have such an ax to grind that they needed to kill him? I mean, he had his little — what? — peccadillos? But he was a nice enough guy." He sat on the bench facing Busch.

Busch removed a ball-peen hammer from a wall bracket and examined it. "Actually, my friend, I need to ask you some questions. Do you mind?" He replaced the hammer.

Bud looked up at Busch. He set the weights down at his feet. "What kind of questions? You don't think I had anything to do with it, do you? Shit, man. Do I need a lawyer?"

Busch shook his head. "Mr. Schweitzer, you collect baseball trinkets, don't cha?" He looked apologetic. "I gotta make it sound official."

Bud frowned. "Well, I collect sports memorabilia, if that's what you mean. What's that got to do with anything?"

"I recall hearing you go on and on about a bat — a baseball bat — that you claim is a collector's item. Am I right?"

"Well, yeah, my Stan Musial. It's a beauty. You want to see it? I still don't understand what this has to do with anything. Level with me here, Buschie. What's this all about?" Bud got up from the weight bench and walked toward a pile of worn tires stacked in a corner. "Normally, I keep this baby on display in my trophy room, but it's been here in the garage for a while."

Busch was now getting somewhere. Honey had told him she recalled Barfright saying he was going to Schweitzer's place to see the famous bat, just before the murder. He said to Bud, "The coroner says Danny's death was due to blunt force trauma. Hell of a way to go."

Bud stared at Busch. "That's why you asked about my Stan Musial? You think there's blood on it or something? Damn it, man, you aren't very subtle. And you ain't going to find no blood on my pride and joy, I promise. I was showing it to Danny the afternoon of the day somebody killed him. I'm sure the others will tell you that Danny was coming to my place to see the bat that afternoon."

"That was mentioned. Yeah."

"Well, they were correct. Danny left in a hurry, though. Said he had to get home before dark. He was going to stop at Dunkin Donuts on the way home. Well, in all the rush, I neglected to put the bat away. I left it here in the garage near the tires. It would normally be in my trophy room…"

"I'd like to see it," Busch said.

Bud reached down into the center of the tire stack. "What the hell? Is this some kind of joke?" He stuck his head in the opening to get a better look in the low light.

Busch walked closer. "What are you talking about?"

"My Stan Musial. It's gone. It has to be here, but it's not." Bud had a look of panic on his face. "Buschie, level with me. What's going on? Did you take it? Is this a cop trick?"

If Bud was Danny's killer, the coach was also a damn good actor, Busch thought. "Look, Bud, it's not my job to tell you all about this investigation. But blunt force trauma and you bragging to all the Buddies about a baseball bat. I'm just checking out leads. Like I said, due diligence. So, where is your prized possession?" He shot Bud a look that showed he meant business.

Bud was sweating. "Buschie, honest to God, I don't know where my Musial is. You gotta believe me. I'm telling you it was here!" He stopped to take a deep breath. He looked at Busch. "I need you to believe I had nothing to do with what happened to Danny. I swear it on my mother's grave."

"Let us keep your mother out of this. Okay? You didn't answer my question. Where's the damn bat?" Busch scrutinized a face drowning in sweat.

Bud yelled, "Look, I don't know where my bat is. Ya' hear me? If I find the son of a bitch who took it, he's dead." He caught himself before he said worse. "You know what I mean. I mean, he ain't really dead. I ain't capable of killing anyone. But he's gonna be sorry he took my Musial."

Busch almost believed Bud was upset about losing his bat. "When's the last time you saw the bat here?"

Bud glanced at Busch and seemed to struggle to control his anger. He turned his eyes to a vintage cathedral radio on a high shelf, still tuned to AM-950, now playing an old Eric Clapton favorite, "I Shot the Sheriff."

Bud's face lit up and he turned to Busch. "Wait! I just remembered something. The night Danny was killed, Nathan was here." His eyes darted to Busch. "You remember when I mentioned one Tuesday that I ordered too many pavers for my patio project? Well, Nathan said he could use them. I'm not sure what for. I told him he could have them just for hauling them away. He came over

138

that night for the pavers. I had about a hundred of them stacked just outside the garage."

"So, Nathan was here?" Busch knew Nathan had been a soldier and was more than capable of murder.

Bud rambled, smiling idiotically. "Nathan came over driving that damn Gremlin. Honest to God, that's an ugly car. Before he started loading the pavers, we came here, into the garage. We shared a couple of the beers I had set out to drink with Danny." He saw Busch's eyes blink. "Yeah, I remember now. Nathan saw the bat by the tires and asked about it. When I told him it was the Musial, he took it outside and held it up to the light. We chatted for a while over a beer after he loaded all the pavers into the back of his Gremlin."

"Gremlin? I thought he owned a Range Rover."

"He does, but he is so proud of that Range Rover, he never takes it out of his garage. Besides, it is one of those African bush rovers. It's uglier than his Gremlin."

Busch said, "You may be right. Nathan is a 'car guy,' and you know how they are. Anyway, you say he took your bat outside?"

"Yeah. He was fascinated that I had a Musial. After he pawed it a while and took a couple of swings, he put it back down. At least, I thought he did."

"So, he brought the bat back?"

"I think so. My Musial was standing right here in the corner, where I left it. I think so." Bud looked nervous. "I had a few beers."

Busch nodded. "So, Nathan knew where that bat was the day someone clobbered Danny. Did anyone else know?"

"Everyone knows I have Stan Musial's bat, and they know I keep it on display in my trophy room."

"But Nathan saw it in your garage?"

Bud nodded. "But wait. There's more. Just a couple of minutes after Nathan left, I was in my kitchen, washing my hands. I always wash them for at least twenty seconds. Nathan stuck his head in the door to tell me he forgot his gloves and was going to grab them from the garage. I told him no problem. I stayed in the kitchen. I wasn't finished Pureling. I guess he went to the garage for his gloves. He didn't come back. He just took off again." He looked at Busch. "Do you see what I'm getting at?"

"You think Nathan stole your bat?"

"Nathan knew where the Musial was. The last time I saw it was when he was here to pick up my pavers."

Busch glanced around the garage again, and then aimed his eyes at Bud's sweating face. "Schweitzer, I got a feeling you're not telling me everything. But I got enough for now. You better get your story straight. As far as I know, you're the last one to see Danny alive. That makes you a prime suspect."

Bud forced a smile. "Buschie, you know me. Do you think I could kill Danny?"

Busch wished Bud had not grinned like that. "Anyone can kill if they are pushed hard enough," he said and walked from the garage.

As he walked back to his pick-up, Busch thought he heard Bud groan, "Damn you, Danny! You deserved to die."

Chapter 33

The phone rang. Amber shook herself out of deep sleep and looked at her watch. Nine a.m. on the dot. *Well, not as early as I thought, but I sure as hell need more rest.* She was hungover, and her mouth tasted like mice had been nesting inside. "Hello?"

"Ms. Bock? My name is Porter Stout, Esquire. I'm the attorney for Danny Barfright."

Amber sat up in bed. "Lawyer? For Danny?"

"That's right. Mr. Danny Barfright. I have a matter to discuss with you. Could you come to my office this morning?"

"Well, sure, but please, I need about an hour."

"That's not a problem. My address is 1129 Main Street in Spanish Springs. See you soon."

Amber showered and dressed quickly, applying far less makeup than usual so she could leave on time. *Why on earth would Danny's lawyer want to see me?* She put down a dish of food for her cat. "Sorry, Pumpkin. Mommy's gotta go out early. Be a good girl." She stroked the soft orange fur, wishing she could enjoy her morning coffee curled up with the cat. That was her favorite way to start the day. With a sigh, she headed for the door.

Her little Mustang, bought used with way too many miles on it already, stood waiting for her like a faithful steed. She loved that pony car. It made her feel special and sexy, even if it was old. The engine purred and whisked her across town in plenty of time for her meeting. She patted the car before she locked it, and then looked around for the address. A directory outside the building listed Porter D. Stout, Attorney at Law, on the second floor. She climbed the steps and quickly found Stout's office.

The receptionist called her boss. "Amber Bock has arrived, sir."

Stout came out to greet her. "Thank you for coming, Ms. Bock. Please come in."

Amber followed him into his office and took the seat he indicated.

Stout pulled out a manila envelope. "Ms. Bock, Danny Barfright — he was my client. A firm in the Cayman Islands handled his business dealings, but he entrusted me to handle his personal affairs. Mr. Barfright made some shrewd investments. He also wisely made me the executor of his will. The latter is why I've asked you to come in today."

"Danny's will?" Amber looked confused.

"That's right. You are the sole heir to Mr. Barfright's estate."

"Estate? Danny Barfright?"

"Yes. Most of Mr. Barfright's wealth is held in an offshore bank account — a numbered account on Grand Cayman Island."

"I don't understand. Why did Danny leave money to me?"

"That is not something I'm at liberty to divulge. Let us just say your benefactor felt you deserved to have this money."

Amber sighed. "Okay, I guess. How much is it?" She couldn't imagine it would be very much.

"Several million. You'll be receiving a full accounting soon."

"Million?" Amber was stunned. "You said several million?"

"Yes."

"Millions?"

"Yes. For the moment, however, I can release only fifty-thousand dollars to you. I strongly advise you to keep the balance in the current account and draw on it as needed. We can arrange regular payments if you wish. A monthly annuity, so to speak." He picked up the check from his desk and handed it to her.

Amber stared at the check, still in shock.

"Is there anything else I may do for you?" Stout asked.

Amber stared at the lawyer. "You can't tell me why Mr. Barfright left all this to me?"

The lawyer smiled sympathetically. "No. I'm afraid I cannot."

"Thank you," Amber said and walked to the door.

When Amber arrived back at her car, she examined the check again, trying to catch her breath. "Millions?" *Why, Danny, did you leave this to me?*

Chapter 34

Amber's meeting with Porter Stout was done by eleven o'clock on Tuesday morning. She was still stunned. "What the hell just happened?" She needed time to digest this. She saw her favorite restaurant on the square. She hurried over and treated herself to Nova Salmon Benedict at TooJay's. *I guess I can afford that now.* She looked at the check under the table and decided the safest bet was to take it to the bank.

At the bank, she stumbled writing the deposit slip for fifty-thousand dollars. She opted to keep four-hundred dollars as 'mad money.' *I never had 'mad money' before,* she smiled to herself.

It was still early for the Beer Buddies, but Amber could not think about going back home. *Maybe I'll stop by the bar early and share this news with the guys. They cared about Danny. Hell, they knew him much longer than I did. Danny could be unpredictable, but this is just unbelievable.*

When Amber walked into World of Beer, most of the gang were already at their favorite table. *Wow, they come earlier and earlier each week.* She smiled at this motley crew for whom she had come to care. "I have to share some wonderful news I just got from Danny's lawyer. Danny left me money in his will."

Margarita asked, "How much?"

Amber was surprised by the greedy look in Margarita's eyes. "I don't know the total yet."

Margarita chuckled. "Not that much, I bet. They're all cheapskates."

Amber replied, without thinking, "Oh, no, a lot." She realized she sounded as if she was celebrating Danny's murder. "Of course, I'd rather have Danny here than the money."

"Of course, you would," Margarita said, showing more interest.

Sam shrugged. "Well, you were his girl. So, it's not so much surprising that he leaves it to you."

"Yeah, good payout, sister." Bud grinned.

"No. No. It wasn't like that with Danny and me. Sure. At first, I was attracted to him, but he always treated me like he was a sweet uncle." Amber looked at Margarita. "No, Danny was totally into Mags here."

"Strictly business between Danny and me." Margarita pursed her lips and waved her beer glass side to side.

Amber was surprised at Margarita's remark. Was it true? She assumed Danny had the hots for Margarita, but maybe it wasn't mutual. She remembered the fight she overheard between them. Maybe their relationship had crashed and burned, and she was the benefactor of Margarita's bad luck.

Margarita shrugged. "Some broads know how to milk a man's wallet."

Amber thought of protesting. Instead, she decided to buy the Buddies a round of drinks. In all the times she had been with them at the bar, she had never been able to do that. Money was always tight. The guys kept a drink in front of her to keep the 'sexy babe' with them. Buying drinks now, she thought, might smooth the rough edges.

Seeing that Honey was busy at another table, Amber went up to the bar to order. "Hey, Pete, I'd like to treat my friends."

"Sure, Amber." Pete turned to get the order ready.

Amber watched him set up the tray with her back to the table.

Margarita's voice cut through the din in the bar like a sharp knife. "I'm not buying that crap. Little Miss Innocent wasn't sleeping with Danny? My ass."

Bud replied, "Danny was a dog. He'd never let a piece of ass like that go untapped."

Margarita's voice rose even higher. "Hell, it looks like little Amber had the biggest motive of all of us for murder. She had

Danny wrapped around her little finger. As soon as he wrote his will, I bet she knocked him off."

Bud smirked, "The way she dresses, she was gunning for him."

Margarita laughed, "Yeah, but at least Amber's out front with it. Some of us 'boys' are not."

"Shut up, bitch," Bud shot back.

"I'm not the bitch," Margarita asserted. "I'm not the one who got Barfright's dough."

Amber's heart sank. *I thought they cared about me. They don't even seem upset that Danny's dead.* "Pete, can you do me a favor? Please, take the drinks over to the table for me? I have to leave."

"No problem, Amber," Pete said.

Amber left money on the bar and slipped out the door.

Only Sam saw her go. He shook his head sadly.

Margarita poked Sam in the ribs. "That little bitch had the best motive in the world."

"And you did not?" Sam said, so softly Margarita didn't hear him.

Chapter 35

Tossing and turning. Turning and tossing. There was no way Busch was going to get his beauty rest tonight. For hours he watched the clock, and the minutes, tick away. It was now almost 3:30, and the sunrise of another day was imminent. Whether it was those damn Yankees who were off to as bad a season as 2016 or maybe even Amber's abrupt departure last night — it didn't matter. He could not get to sleep. He steeled himself to get up, brew a pot, and suck on his first cuppa Joe.

Busch wandered through the dark bedroom to the bathroom and sleep-walked through his daily shit-shower-shave routine. He wrapped a towel around his waist, went through the house to the kitchen, and put on a fresh pot. He sat at his desk, poring over his notes and jotting down notes of things he needed to talk to Amber about.

Amber had to have been both hurt and frightened. She must have overheard the others speaking about her with contempt, insisting she was sleeping with Danny. All of them, supposedly her friends, were willing to point the finger at her for Danny's murder.

Busch could not visualize Amber killing anyone, but Danny had seemed to be a sucker for Amber's sweet façade. He had shown a more tender side for her, softening his voice and avoiding sexist remarks when he spoke to her. One time, he had even driven her home, protecting her from a drunken Bud. But a ton of cash could turn someone into a murderer. It wouldn't be the first time a beautiful, seemingly sweet woman, like Amber, killed someone for a lifetime of ease. As much as he hated to admit it, Amber was a logical suspect.

Certainly, the others now considered Amber to be a suspect, more than one pinning the murder on her 'surprise' inheritance. Yet she claimed she had just learned of her good fortune moments before she showed up at the bar and announced it to her friends. Did he believe she did not know Danny named her in his will? Too many questions. He needed to speak with Amber. Busch picked up his phone.

"Amber, I hope I didn't wake you."

"No. I didn't sleep much last night. But that should come as no surprise."

"I know what you mean. Neither did I. We should have stayed and kept drinking."

"Nah. At least I don't have a hang-over this morning. So, what can I do for you at this ungodly hour?"

"Ungodly hour? Hell, it's almost eight. The day's half gone." Busch chuckled. "We need to talk. When can I come your way?"

"Uh-oh, that doesn't sound good. How about you give me some time to put on my face? Maybe you can come to my place at what, say, nine o'clock? I live in Chastewood Villas. Can you find it?"

"I'll put it in my GPS. Half an hour will give me time to get dressed and throw in a load of laundry before I leave."

"Buschie, we need to find someone for you. You shouldn't be doing your wash alone. Know what I mean?"

"I'll see you at nine."

Busch putzed around some before he left, washing a few dishes, tidying up his kitchen. He grabbed a small load of grimy work shirts from the hamper and tossed them into his new high-efficiency washer. The weekend mechanic wondered if the folks whose cars he worked on noticed his work clothes' improved appearance — but, hey, it didn't matter. He also wondered why he had not the heart to tell Amber that Margarita had twice offered to do his laundry — offers he politely declined.

Moments later, Busch pulled into Amber's driveway, parking next to her rusty, old orange Mustang. That clunker had seen better days. He told Amber, more than once, that it was on its last legs, and the time was fast approaching when he could no longer keep it on the road for her. She would soon have to find new wheels. Now she had the money to do it.

Busch walked past several crepe myrtles bordering her driveway. He rapped on the door of the rented villa. He couldn't help but think that soon Amber would either be in her own home or prison.

Amber opened the door almost immediately. "Come on in, my friend. Coffee's fresh."

Busch smiled. "You're a dear, Amber. It's going to take a bit of java to keep both of us going today."

Amber poured them each a steaming mug. Cream and sugar were ready to go on the kitchen table. She replaced the carafe, picked up both cups, and handed one to Busch. Amber sat at one end of the table, her legs tempting in a short robe.

Busch dropped into the chair at the far end. The rental was comfy, clean, and neat. He poured a shot of cream into his mug and said, "I'm upset by what I heard yesterday from our 'friends.' I want you to know that. I'm trying to put two and two together."

Amber listened silently.

Busch put down his cup. "What's with the others coming down so hard on you?"

"I wish I knew. I thought they were my friends. Why would they hurt me like that?"

Busch lowered his mug to the table and cradled it with both hands. He knew why. Money. "Amber, you know I have to ask you some tough questions."

"Fine. I figured. Shoot."

The wrong choice of word, Busch thought. "Bear with me here. Asking this isn't my choice. Amber, did you sleep with Danny?"

A look of anger crossed Amber's face. She nearly spilled her coffee. "Hell, no, I didn't sleep with Danny. I never slept with Danny. Never been to his house." She hesitated. "He was here one time, and one time only — the other night when he drove me home from the bar. But he didn't even come in the door. I swear, I never met him anywhere there wasn't a bunch of other people around. I think the only place I've ever seen Danny was at the bar on

Tuesdays." She glared at Busch. "And for your damn information, and everybody else's, I don't sleep around."

"Take it easy, girl. I did not say you slept with him. I asked."

"Why would you even ask me that? What would make you think that I had?"

"Well, you tell me. Why would Margarita go behind your back and say that you slept with him? And why did the others not challenge her?"

A shadow of hurt colored her words. "Look, Deputy, I wish I could answer that."

Busch noticed she used his official title and not the name she always called him. "And that would be?"

A glint of fire lit up her eyes. "I can tell you what I think. I wouldn't be surprised if it was Margarita and Danny, who were bumping uglies. Hell, those two appeared to be made for each other." She took a breath and spoke more calmly. "Let's face it; they had some kind of business relationship. Who's to say the little deal I overheard them arguing about the other night didn't start in the sack?"

"So, you think Mags was just deflecting suspicion from her to you?"

"Makes sense to me. And from what I overheard, whatever deal those two had together, well, it sure better not have gone sour. I mean, Margarita sounded totally pissed-off at Danny. Hell, she threatened to kill him. I heard her say that."

"Did you tell anyone? Why didn't you tell me?"

"I mind my own business. Unlike some of these nosey bodies."

Busch was skeptical. "Well, Mags and Danny, both retirees, in some kind of business deal sounds a little cockamamie to me, but I'll think about it. I want to give you the benefit of a doubt."

Amber replied, "Thank you, Deputy."

"Let me ask, do you happen to have a copy of Danny's will?"

"No. Why would I have a copy?"

"I thought maybe his lawyer gave you a copy yesterday when you got your good news."

150

"No. I never saw it, and I never thought to ask Mr. Stout for a copy. I suppose I should."

"Well, I'm sure he's going to take it to the courthouse. You know, probate it and all. But that could take a while. Eventually, it will become public record. I don't want to wait for eventually. I'd like to take a look at it right away. Do you mind asking him?"

"Why not? I've got nothing to hide. Besides, maybe there's something in there that will give me a clue as to why Danny would . . ." Amber's voice trailed off and a tear formed in her eyes. She swallowed. "I don't understand, Buschie. Why would he leave me his money? Why me? Do you know how this is going to change my life?"

"Hey, count your blessings," Busch said in a softer voice, seeing Amber's tears. Some might not believe the tears were real, but he thought they were. "Amber, I'm sure Danny had an excellent reason to do what he did."

"Do you think I slept with him?"

Busch studied her face. "No. I think the others are wrong. I don't believe you did." He drained his mug. "Oh, Amber, one more thing, if you don't mind my asking? Was yesterday the first time you were ever at Danny's lawyer's office?" Her visit to the lawyer was something he could easily verify.

Amber looked at him. "Why do you ask? That's a strange question."

Busch wanted to be honest with her. "His records will verify whether you were there or not."

Amber nodded. "He wasn't my lawyer. So, no, I was never at his office before yesterday." She looked at him. "I swear I didn't even suspect Danny had a lawyer here."

"It's no big deal. I just had to ask." Busch stood and carried his empty mug to the sink and rinsed it. "I better be going. Thanks for your time." He looked at Amber and wished he could cross her off the suspect list. "What's on your plate for the rest of this gorgeous Florida day?"

"Don't make me tell you," Amber said.

"No secrets," Busch replied.

Amber smiled. "For the last two weeks, my mother has been visiting from California."

"Your mother is here? Can I talk to her?"

"She was down in the Keys a few days. She just got back. Maybe you can see her a little later today. We're going to the Mercedes dealer up in Ocala. You're good at working on foreign cars, too. Right?"

"Gotcha covered, Amber. Gotcha covered. I'm happy for you." Busch turned to walk toward the front door. "I can show myself out." A Mercedes, he thought, spending Danny's money already. He shook his head and turned back for a last look. "If you think of anything else, call me. And please, don't try to leave the state."

"Do you think I'd do that?"

"No. I have to say that." Busch left by the front door. He climbed into the pick-up and took off for his garage. He drove too quickly as if Danny was alive and chasing him. *Could I be wrong about Amber? Danny is gone a few days, and she's out buying a Mercedes. I was ready to cross her off the suspect list, but now?*

Chapter 36

Danny's murder made his week a hectic one. Busch was still processing the fact someone had violently snuffed the life out of one of the Beer Buddies. Danny had been a drinking buddy, not a close friend. It didn't matter. When someone you drink with every week gets murdered, its reality invades every moment of your life. Worse still, Busch might know the perp. There was much to process. He was relieved that the weekend had arrived, and he could look forward to chilling at his garage. Although he still had much work to do on the case, he would have time to think.

Busch climbed into his pick-up, travel mug in hand, tossed his cell phone onto the dash, and headed to the garage. The drive took about twenty-five minutes, long enough for him to tune in to NPR for some continuing education courtesy of "Click & Clack, The Tappet Brothers." If anything could make him chuckle today, it would be his fellow car junkies on *Car Talk*. He vowed, not for the first time — someday, he would visit Cambridge, their fair city.

The ring of the phone yanked him out of his reverie and back to the present. He reached for it on the dash and thumb-pressed the green icon. "Yo, Busch here."

It was Nathan. "Hey, buddy, I was wondering if you're going to be at the shop today."

"It's Saturday, right? Yep, headed there now. What can I do for you?"

"Something's not right in my rear end." Before Busch could respond, Nathan regrouped. "No, no, no, I mean the rear end in my Range Rover. The thing's got some miles on it, as you know, but I have no choice — got to keep the beast on the road for a couple more years. Do you mind looking at it?"

"Not at all. I have some other work waiting for me, but will be glad to take a look."

"Great. I should be there within the hour. And thanks, pal."

No sooner than the call ended, Busch slowed to make the right turn from Shady Lane onto Goah Way, where he promptly arrived at his tasteful new sign: *The Pit Stop, B. P. Frapp, Proprietor.* The garage was his sanctuary and hobby shop. He pulled into his reserved space in the parking lot.

Inside the cramped office, he turned on the window air conditioner and started a pot of coffee. Though he would deny he was a neat freak, nothing was amiss on his desk. It looked more like the desk of a law firm receptionist than the desk of a mechanic. He picked up and sharpened a pencil, just one, returned it to the desk drawer, and then walked through another doorway into the adjoining garage. Busch got happily to work.

He had just finished replacing a headlight and tail lamp on an aging Triumph Spitfire when Nathan Lambic pulled up out front. Walking in through the office and directly to the garage, Nathan roared, "How's it hanging, Busch? You havin' fun here in your junker bunker?"

Nathan is trying to lighten the mood. He knows I'm knee-deep in a murder investigation in which he's a suspect. "You nailed it, my man. This is where I come for work as well as for R&R whenever I get the chance. Tell me, what's with the Range Rover?"

"I keep hearing a rumbling sound in the back end. It happens when I'm on a curve or turning a corner. I don't know what it is. Maybe the differential. I don't want to put a lot of bucks into this thing just now, but if it's a must, I will. Thanks for looking under the hood, so to speak."

"That's why I'm here. I'll check it out this morning, but it'll take me a bit. If you need wheels, you can take my truck, so long as you have it back here by two. I should be finished by then."

"Gee, thanks. That does help." Nathan scratched the back of his neck. "I was about to go to Lowes when it occurred to me to call you this morning. I broke an axe handle and needed to pick up a new one."

Busch nodded, making a mental note to check out Nathan's broken axe before he had a chance to get rid of it. "I might be able to fix that for you," he said. "Keep it for me."

"Sure thing," Nathan stammered.

The weekend mechanic reached over the tool bench along the sidewall and replaced two screwdrivers. After wiping his hands on a towel hanging from his belt, he turned and walked toward the office.

Nathan followed.

Busch tensed at the man's closeness, a soldier in various combats, but decided to play it cool. "Hey Nathan, you care for a cup of coffee for the road? I just brewed it."

"Thanks, but no. I've already had three cups this morning."

Busch was uneasy. He wanted Nathan to leave. "Okay. See you later. I'll work on your car as soon as I can."

Nathan nodded. He had his hand on the doorknob when he turned back to Busch. "I've been meaning to ask you for a long time about 'The Pit Stop.'" He emphasized the three words, *The Pit Stop*. "Where did you come up with that name?"

A grin broke out on Busch's face. "Funny you should ask. I'll spare you the details because we both have stuff to do this morning. Pit Stop, named after a deodorant. It's a long story."

Nathan didn't laugh. He glanced at the wall clock. "I don't have time today." He left.

Busch found the keys in the ignition of the Range Rover. He fired it up and drove toward Morse Boulevard. Since Nathan described the unsettling noise happening on curves and corners, he checked it out on The Villages' roundabouts and the Lake Sumter Landing square. His route took him on Morse south to Stillwater Trail, then west toward Buena Vista Boulevard interrupted by a 540 at the Canal Street roundabout, then north on Buena Vista and right onto Old Mill Run. After two circuits of the square at Lake Sumter Landing, he drove back to The Pit Stop.

There was no mistaking it. Nathan was right. The noise only happened when the vehicle rounded a curve or turned a corner. With each change of direction, there was an unusual sound in the rear section.

Busch pulled to a stop and hopped out of the car. He dropped to the ground and looked under the chassis toward the differential. He examined the exhaust pipe and tires. "Nothing amiss that I can see." He scratched his head. He lifted the tailgate and stared in disbelief.

There it was, rolling around in the cargo bay — a baseball bat. Busch picked it up with latex gloves he kept in his pocket. "Shit." He focused on the gleaming ash barrel, and then he saw it: Stan Musial's autograph. Bud was right. Nathan stole the bat. Nathan was Danny's killer.

Chapter 37

It was still early, but Busch had already downed several cups of coffee. He was excited. Tuesday would be a day of reckoning for the Beer Buddies, especially for one of them. He knew that he still had to keep an open mind about Nathan's guilt, but there had always been something fishy about him. He had to admit that he'd never fully trusted Nathan, but could never put his finger on why. The bat in his car was evidence, but only circumstantial. He needed much more before going to Tuborg or the FBI.

Busch carried his fourth java, phone, and a yellow pad out to the lanai and sat at the bistro table. He wrote the names of all the Beer Buddies on the page. Not wanting to suspect his friends, he hoped Blue was right and the crime was the work of the Cereal Killer. He thought it would be a slam-dunk to close this case, but it gnawed at him that something wasn't right. And now, he had the bat.

The early morning hacks were making their way along the cart path to the sixth green, chattering away — but it didn't matter. He lived here for the view and all that came with it. That included not only the chatter, but an occasional dimpled Titleist or Srixon in his yard, courtesy of some duffer's errant shot. Life was good as long as he didn't get konked by a golf ball before he solved this case. It would feel great to solve it.

But was Nathan a good suspect? Nathan never let out precisely what he did pounding around the Dark Continent for so many years. He was always vague, clammed-up when it came to questions about his past. He was a man who made a mystery of forty years in Africa. That alone raised many questions. The bat raised more.

As he pondered what he knew about his Beer Buddy, Busch doodled. Doodling always helped him think. I need more, he thought. He decided to make sure Nathan showed at the Beer Buddies this afternoon.

Busch dialed Nathan's number. After several rings, it went to voice mail. "Buddy, this is Busch. I want to make sure you'll be at the bar this coming Tuesday. I found something that I think will interest you." Would that frighten him off? "Would you believe I picked up a pristine owner's manual and pair of window crank handles for a vintage 1970 Gremlin?" That's better, he thought. "Anyway, they're yours if you want them. I'll have them with me on Tuesday." Sweeten the pot a bit. "By the way, the owner's manual bears the handwritten inscription, 'Jimmy Stewart, 1102 North Roxbury Drive, Beverly Hills.' Don't ask how I came by this gem. Later."

Busch held the phone, eager to see if Nathan called back. He searched the photos on the phone and found the 'Stan the Man' bat. The detective in him could not wait to see Nathan's face when he whipped that bat out in front of everyone. "Case closed!"

Chapter 38

Over the weekend, Busch wrapped up work on a 1969 Corvair. Its owner asked him to find and get rid of every last rattle, but surely its owner should have known that no Corvair was ever rattle-free. Busch put so much effort into trying to ferret them all out that now it was he who was rattled. He rotated all four white-walls and replaced what had to be the original air filter. He'd only bill the owner, a long-time friend and customer, a modest charge, as the real value of the time he invested in tracking down rattles far exceeded the value of the car.

On Monday morning, Busch felt more relaxed after spending his weekend in the shop. Putting down the newspaper, he glanced at the clock. With a yawn and a stretch, he walked from the lanai to the bathroom, showered quickly, and donned his uniform.

Hungry, he opened his fridge and groaned. He had been so wrapped up in the Barfright investigation that he was long overdue for a grocery trip.

Faster than a politician can make a U-turn, Busch was off to the Winn-Dixie at Lake Sumter Landing.

The store was not crowded. For that, Busch was grateful. He was able to make his rounds without bumping into anyone who might delay him, wanting to discuss the case. He pushed his almost-full cart to the only open check-out lane. He was unloading when he stopped cold. In the line in front of him was none other than Honey, with fewer than half a dozen items. Struck again by how young she looked, Busch spoke up. "Fancy meeting you here. How are you doing?"

Honey gushed, "Oh, hi, Buschie. It looks like you're buying groceries for two."

"Not really. I guess I should come here more often. What are you up to today?"

Honey pointed to her cart.

"Silly me," Busch said. "Anything else?"

"I was planning to do laundry as soon as I got home." Honey smiled at Busch. "But now, I'm thinking laundry can wait on a gorgeous day like this." She gave him a hopeful look. "I might just head up to the square for a cup of coffee. Care to join me?"

Busch was not one to disappoint a pretty lady on a sunny day, and he did need to speak with Honey. "That would be nice. How about watching my stuff here for a second while I return a couple things that need refrigeration. I don't want them to be out in the heat too long." He picked up the gallon of milk and a pack of chicken breasts from his cart and took them back up the aisles.

"Most people wouldn't have run to put them back in the right places," Honey said when he returned.

"I had to do that," Busch replied. "I guess it's just my nature."

After they both checked out, they placed their groceries into their cars.

Busch walked over to Honey's car. "Are you ready?"

The two strolled together down Lake Sumter Landing to the square, making small talk.

"Starbucks okay?" Busch asked. "Smell that coffee!"

"Sure."

Of the hundreds of permutations of coffee drinks at Starbucks, their two orders to the barista were identical: dark roast of the day, extra bold, *grande*, leave room for cream.

Busch picked up the tab.

"Thank you," Honey said.

Busch led her to an empty table on the patio in front of the store. "I can't believe we both ordered the same drink," he said, chuckling at the coincidence.

Honey laughed.

"With all the fancy brews they have at this place, I thought you'd ask for one of those concoctions that takes ten minutes to cook up," Busch said, "yet you got the same damn thing as this old sailor."

"Nothing fancy about me, including my fondness for a simple cup of strong coffee."

Busch nodded. He always liked Honey and wondered why someone like her was satisfied working in a bar. "So," Busch began slowly, "you know I've still got this investigation thing going."

Honey stopped sipping her coffee.

Busch continued, "It bugs the crap out of me to know that one of our friends got knocked off." He waited for a reaction. "I guess you knew I'd have to talk to you at some point." He still did not see any overt reaction. "Yet, you invited me for coffee this morning."

"You suggested Starbucks."

"But you let out that you were going for coffee and invited me along."

Honey took a sip of her drink. "Busch, I have nothing to hide. There is not a reason in the world that I should worry about how your investigation is coming along." She looked him in the eye. "I mean, why should I be nervous? I am just here to enjoy your company. And this fine cup of coffee."

To passersby, Busch and Honey probably looked like a couple. Their conversation was quiet and calm. No one would conclude that this man in uniform was interrogating this young lady as part of a murder investigation.

As Busch enjoyed the fresh air and Honey's company, he noticed a lone figure sitting on Panera's front porch. He watched the man out of the corner of his eye. Was the guy spying on him? Maybe he was just ogling this attractive woman. It was too far to see the man's face. He put his concerns aside and picked up his conversation with Honey. "Listen. I want to be honest with you. You're not high on my list of suspects."

"Thank you."

"I wanted to get that out of the way. But some others said you hated Danny or at least had a strong distaste for him. That's no secret." He lowered his voice. "The question is, did you hate him enough to want him dead?"

Busch's directness caught Honey off guard. She fiddled with her coffee cup, but recovered quickly. She looked into Busch's face. "It's true. I didn't like him, which is why I wanted Danny to be my big ending. But that doesn't mean I wanted Danny dead."

"Your big ending? I'm afraid you'll have to explain that one to me."

"Well, I kind of figured Danny was like all men, just worse. My instincts for men are usually spot on. But in Danny's case, I guess I just read him wrong. You see, he was supposed to be the last chapter in a book I'm writing . . . about relationships. I couldn't seem to find an angle I was looking for, and then one day, Danny spoke up, and things suddenly fell into place."

Busch fell back into his chair. "So, you're writing a book? I didn't realize."

Honey leaned closer. "Yeah. Please don't tell anyone else," she urged.

"Well, good luck with . . . uh . . . your book." *I knew there was something about her—but this?* Busch felt as if he'd been punched in the gut. "You can fill me in on the book later, but what about Danny?"

Honey looked around. "Two or three weeks ago, at the bar, Danny asked me over to his place."

Shit. Another revelation Busch didn't want to hear. "You went?"

"Give me a chance. He asked me, and I wasn't shocked. I was only surprised it took so long for him to hit on me. The invitation was the perfect opportunity for me to follow up on the angle I was working on in my book."

Holy crap, Busch thought, unable to take all of this in.

Honey continued, "Of course, I accepted. I did not doubt that he was going to put a move on me. And my game plan was that I'd give him nothing but a cold shoulder. I figured at that point, he would either go all 'lovey-dovey' on me or try to get physical. You know, he would become an angry, horny bastard, just like all the rest of them."

A wounded expression showed on Busch's face.

Honey added, "Present company excluded, of course." She sipped her coffee.

Busch smiled weakly. "So, what happened at his house, if you don't mind my asking?" He added, "You can spare any intimate details."

Busch's coffee companion sat up, coughed, and smacked a napkin up to her face.

Busch handed his clean napkin to her for back-up.

Honey looked at Busch and spat out, "There were no *intimate* details. As it turned out, Danny was the perfect gentleman." Honey cleared her throat.

"What do you mean?" Busch pressed, finding this hard to believe about Barfright.

Honey crossed her legs. "Well, our friend, Danny, I can report to you, was a charmer the whole evening. We sat out on his lanai, sipping an excellent Merlot. I never took Danny for an oenophile, but, by god, he was."

"A what?"

"Oenophile, a wine expert."

"Oh. And a gentleman?" Busch shook his head.

Honey nodded. "Yes, he was. The mystery of why he invited me to his home unfolded after we had our first glass. He said he wanted to apologize to me for the behavior of the gang back at the bar."

"Danny said that?"

Honey nodded again. "He said he wasn't trying to make excuses, but he wanted me to know that the Buddies were just...," she paused to make air quotes, 'Harmless old codgers.' Present company excluded again." She smiled at Busch.

Busch sighed. "Old codgers?"

Honey smiled at him. "Old codgers, who grew up during an earlier time. Guys who said or did things all their lives that just aren't acceptable in today's world. He said that some of the boys found it hard to change their ways."

"Danny said that?"

"Yes. Danny went on to say how he knew their behavior wasn't right and that they shouldn't do and say some of the things they do, but they never mean any harm. I was amazed. I never expected that from him."

Busch was surprised, too. "This doesn't sound like Danny. Was that all? He asked you to his house so he could apologize for the Beer Buddies?" Busch was incredulous.

Honey's eyes teared up.

"I didn't mean to upset you. But it looks like there's something else going on here." Busch's voice trailed off.

Honey shifted in her chair.

"Do you want to tell me about it?"

Just then, the figure at Panera bread caught Busch's attention again. He was sure the guy was sneaking peeks at them. It was hard to see his face hidden by a newspaper from a distance, but Busch thought he looked familiar.

Honey interrupted his thoughts. "Yes, there is more, Buschie." She used her fingers to rotate her almost empty coffee cup on the table. "Danny went into this spiel about single mothers, like me. He rattled off statistics about how many young women across America are raising children without a dad in the house, how they work more than one job just to keep things together. He said they had a tough time making ends meet, while still trying to be good moms to their kids. His unexpected sensitivity floored me."

While Busch found this hard to believe, he was enthralled by her voice, the gentleness of her demeanor as she went on with her recollection of Danny's 'spiel,' as she called it. "Do you have any idea why he felt the need to tell you all this?"

Honey looked uneasy again. "I told you there's more." She took a deep breath as if she were trying to muster the strength to continue. "Danny said he found out that I was raising my twins, Justin and Jason, as a single mom. He said he knew parenting my twin boys was a tough job on a barmaid's income. He was right about that. It's tough making ends meet. But a mother's gotta do what a mother's gotta do, I told him." She looked at Busch. "I couldn't understand why he was telling me all this. I figured the wine mellowed him out."

"Well, where was all this going?" Busch was genuinely curious, but his attention was drawn to the male figure on the Panera porch once more.

Honey pushed the chair back. "You know, I have mixed feelings about sharing all of this with you." She wadded her napkin and dabbed at her eyes. She did not look at Busch as she told the rest of her story. Her voice was soft, almost a whisper, but intense. "Danny, out of the blue, said he wanted to help me out. He told me that he wanted to start by being more generous with tips. You know, my tips at the bar. And boy, was he ever more generous. Like the rest of you, Danny always threw a couple of bucks on the table, not chintzy, but modest."

Busch felt embarrassed. No one could accuse him of being a big tipper.

"But since that night at his house, every single time he came into the bar, he slipped an extra hundred-dollar bill under his napkin for me. A HUNDRED DOLLAR BILL! Do you have any idea how much that helps?"

"I had no idea Danny was doing that."

"Nobody did. Well, let me tell you, that man had a heart of gold. He was warm, and he was tender to me after that night. It was like he was a changed person." Honey's lips quivered. "Why would anyone want to take his life like that? It's beyond me. It's so unfair."

Busch frowned. Honey shared a good story. Did he believe her? Could she be making this up to get taken off the suspect list? "Well, somebody wanted Danny out of the picture, and now he's history."

"Buschie, I'm sorry I got all choked up just now. This thing has me shook. It's not just that my kids will miss out on those big waitressing tips now that Danny's gone. I'm having a hard time dealing with all this. I never knew anybody who was murdered." Honey scrunched her napkin into a tight wad and stuffed it into the empty coffee cup.

"I understand. I'm sure you're not the only one of us trying to make sense of all this."

Honey glanced at her watch. "Hey, can we head out? I promised the boys I'd take them swimming this afternoon. Laundry will have to wait."

"What about the book?" Busch asked.

Honey looked alarmed. "Danny was supposed to be the material for my last chapter, but he ruined it for me."

Busch stared at her. Was a ruined book a motive for murder? "What do you mean Danny ruined it?"

Honey shrugged. "I was looking to write about a rat."

You exterminate rats, Busch thought.

Honey put her hand on his. "Please, don't tell the others about my book. Not yet. I have to find a new ending."

"Let's go. It looks like I'll be spending this afternoon writing up my report."

Honey could not have known what he'd put in his report. Having been in law enforcement longer than he cared to remember, a detective for more than half of those years, Busch was trained to investigate, observe, ferret out details. And observe Honey, he did. It was something in her voice and her story. For starters, he knew, not once, not ever, did Danny Barfright leave Honey Lovejoy a hundred-dollar tip. At least not at the Beer Buddies table. It never happened. She was a liar. She lied to everyone about being a barmaid when she was secretly writing a book. Did she lie about being their friend? He felt disappointed. He moved Honey higher on his list of suspects.

As he turned onto Lake Sumter Landing, bound for the Winn-Dixie parking lot where he'd part ways with Honey, Busch got a better look at the lone figure on Panera's porch. He was still there. The newspaper he held up didn't fully cover the side of his face.

Chapter 39

B usch told Honey he had to go back into Winn-Dixie under the pretext of picking up the milk and chicken breasts he'd left there earlier.

"I'll see you tomorrow afternoon," Honey said. "I trust you to keep things between us about my book."

As soon as he saw Honey speed off, Busch exited the store and made a beeline for Panera, hoping to find Sam Adams still on the porch.

Walking to the front door and onto the porch, Busch feigned surprise at seeing his Beer Buddy sitting alone at a table. "Sam? Fancy me finding you here on this gorgeous day," he began. "You been here long?"

Sam looked nervous, but answered calmly, "Time on my hands, you know."

"Mind if I join you?" Busch did not wait for an answer. "Let me grab some high test, and I'll be right back. I needed to talk with you anyway. You understand."

"Whatever. I got nowhere to go. I'll be here." Adams smiled.

Busch returned with his second *grande* brew of the morning and sat across the table from Adams. Fortunately, their table was on the small part of the porch, north of the main entrance, where no one would invade their private space.

Busch began. "Let me cut to the chase, Sam. I got the Barfright killing on my mind, as I'm sure all of us do. Captain Tuborg assigned me to investigate it."

"So, I understand. How's your investigation going?" Sam asked, looking Busch in the eye.

Busch fired his first shot. "So, Sam Adams. Is that your real name?"

"Yeah. It used to be Adamowitz. Nobody could pronounce it, so immigration changed it to Adams, after the beer. That always brings a laugh."

Busch looked up. "After the beer? Not the Revolutionary War patriot?"

"Him, too."

"You were in the clothing business?"

"You know I owned a bra factory. It went bust."

Busch cocked his head. "It went bust?" Without laughing, he looked up again. "Oh, I get it. But I need this for the record."

Sam looked perplexed. "Yes, foreigners. The damn Chinese got their hands on my bras."

Busch saw a twinkle in Adams' eyes and a smirk on his face. He's a crazy old man, he thought, always telling the same stupid jokes. "Yeah, sure. They're taking over the world," he replied. "All my clothes are made in China. Look at the labels."

"Exactly," Sam said and gazed out at the sky. "My bra business went bust."

Busch asked, "How old are you, Sam?"

"Older than my teeth," Sam replied. "I'm eighty-three."

"No shit! You look pretty fit for a guy that age? You work out?"

"A little."

"I hope I'm as fit as you at your age. You lift weights?"

"Once in a while." Adams shifted in his chair uneasily. "I'm from Brooklyn. A Jew where I lived, we had to be strong."

"Brooklyn? Ahh, I spent a couple of weeks at the Brooklyn Navy Yard years ago. Odd, I worked on a murder case there, too. I was on active duty, a Hospital Corpsman Third-Class, medical photographer, at the time. Humph! Memories!"

Sam sat up. "The Navy Yard? It's a dilapidated mess these days. They need to let it fall into the bay."

Busch nodded. "So, tell me, Sam, did you hate Danny?"

Sam recoiled as if a lightning bolt had hit nearby. "Who told you I hated him? I don't hate anyone — except the foreign bastards who got their hands on my bras."

"Did you hate him?" Busch repeated.

"I hardly knew this boy," Sam said, almost in a whisper.

"You met with him every Tuesday at the bar, and you say you hardly knew him?"

"We chatted. We told jokes. Danny flirted..."

Busch cut in. "All the guys flirt. Was there something wrong with Danny's flirting?" Busch leaned on the table.

"He was different. He said nasty things to the girls. I mean, we all throw the bullshit. He was crude at times." Sam peered at the cop. "You know what I mean?"

Busch sat silent, waiting for Adams to continue.

"We all flirt with the girls. It is one of the last pleasures left to us."

The detective recognized the 'old fart' routine when he saw it. "But Barfright went too far? Is that what you mean?"

"Yes. I sometimes thought so."

"And that's why you hated him?"

"Who told you this? I didn't hate him. He was someone who I would not want my daughter to marry. That's all."

Busch noted Adams' expression — irritation. He switched gears. "Do you own a baseball bat?"

"Baseball bat? Me? I don't even like baseball."

"A Brooklyn boy who doesn't like the national pastime?" Busch tapped his cup on the table. "Man, I cried when the bums left Brooklyn."

Adams shifted in his chair.

Busch picked up his pen and jotted something on the napkin. He was careful to keep his notes secure from Adams' curious eyes. He then sat back in his chair and struck a relaxed pose. "So, you weren't a Dodger fan as a kid?"

"My father was very, very strict. As soon as I got home, it was homework and chores. He didn't know baseball from Poland..."

"I thought I picked up a bit of an accent," Busch said.

Adams froze. His eyes darted to, and then away from Busch's face.

Busch had seen this kind of reaction a lot during his career. It was common among those who feared further questioning. He kept on. "You ever play baseball? You look like you've got strong arms," Busch said. "And you're eighty-three?"

"Why would I lie? If I lie, I should make myself younger. No?" Adams shrugged. "I worked in my uncle's factory as a boy. I took it over — the bra company."

"The one that went bust," Busch said and let out a chuckle. "Pretty funny. You do have an alibi for the night Danny was killed, I suppose?"

"I was home, watching television."

"What were you watching?" Busch picked up his pen. "Were you by yourself?"

"Who should I be with?" Sam asked.

"No female companionship?"

"No. These ladies are too old for me," the old man replied and cackled.

Busch didn't laugh. "What about Honey?"

The question caught Sam off guard. "What about her? That lovely girl would never look at an old cocker like me."

There it is again. The 'old fart' routine. Why don't I buy it? Has Sam ever done one thing to make him a person of interest? Other than bad jokes and the geezer routine? "So, do you like her? Honey."

"Who wouldn't?" Sam cocked his head. "I see how you look at her."

Busch was surprised he'd noticed. "Barfright liked Honey, too. Didn't he?"

"I wouldn't know."

"He was always flirting with her. Wasn't he?"

"I guess. Yes, we all do."

"But he went too far, didn't he? You said that."

Sam shifted in the seat. "Yes. I thought so."

"Did Honey think so, too? Did she talk to you about it?"

"Not that I recall. No, I think Honey took it like… a man. I think it was a joke to her."

"How do you know if she never talked to you about it?"

"I *don't* know that. But our Honey is a nice person…"

"You know her, though, right? How well do you know her?"

"What do you mean?"

"You have a relationship with her?" Busch pressed on. "Damn, Sam, nobody ever knows what someone else is capable of doing if you push the right buttons. The sweetest young woman can become a killer."

Adams sat up and replied angrily. "You suspect Honey? You're wrong. She wouldn't hurt anyone."

Busch was impressed. *Why is he trying to protect her?* He pulled the top from his cup and drained his coffee. "I've been doing this for a long time, Sam. You'd be amazed at what people are capable of doing. Thanks for your time."

Sam remained seated. "Honey did not do it," he said, crumpling his napkin and stuffing it into the empty cup.

Busch sighed. "I suppose you know who did?"

Adams stared at Busch. "No. I'm not the detective here. I just don't think such a hard-working young girl with two children could do such a thing." He sighed. "She would not risk losing her children. No?"

Busch got to his feet and smiled. "Well, just keep our conversation to yourself, old man, okay? And don't plan on leaving town. I may have more questions for you later."

Sam nodded.

Busch started to leave, and then turned back. "By the way, what show were you watching that night?"

"Show?"

"On TV."

"Oh. Some police show. *Law and Order.*"

Busch smiled and turned as if to walk away. He then turned back. "You were watching TV all night? You never went out?"

"No. I was home alone. Like every night."

"Pretty weak alibi."

Sam smiled. "I guess, with a weak story like that, I must be the killer."

"I gotta go," Busch said. "I've got the actual killer to find."

Sam, walking as if his back ached from sitting too long, followed Busch off Panera's porch. "You know," he said, "the person you should be talking to is Nathan Lambic."

"Lambic? Why should I be talking to Nathan?"

"I'm not saying Nathan did it, but he had as good a reason as any. Barfright was an arms dealer. His outfit sold defective ammunition to Lambic's army friends in Africa. He hated Barfright."

Busch walked away again, but stopped. He turned to Sam, who was right behind him, hands in his shorts pocket. "How do you know all this stuff about arms sales in Africa?" he asked.

"I have an Israeli friend. The guy is in intelligence. He told me, and I, after some drinks, spilled the beans to Nathan. I tell you, he was livid."

"Why are you telling me all this?"

"Look. I like Lambic. He's my Beer Buddy, like you. But you were about to pin Danny's murder on Honey or me. I am not going to stand trial for murder because I kept information about a drinking pal hidden. I don't think Nathan killed anyone, but he sure as hell had a better reason than Honey or me."

Busch didn't know what to do with this new information. This case was getting more and more complicated. He had to think. "That's it for now, Sam, but remember, nobody hears what we talked about."

"Got it," Sam said, turned, and walked toward the lake.

Busch rubbed his chin and chuckled to himself. "His bra factory went bust. That is pretty funny. So, why aren't I laughing?" All paths lead to Nathan. He had the bat in his car, and now Sam provided the missing piece, a motive. If Danny sold defective guns in Africa, Lambic might want to settle the score.

Chapter 40

The Freightliner tractor had been on the road for three and a half hours when it pulled into the yard in Orlando. The small Hispanic driver backed the trailer up to the loading dock, not expertly, but well enough that he made it on his second try.

Nobody was around. One other trailer, uncoupled, was backed up to the dock.

The driver got out of the cab and went through a metal door to the warehouse's interior. After a few minutes, he came out. He took a cell phone from his shirt pocket and started to dial. He stopped, then looked around, as though sensing danger. He went to the abandoned trailer and opened the rear door just enough to step in. He inspected the inside. There was nothing there but a few folded tarps. Satisfied with what he saw, he stepped back onto the dock and continued dialing. After a brief conversation, he put the cell phone back in his shirt pocket and pulled out a cigarette pack. He sat on the edge of the dock, lit a cigarette, and smoked.

After about ten minutes, a Ford van pulled into the freight yard and parked beside the Freightliner. Six men jumped out. They got up onto the dock and started unloading crates from the semi. A few had guns.

Without warning, six police cars, lights flashing, raced into the yard. They screeched to a halt in front of the dock. Doors opened. Men in dark blue jackets emblazoned with 'FBI' in gold lettering, black Kevlar vests, and helmets burst out, guns in their hands.

Someone with a bullhorn blasted, "FBI, show me your hands."

The men unloading the semi scattered like roaches on a chicken bone when the lights came on. It was no good. The cops were everywhere. Three of the mobsters drew guns. They dropped them to the floor, surrounded by the armed FBI officers.

Only one man escaped.

Juanito, the young Hispanic driver, ducked into the derelict trailer parked against the dock and closed the door behind him. He snuggled into the corner of the trailer and pulled a tarp over himself, leaving only a small crack to peek out. He waited for what seemed like an hour, but was probably much less.

There were sounds outside the trailer, cars moving away.

I made it, Juanito thought. To be sure, he waited a little longer.

Then the door opened, and a man walked in.

Through the peephole, Juanito saw the man was tall and wore black sunglasses and a black fedora. He had experience with the FBI, and this man stunk like a G-man.

The man with the sunglasses turned to the tarp under which Juanito lay crouched. He raised a large gold badge and said, "This is Supervising Chief Inspector Detective Oscar Blue of the FBI. Come out and raise your arms. You are under arrest."

Juanito rose, but he did not raise his arms.

The man with FBI letters emblazoned in gold on his jacket was not armed.

Juanito charged, shoving the FBI agent aside. He dashed out of the trailer through the opening where Supervising Chief Inspector Detective Blue had just entered.

Assistant Supervising Chief Inspector Detective Guinness, waiting outside beside the door, raised her arm and caught Juanito with a vicious elbow on the bridge of his nose. He hit the dock. Lights out. Guinness was on him like a hungry bulldog on a lamb chop. She cuffed Juanito and loaded him in the police cruiser before he was fully conscious.

---  ---

Later that day, Juanito sat handcuffed in the interrogation room of the police station. Blue and Guinness positioned themselves across from him.

Blue stated, "We have you cold. Is there anything you want to tell us? It will make everything go smoother for you, if you give us a statement."

Juanito rubbed his nose. It felt broken. "I'm no say anything to you. I want my lawyer."

"You can call your lawyer at any time. We do not need a confession, Juanito. We busted everyone at the pier in Miami," Blue said.

"I no say nothing. I want my lawyer," Juanito repeated.

Blue nodded. "We followed your truck all the way here, to Orlando. We have camera footage of you unloading the drugs. We know more about this operation than you do. The only reason we're talking to you now is that we're required to do so. You're going to do eight to twenty in federal prison."

Guinness showed her teeth. "They like cutie-pies like you in the pen."

Juanito cried, "Wait a minute. What if I give you something? Maybe I get a lighter sentence?"

Blue smiled. "I just told you, little man, you have nothing to give. We know you work for Gaspo. We've got the head of the Miami and Orlando operations, and we have everyone who was in on this operation. You have nothing we want."

Juanito's head sank.

Blue said to an unseen microphone somewhere in the room, "Come get this guy. He wants to make a call."

The door to the interrogation room clicked open. A uniformed officer came into the room and took Juanito by his arm. As they started to leave, Juanito's head popped up. His eyes brightened, "Wait a minute. I got something you don't have."

"Hold it," said Blue. "What do you think we need?"

Juanito smiled slyly. "I got a murder one. Gaspo didn't do it, but he ordered it. He paid a guy for a hit in Florida. You gotta give me something for a murder rap on Gaspo."

"You've got nothing. Take this thug away." Blue waved his hand.

"Wait! I got the name of the mark, the hitter's name, and the place of the murder. I got enough for you to sweat a confession out of the killer."

"What's the name of the killer?" said Blue, looking nonchalantly at his nails.

"I not give you shit until my lawyer brings me a deal."

Blue looked at Guinness, and then back to Juanito. "Take him away," said the Supervising Chief Inspector Detective. He barked an order to his officer, "Get me the phone. I have a call to make."

Chapter 41

Amber headed for the bathroom and a long, hot bubble bath. In five minutes, she would be leisurely lying in the tub with a glass of chardonnay and her Bose speakers playing the sultry songs of Sade. Perfect. Just as she poured her wine, the phone rang. *Damn it. I don't want to talk to anyone this afternoon.*

"Amber, honey, what time will you be here? I'm telling you, my hair is one big mess today."

Amber recognized the voice. "Oh, Dominic? Is that tonight?" In all the excitement, she had forgotten the appointment.

"Of course, it is, Sugar. You promised to be here early to do my makeup and hair," Dominic whined.

"What time does it start?"

"At seven o'clock."

Glancing at her wall clock, Amber said, "Damn. It'll take a few hours to get there." She stared ruefully at the tub. "Okay, I'll change and get on the road."

Amber dreaded making the trip, but she had promised Dominic well over a month ago. Before this mess, she had planned to be in Miami on business anyway, so it was the least she could do to support her best bud. She knew how important this event was to him. Last year he was runner-up in the Drag Queen America Beauty Pageant. All year, he had honed his routine for the talent part of the contest. She couldn't let him down.

Amber quickly donned leather pants and a low-cut black lace blouse. With a quick sip of wine, she grabbed her bag and hurried out the door to her car. "Our last ride together," she said affectionately to the orange Mustang.

Amber was grateful to Busch that the car made it down the thruway with hardly a cough. She wondered if she would be wealthy enough to keep the 'Stang and the Mercedes.

The pageant took place in The Sea Breeze Plaza, a gorgeous hotel near the water. As Amber walked through the lobby, she noted eyes in the room followed her. She couldn't stop. Her friend needed her.

"Amber, honey, over here!" Dominic waved to her from the bar. "Sweetheart, you've got your work cut out for you today." He whisked her off to the contestant dressing room.

In all stages of dress and undress, fifty men crowded the room, all trying to get their makeup and hairstyles ready before squeezing into evening gowns.

"Lovelies, my friend Amber is here for support," Dominic announced.

A chorus of men welcomed her.

"Those beauties real?" A guy pointed to her breasts.

Amber laughed. "All mine, honey." In any other group of men, she would have felt flattered or annoyed. From these guys, she considered it artistic envy.

Dominic sat on a stool. "Oh, Amber, you need to hurry."

Amber applied the makeup like a pro. She then stood back to admire her work. "Looking pretty, if I say so myself," she smiled.

Dominic looked in the mirror. "My hair, Sweetie? Can you save it?"

Amber ran her hands through Dominic's thick, black hair. "Oh, Dom honey, you're right about your hair. Bad hair day for sure. You been rolling in the sheets or what?" She wielded a hot curling iron and wrestled his unruly strands into adorable curls that framed his face. "Take a look, Sweetie."

Dominic smiled at his reflection in the mirror. "Sugar, you're the best. Now, if I could only have those boobs of yours!" He laughed as he stuffed falsies into the lacy push-up bra.

"Not bad, Dom." Amber smiled. "Where's your gown?"

Dominic opened a sateen garment bag and pulled out a stunning red dress. Slipping it carefully over his head, he signaled Amber to zip it up in the back.

"Can you breathe?" Amber asked, laughing.

"Probably not, but who cares?" Dominic pirouetted a few times to show off the outstanding results.

Amber nodded her approval. "At least that thigh-high slit will let you sashay across the stage."

"That is the idea, Miss Amber."

"Listen, Dom, I'm going to grab my seat so I don't miss the action. Break a leg, Sweetie." She kissed him carefully on his cheek to avoid messing up the makeup.

"You're the best, Amber," Dominic said, waving.

Amber found a seat with a good view of the stage. She noted in the program that after the evening gown event, talent performances would take place. *This should be fun*, she thought.

The band leader raised his baton, and the music swelled through the room.

Amber recognized the old Sinatra standard, "This Is All I Ask."

As the grand procession of contestants in evening gowns glided across the stage, a baritone's smooth voice crooned, "Beautiful girls, walk a little slower when you walk by me . . ."

Amber applauded with the rest of the audience. *They look stunning in their evening gowns, especially Dom in that red dress. Dominic rules.*

A tall contestant near the end of the procession caught Amber's attention. He was beautiful except for his bulging biceps. Those arms looked familiar. Something about him looked familiar, but she could not place him. *Maybe he's a friend of Dominic I met once?* She rifled through the program to see if she recognized a name. That proved a waste of time. No one in the contest used their real names. Dominic Diaz was Dominica Divine. *It's probably my imagination.*

Dominic slayed it during the talent portion of the contest. He had changed into a red patterned leotard. Twirling flaming torches, Dom danced and then slithered on his back across the entire stage toward the judges' table, still twirling the flaming torches. He winked at the judges for the act's climax and then slowly, suggestively, seductively, swallowed the torch's flames.

The audience went crazy.

The familiar-looking guy was on next. He wore a flowing white chiffon one-piece jumper that worked perfectly with his long, dark wig. *Those biceps, though. Ugh. Throws off the whole look. He could use some help with his wardrobe. I should tell Dom.*

Sitting down on a high stool, the contestant strummed a guitar and sang in a strong, hauntingly beautiful falsetto Adele's, "Someone Like You."

Impressed by the rendition, Amber looked up the singer's name in the program. Lavender. Lavender Schweitzer. *Oh my god! That's Bud Schweitzer! I wonder if the Beer Buddies know!*

Chapter 42

Busch drove his F-150 into the World of Beer lot moments after the 2 p.m. news. He recognized the cars in the parking lot. His friends were inside. A couple of them were well into their second beer, judging from the empties on the table. He walked over to Nathan and placed a brown paper bag in front of him, whispering into his ear, "Check this shit out when you get home. And remember, no questions."

If skeptical approval is a facial expression, that was Nathan's façade. He nodded and placed the bag on the floor near his feet.

Busch looked toward Honey. She went off to the bar and returned with a mug of one of his favorites, *Erdinger Weissbier*.

As was often the case lately, the babble at the table was all about Danny's murder. Schweitzer was laughing up a storm, almost giddy, and egging his friends on. "Buschie here figures it was one of us. I think it was Nathan over there."

Nathan dismissed Schweitzer with a wave of his hand and raised a frothy mug to his lips.

Tony tossed the crust of his pizza slice onto a plate. "What the hell makes you think it was Lambic?"

Bud leaned over. "Well, I'm glad you asked. Buschie says it was one of us, so we might as well finger someone to get this shindig started. And I'd rather it be him than me or any of you other guys." He burst into laughter.

Busch picked up on the conversation. "Yeah, Lambic, why should anyone give you the benefit of the doubt? You kinda look guilty to me."

Nathan squirmed in his seat. "You got nothing on me, flatfoot. Nothing at all. Go ahead and speculate all you want, you drunk bastards." It was his best Bogart imitation, a hit at parties.

Busch wouldn't let it go and peered at Nathan. "I just got here, and speaking for myself... I'm not drunk, not now, not ever. So, go ahead, convince us you're innocent."

Nathan's face reflected his dislike of the accusations. He growled at Busch, "You have nothing on me. Nothing at all. Not one stinking piece of evidence. So, lay off."

Busch was quick on the draw. "Well, I'm not so sure about that. You stole Bud's Stan Musial, and you can't deny it. It was found in your car. I was the one who found it."

Nathan looked surprised. "Bud's Stan Musial was in the back of my Gremlin?"

"No. Your Rover."

Nathan looked more surprised. "Oh, yeah, I remember now. But I didn't steal it."

"No? It flew into your trunk?" Busch looked skeptical.

Nathan looked like a trapped hippo. "I borrowed it the day I picked up his pavers because I wanted to get the thing appraised. I was doing it for my friend, Bud, because he didn't know the actual — other than the sentimental — value of the bat."

"A likely story," Busch muttered.

"No, really. I had every intention of returning it. It just slipped my mind until you just mentioned it." Nathan looked Busch straight in the eye. "I'm a soldier. Highly trained. If I used it as a murder weapon, do you think I would have let you work on my car?"

Busch sucked in his breath. That argument made sense.

Nathan's hands straddled the table. "So that evidence is crap. It gets you nowhere. I didn't do it."

Busch saw Nathan was perspiring. As much sweat beaded on his forehead as beer foam did in his mustache. The detective in him wasn't ready to yield on Nathan Lambic as a suspect. "Sam over there, he let you in on Danny's little secret, didn't he?"

"What little secret are you talking about?"

"You know damn well what little secret. Danny was an arms trader. In Africa, no less. Ring any bells?"

"You told him that?" Nathan shot at Sam.

Sam shrugged. tapping his earpiece on the table.

Busch continued, "And it was Sam who told you that the arms Danny boy was trading were not reliable. He said you knew that. It was your friends, your allies so-to-speak, that were killed when their rifles misfired. That is all true, isn't it?" He was going in for the kill.

Nathan glared at Sam, and then turned his gaze on Busch. "You think you're so smart, Deputy Busch. Yes. All of that is true. But that does not mean I killed the punk. Yeah, I detested Barfright, and what he did over there. I saw the horror of it. I still have nightmares. If you think all that amounts to a motive, so be it. But it is a long way from proof. And I am telling you all — you're looking at the wrong guy. I didn't do it."

Busch wasn't convinced. "You had as much, if not more, of a motive than anybody else here. So now that we have your motive signed, sealed, and delivered, where were you the night somebody murdered poor Danny boy?"

Though he never thought it would come to this, Nathan Lambic was ready. He took a deep breath, and then he raised his head and announced, "I was at the hospital."

"At the hospital, were you? What were you doing there, getting an alibi implant?" Busch joked, ready to clamp on handcuffs.

"Yes, Deputy Smarty Pants. I was at the hospital. That evening, right around dinnertime, Honey called me, upset, screaming into the phone. One of her twins, Justin, had fallen off his skateboard and was not 'oriented.' I think that is the word she used."

"Umgebracht," Sam offered. "It means . . . I don't know how to translate it into English."

Nathan glared at him. "Honey pleaded with me to come over. I raced there. Justin had a knot on the back of his head the size of a cue ball, and he was acting weird. We ran him to the ER, and I ended up staying with him all night while she took Jason back home."

"How was the kid?" Amber asked.

"Justin turned out to be okay, other than a mild concussion. But they didn't discharge him until nearly eight o'clock the following morning."

"And you stayed with him the whole night?" Busch was skeptical.

Nathan nodded. "Yep. I was with the kid the entire time. All night!"

Margarita put down her beer. "Yeah. I remember something like that. Honey was all upset when she came in that day and told us about Justin's accident. She was relieved he was going to be all right. But she was worked up about the kid not wearing his helmet. She told us he was in the ER all night, but never mentioned you was involved, let alone that you stayed with him the whole time."

"Whether she mentioned me is neither here nor there. That's where I was. I'm sure my cell phone records will confirm my whereabouts. I must have talked to Honey on the phone at least a half-dozen times that night. I don't think either of us got any sleep. Besides, you can ask the ER Nurse, Bea Naughty. I think that was her name. She'll remember me."

"Bea Naughty? I know her. I wouldn't mind checking her vitals," Bud said.

Nobody laughed.

Honey, who had been standing at another table taking orders, came over.

"Was Nathan with Justin all night when he got hurt that night on his skateboard?" Margarita asked.

Honey looked at Nathan. "What Nathan said is true. I don't know what I would have done if Nathan had not come to my rescue that night. Thanks, Nathan."

Busch stared hard at Honey. *Nathan pulls a flimsy alibi out of his hat at the last minute, and Honey corroborates it all. His explanation also clears Honey. Unless they rehearsed this story together, it'll pan out. Justin's ER records and Nathan's phone records will confirm their claims. It's back to square one. Damn!*

Chapter 43

It's in the details. It's always in the details. Busch's typical breakfast for years was a bowl of cereal and orange juice on weekdays. Yesterday he cracked the seal on a fresh, new box of Rice Krispies. Something about the cereal — he couldn't put his finger on it — just wasn't right. Since a busy day lay ahead, he pushed it to the back of his mind and went on with things. It didn't matter. Now, a day later, the Rice Krispies weren't right again. This time, it bothered him, and Busch could not let it go. Today, like the clap of a mousetrap, it came to him: *Snap, crackle, but no pop. Real Rice Krispies are supposed to snap, crackle, AND pop. These pop-less kernels are frauds.* He was done with them. He would move on to Honey Bunches of Oats tomorrow morning. He tossed away what was left, grabbed his mug of coffee, and darted out through the back door. *Details. Always in the details.*

In his pick-up, driving to The Purple Pig at Lake Sumter Landing, Busch grabbed his phone and called Bud Schweitzer. His investigation had produced a myriad of troubling leads, but still no culprit. Now, he reluctantly needed to talk to a friend high on the suspect list.

The call went to voice mail. "Bud, it's Busch." He looked at his watch. "It's about eight-thirty. I'm on my way to Sumter Landing. I need to talk to you. Call me as soon as you get this. You have my number. Thanks." *And buddy, I've got your number, too.*

Busch was lucky to find a parking spot on Canal Street. A quick jaunt into The Purple Pig was all it took, and he returned to his truck with just the right card for Honey. It was a scratch and sniff and even smelled like beer. He planned to give her the card to make up for his earlier questioning. Before pulling away, he called Bud again. "Schweitzer, I really do need to talk to you, preferably before this afternoon at the bar. Call me ASAP. Thanks. Oh, this is Busch."

The detective returned to the local sheriff's office for a couple of hours to tend to neglected files. He detested paperwork, a waste of good investigating time, but recognized it as a necessity. Sometimes, you might even find a detail that solves a case.

Three times again, he called Schweitzer, and ended up leaving a message. He thought it odd that Bud was not returning his calls. *It would be best to talk to Schweitzer before we run into each other at the bar later. If there is a confrontation, why risk others?*

Busch raced through several online databases, downloaded a file or two, and printed out two curious reports. He found that Schweitzer was cited in Miami-Dade County twice in the past seven weeks for speed violations. The citations probably had nothing to do with the murder investigation, but it was an 'i' without a dot, in a case with many uncrossed 't's.' *Just one more angle to check out. Schweitzer never said a word about being in south Florida. Odd, he didn't mention that.*

Busch left the office just before noon, and after serving several no-show warrants and a jury summons in Spruce Creek, he drove to the Sonic and grabbed a burger. He made one final call to Schweitzer, but left no message.

Chapter 44

After Busch's embarrassing attempt to implicate Nathan Lambic in the murder of Danny Barfright, he felt frustrated. He wondered how they would treat him when he returned to the Beer Buddies get-together at World of Beer. By the time he pulled into the parking lot, the sky had opened to a downpour. He made a run for the bar, but got soaked. It didn't matter; he had work to do, wet or dry. As he made his way to the table, he found all of the Beer Buddies waiting for him. He waved to Honey.

The Beer of the Week, according to the sign over the bar, was *Hellraiser Dark Amber*. Busch ordered the *Hellraiser*, delighted he could enjoy a drink on duty and still keep his no-alcohol proclivity under wraps.

"You look like you just got out of the shower, Buschie. Didn't your mother teach you to dry off before you got dressed?" Bud quipped.

"Schweitzer, you're not answering your phone. What gives?" Busch spoke in a severe tone.

"Did you try to call me?"

"I've been leaving messages for you for days."

Bud smiled at the others. "Sorry about that. My damn Android is back in the shop. The thing wouldn't hold a charge. I've been without a phone since yesterday afternoon, and I'm really missing my Angry Birds."

Someone tittered in the background.

Bud smiled at Busch. "What'd you need me for?"

"You know. The investigation continues. Just a few questions for you. Can we scoot to another table for a minute?"

Bud looked puzzled. "Why can't we just talk here?"

"It's better if we have some alone time if you know what I mean. Grab your beer, and let's take that table." Busch pointed to an empty table about fifteen feet away.

Bud stood up, beer mug in hand, and walked behind Busch. Turning, he addressed the Buddies, "See you chaps in a minute or two. I guess I'll find out what Buschie has on his mind."

The others watched somberly as the scene played out before them. Nathan sipped at his beer, his eyes aimed at Busch. Margarita shook her head and mumbled something that sounded like 'shit crick.' Sam knocked back a swig and, lowering his half-empty mug to the table, licked his lips. He watched Busch's lips. Tony stopped chewing his pizza and joined Sam watching the interaction between Busch and Bud. "You think Busch is going to try to pin the murder on Bud?" he asked Sam.

The conversation between Busch and Schweitzer was calm at first; then became heated. Everyone heard Busch shout something about a "cock-and-bull" story when Bud again tried to convince him that Nathan stole his Stan Musial bat. Then it got quiet.

"I wonder what's happening?" Margarita asked.

Suddenly, all hell broke loose.

"The hell you are, you son of a bitch," Bud yelled and stood up.

Busch jumped to his feet and walked around an empty chair. "Put your hands behind your back," he ordered, flipping open a pair of handcuffs.

"Buschie, you can't be serious. What the hell are you doing?" Bud shouted, but offered no resistance. "I'm innocent. I didn't do it."

The Beer Buddies were a captive audience, their eyes glued to the confrontation. Tony spoke up, "Busch, what in god's name is going on?"

Busch clamped the cuffs onto Bud's wrists. "You just watch." Turning back to Bud, he announced, "Bud Schweitzer, I am placing you under arrest for the murder of Danny Barfright."

"Are you kidding?" Margarita exclaimed and burst into laughter.

Busch next articulated words all too familiar to anyone who watches TV. "You have the right…"

Amber stood and said, "There's gotta be a mistake here. Buschie, please calm down. Talk this through."

Busch would have none of it. He continued reading Schweitzer his rights, "You have the right to remain silent. Anything you say can and will…"

"Guys, guys, guys," Tony shouted, "If this is some kind of joke, we get it. Stop already."

"No joke," Busch said. "You have the right to an attorney, and if you cannot afford an attorney, one will be provided for you." He completed the *Miranda* warnings making a mental note that six witnesses had seen him do it. He heard Honey standing at the bar weeping into a Kleenex. He'd talk to her later.

The others stared morosely as Busch followed a now handcuffed Schweitzer toward the door.

Amber gave it one more try. "Buschie, can't we please talk about this? This whole thing just isn't right. Please? We're all old friends here."

Busch stopped, placed his hand on Schweitzer's shoulder to turn him toward Amber and the Beer Buddies. The protocol didn't require him to explain to bystanders what he was doing, but these were his Beer Buddies. "Look, guys, Danny's dead. Schweitzer drove his cart along the same path the night somebody killed Danny. He admits he followed and saw him at Dunkin Donuts." He paused to let that sink in. "Danny, poor soul, was killed by a devastating blow to his head by a heavy object. I went to check on Bud's Stan Musial bat for obvious reasons. Danny had seen it shortly before at Schweitzer's house. Our friend here, after he knew we were looking for a bat, claimed somebody stole it. He tried to put it off on Nathan, claiming he was the one who took it." He paused again. "Well, it turns out that Nathan had our friend's Stan Musial. After intensive questioning, Nathan said he was only borrowing it and offered a perfectly reasonable explanation. Nathan also had an alibi, didn't you?" He looked in Honey's direction.

A red-faced Nathan nodded his head. "It's the truth."

Honey nodded.

A look of disappointment blanketed Busch's face. The case was frustrating enough. "So, Nathan has an alibi. And that's one thing that our mutual acquaintance, Bud here, doesn't have." Bud shook his head. "If he had an alibi, he would have told me by now." More dramatic than they had ever seen him, Busch announced with fanfare, "Friends, meet the cold-blooded killer of Danny Barfright."

"No . . . No, wait. I can explain. I do have an alibi." Bud choked up.

"The hell you do," Busch shouted. "How many times have I asked? And what have you told me? Nada, big man, nada!"

Bud looked down at the floor. "I never dreamed that I'd be a serious suspect, Buschie. I hated lying to you, but I was too embarrassed to say where I was that night."

Busch had a bad feeling about this. "Okay, Schweitzer, There's no time like the present."

Bud took a deep breath. Then another. "I was in Miami the night someone else killed Danny." He hesitated. "I was at a contest."

"Oh, brother," Busch moaned.

Schweitzer stammered, "I was a contestant."

Busch grabbed Bud's arms. "Now, I've heard everything. What was it, a chili cookoff?"

Bud shivered. "I was in the Drag Queen America Pageant." He burst into sobs. The big man trembled like a child caught in a naughty act.

Tony tipped his head to the side, staring at Bud as though he had just witnessed an unbelievable act.

Margarita guffawed and said, "I knew it. I knew it."

Sam sported a look of concern that replaced his usual toothy grin.

Busch shook his head, batting his eyes furiously. "You what? You want us to believe that you were a drag queen contestant? Is that your alibi?"

"I can prove it," Schweitzer said in a low voice.

"We're all waiting, Miss Schweitzer. Go ahead, prove it."

"I won second place in the beauty contest. I got fifteen dollars."

Busch laughed. "That's your proof? Fifteen dollars?"

Bud shook his head. "Wait. It was only a preliminary, mind you, but I can prove it. I'll show you my trophy."

Amber jumped up, shouting, "Yes, yes, yes! Bud's telling you the truth. I was there. I was in Miami. I saw him!"

Busch whirled on Amber. "You have got to be fricking yanking my chain. Amber, you went to see Miss Schweitzer in a drag queen contest?" *What the hell is going on? Is she making this up? Are all these people insane?*

Amber walked over to Bud. "No, I didn't go to see Bud. I didn't know he was in the contest. I went to Miami to help make-up a friend who was also competing." Then, she added, almost as an aside, "Damn, Dom looked hot when I finished with him."

Busch held his head with his hands. "I have a headache."

Amber continued, "I decided to go to the contest and root for my friend. That's when I saw Bud. He was stunning in a gorgeous white chiffon jumper. At first, I wasn't sure it was him. But his muscles gave him away."

The Beer Buddies erupted in shouts of joy, applauding their friend's dismissal as the prime suspect.

A smirking Honey dropped a quarter into the jukebox.

The rest of the buddies rushed to Bud.

Busch groaned as he reached for his handcuff key.

Once free, Bud laughed and shook his hindquarters in perfect rhythm to "Dancing Queen" like none of his buddies ever dreamed he could.

Deputy B. Pillsbusch Frapp felt like he needed a beer. Maybe even a six-pack. As he stared sullenly at the festivities, he realized what he really needed was a suspect.

Chapter 45

For Busch, it was another night with little or no sleep. He was agitated because a cable outage made him both unable to watch *MacGyver* or continue snooping around the Internet for anything he could find on Tony Bellome, another of his suspects. He hit the sack by ten o'clock, but couldn't shake the images thrashing around his brain. *This case is driving me crazy*, he thought after replaying his jumbled arrest of Bud Schweitzer.

Busch tried to steer his mind back to his younger days, his life as a sailor — good times, wild times, with his shipmates. But there were memories of bad times, too. Blackouts after too much drinking; the time he passed out on the beach during shore leave. And the horrifying explosion in the engine room when he stared death in the face. Had it not been for his buddy, Slim, he would have died that day. That memory haunted him as a recurring nightmare, always leaving him with cold sweats.

Now haunted by the need to solve this case, Busch did not want to waste time sleepless in bed. Once he abandoned all efforts to sleep, it did not take long for him to get on his feet and rolling. He made do with only a pair of boxers. *At 3:40 a.m., a cop isn't going anywhere, so why dress?* After brewing coffee, he poured himself a mug and walked out to the lanai. He got comfortable on his chaise longue, seat back in the full upright position.

The neighborhood was asleep. A faint odor of insecticide hung in the air, stirring up visions of the guy from the lawn company in his green jumpsuit dragging a long yellow hose around the house and spraying chemicals into the eaves. It pleased Busch that he lived in an insect-free house. *Now, if I could only get the damn bugs out of my head, I'd be okay.*

Subtle, indirect lighting coming from the neighbor's pool illuminated floating toys, signaling their grandkids' imminent arrival from Idaho. His reverie shattered when his sprinklers popped out of their hiding places at 3:45 a.m., set on their task of keeping The Villages green. *The sprinklers come on automatically — now, that is handy. Would that criminal investigations were so convenient.*

The detective — accomplished as he was from years of experience, and despite the disparaging comments of Supervising Chief Inspector Detective Oskar Blue of the FBI — began yet another thorough review of what his investigation had turned up. Even though recent events had not produced the murderer and had been humiliating, there was a consolation. All-in-all, his investigation vindicated the Beer Buddies and proved they were a decent group of codgers rather than suspects.

Busch evaluated what he knew. Bud Schweitzer had the most laughable alibi he had ever heard. In relying upon it, Bud had to disclose to his friends a secret about his 'other life' that he was terrified would embarrass him. His friends had supported him, and he told them how Danny had threatened to expose him. He admitted following him and running away when he discovered his body. Bud was still a suspect, but he had slipped way down on the list.

Busch thought of Honey Lovejoy. Not much of a motive, and she had an alibi. One of the twins was in the hospital suffering from a concussion the night of the murder. Her story also protected Nathan Lambic, who had been a prime suspect. Nathan had 'borrowed' the Stan the Man bat from Bud without telling him. But, as a result of his kind act of caring for Honey's son in the hospital, Lambic had an air-tight alibi.

Busch came to Sam Adams. He had a weak alibi. He claimed he was home alone watching *Law and Order*. If he was the killer, wouldn't he dig up a better story? Given Sam's advancing years, he wasn't up to the task. More importantly, Busch could determine no motive for the bra maker to want to take Danny's life. He told the guy ribald jokes. I can't see it, Busch thought.

And then there was Amber Bock. After Danny's death, she claimed to have learned that he named her in his will for a sizable inheritance. There wasn't an iota of evidence that connected her in any way to Danny's murder. Still, the motive was strong.

All of that brought things down to Tony Bellome — the old pizza-lover. The more Busch thought about it, the more questions he had. It was time to put the squeeze on the Italian New Yorker. Busch called Tony just before 9 a.m. and arranged to meet him an hour before the regular time the Beer Buddies got together for their happy hour.

Shortly after lunch hour, Busch entered the bar from a bright and sunny Florida day. It took his eyes a while to adjust to the inside lighting. He found Tony sitting in his usual chair at the Beer Buddies table, facing the front door. He noted that the big man wore a long-sleeved, satin shirt the color of a creamy marinara sauce.

Tony waved Busch over.

As Busch got to the table and pulled up a chair, Bellome wiped his eyeglasses with olive oil! Busch thought it best not to ask as Tony, after much rubbing, put on his glasses.

"Tony, my friend, thanks for meeting me early today. We need to talk, and it's best if it's just us. You know." The lenses on Tony's glasses made it difficult for Busch to focus on Tony's eyeballs.

"It's the least I could do. I figured my time was coming." Tony removed his glasses once again then held them up as if to look through them before placing them in his shirt's breast pocket. "So, you think it comes down to me, Busch, is that right?"

"Wow, it doesn't take you long to get to the point, does it? I was ready to chit-chat a bit, but let's get to it, big guy."

"Shoot. No pun intended." Tony guffawed and added, "If you want a 'pizza me,' go for it." He poked Busch. "Get it?"

"This is serious, Tony. I need serious answers."

Tony nodded his head. "I ain't got nothin' to hide. How can I help?"

Busch thought it curious that Bellome did not appear to have his guard up. Not a good sign. Perhaps this old guy really did have nothing to hide. *Why am I always so suspicious? Even of my friends.*

"You know, Tony, I don't think I ever heard why you came to Florida. I mean, your accent is a dead giveaway. You talk a lot about being from Brooklyn. So, do you have family down here?"

"Nope. My kids and grandkids are scattered all around. I was widowed two years ago, just after our thirty-seventh wedding anniversary. The kids came back to New York for it, though, and we had a big party at Agostino's Uptown Olive Hut in Bensonhurst. Celebrated thirty-seven happy years of marriage." He poked Busch in the ribs again. "You ought to try it sometime."

"And just who's saying I haven't tried to find someone?" Busch did not want to be side-tracked. "Anyhow, we're not here to talk about me." He caught Honey Lovejoy's eye and gave her the high sign.

Honey waved and smiled. She then headed to the bar.

Busch turned back to Tony. "So, you hightailed it to Florida after your wife passed. Sorry to hear that."

"Yeah. Sort of. I was already retired, and there was nothing left for me in Brooklyn. The place was turning into a dump, and no family close by. A couple of friends told me about free golf down here and lots of stuff to do. Even though I'm not a golfer, a claim like that — well, it draws you to a place. I came down to check it out, and before you know it, I'm living the retirees' dream in a rented villa. Now, I'm looking to buy a place. I never owned a house in my life, and I got a realtor looking for one. Can you imagine that?" Tony said.

"Yeah. Who would ever buy a house on their first visit to this place? A lot of people. It's a story that's been told here a thousand times. So, you still haven't taken up golf, huh?"

"Nope. I gave it a try, but I already spent too much of my life chasing what I shouldn't a been chasing. I'll leave that little 'fore' plaything to the rest of you happy hookers."

Honey walked over to the Beer Buddies' table, bringing a tall, frosted pilsner of *Golden Road Mango Cart NA* for Busch and a *Birra Moretti* for Bellome. "Hey, Buschie, can I get you anything else right now? I'll have your pizza out here in a jiffy, Tony."

Busch smiled at Honey. "Nah, I'm fine. But thanks for asking."

Honey left, seeing another patron across the bar hailing her.

Turning back, Busch asked, "So, Tony, what line of work were you in before you retired?"

"You know, a little this, a little that. You name it, I did it, or some of it."

"That doesn't tell me very much. Were you in the service industry?"

"In a manner of speaking, yeah, I suppose I was."

Busch was losing patience. "Come on, spill the beans, old man. Are you going to make me comb the database for your rap sheets?"

Tony leaned over, placing his gigantic hands flat on the table and aiming dark eyes at Busch. "It won't do you no good cause there ain't nothing there. Like I told you, I'm clean." His smile reappeared. "Buschie, I'm Italian. I'm from Brooklyn. I was gainfully employed my whole life, and I'm still alive. That should tell you all you need to know about what business I was in. Need I say more?"

Busch leaned forward, lowering his voice, "Are you telling me you worked for the mob, Tony?"

Tony raised an index finger over his lips and whispered back, "I said no such thing, no such thing at all." Then lowering his voice, he rasped, "But I ain't denying nothin' either."

Busch sat back in his chair, deep in thought. He needed to proceed with caution. When he next spoke, he chose his words very, very, carefully. "What the hell is your real name?"

Bellome had a look of confusion on his face.

"I said, is your name really Tony Bellome?"

Tony looked around the room, and then turned back to Busch. "No. Actually, it isn't."

The more Busch questioned Bellome, the more obvious it became: Bellome was now, or had been a mobster. Things were making perfect sense. Busch surmised that when Bellome — or whoever he was — landed in Florida less than eight months ago, he probably changed his name to stay hidden. In The Villages, he'd found the perfect hiding place. No family. No one snooping around. The Villages was the ideal place to hide, especially if his

life was on the line. Busch could not believe he had missed
something so obvious. The guy he was now talking to, this Beer
Buddy he had known for so long, just admitted that his name was
not Tony Bellome. So, who was he? What was his real name?
Setting his half-empty pilsner glass aside and folding his hands on
the table before him, Busch asked, "Care to tell me what your real
name is then?"

Tony looked left, then right. He turned left again, a bit
farther. He peered over his shoulder toward the bar. When the big
man turned back again, he leaned toward Busch and whispered,
"My real name? Sure. It's Anthony Giuseppe Bellome." Then Tony
Bellome laughed so hard the others heard it above the toilet
flushing in the men's room across the saloon floor.

"You son of a bitch. You got me," Busch said, now
laughing, too.

When they both regained their composure, the detective
continued with his questioning. "So, why didn't you cotton to our
friend, Danny?"

"Cotton? Hey, who says I didn't like Danny? I didn't mind
Danny at all. I sort of miss the guy. Don't you?"

*Did he? Danny was a piece of work. There were times I
wanted to shut him up.* "We all miss him. What happened to him is
too damn bad. But doesn't it bother you that his murderer is still
out there, maybe looking for another victim?"

Tony looked at his hands. "Look, I wish you all the luck in
the world to catch the bastard that killed Danny. I'm even willing
to help you find him if there's some way I can. But just because
you now know a little bit about my former life, my earlier 'gainful
employment,' doesn't mean I should be a suspect. I thought he was
mostly a pretty good guy. I'm sorry for what happened to him. But
I had nothing to do with it. End of story. You should stop wasting
your time barking up my tree."

"You wouldn't be threatening me now, would you, Tony?"

"Of course not. No reason to. I will admit to having fun
pulling your chain."

Busch was about to lecture Tony about interfering in an
investigation when Honey returned to their table, bearing a sixteen-
inch thin-crusted, marinara-flooded, cheese-engorged pizza,
covered with pepperoni slices a quarter-inch thick. "You guys look

like you're having fun. Don't let me interrupt you." She placed the pizza alongside a pair of ceramic plates, a stack of white paper napkins, and a neatly folded and pressed linen napkin near Bellome.

Busch looked at the pizza, then at Tony, and exclaimed, "Good God, Bellome! Who are you expecting? The Pope and half the Swiss Guard? There's enough pizza there for…"

Tony interrupted him, stretching his marinara-colored arms. "I got this for all the Beer Buddies, who should be here soon. And Honey — if the boss will let you, why not join us for a bit?"

Honey smiled. "That's real nice of you, Tony. Thanks. But the boss doesn't like us doing that with customers. Why don't you eat my piece?"

Busch had a retort for that, but exercised a morsel of self-restraint and just bit his tongue. Honey's piece would go to Tony without further comment. "Why the pizza party?" he asked. "Are we celebrating something?"

Tony smiled. "I got my reasons." He got up and left the table.

Everyone has secrets, Busch thought. He resolved to find out more about the mysterious Tony Bellome's background, even if it killed him.

Chapter 46

After Tony left the table, Busch sulked, drowning his chagrin with a pint of *Guinness Kaliber*. It wasn't as if there were no legitimate suspects among the Beer Buddies. He had a sailor's hunch the killer was still within reach.

The afternoon wore on, but he wasn't about to quit. After he finished the delightfully smooth *Kaliber*, he ordered another beer from the new menu and reconsidered the facts. It would be easy to drop the investigation and accept the snooty FBI detective's conclusion that it was a random killing by the Cereal Killer. Surrender was not in Busch's DNA. He would make one more pass at finding the murderer. He waited until the others arrived and asked Margarita to accompany him to the room behind the bar.

Margarita smiled. "Whatever you say, Buschie." She picked up her glass and followed him after winking at the others at the table.

Once inside the small room, Busch turned to Margarita and said, "And as for you, Margarita Gose," he pointed his foamy mug of *Clausthaler Premium Lager* toward the blonde bombshell. "We still haven't heard where you were when Barfright bought the farm." He moved closer to her. "The backend of a pool cue would carry enough weight to crush a man's skull, and we know you handle your stick like a pro."

"Hold on to your brown ale, Busch!" Margarita retorted with a wicked smile. "You're way off base, casting accusations of murder at me." She stood up and began circling the table. "Sure, I had reason to hate Danny. He tried to get me to grab his stick every time we were alone. I was not going along with him. He knew he disgusted me, and it drove him crazy. Besides that, why would I kill him? Danny was working on a little side deal involving some friends of mine. It was worth a ton of dough. Too bad. The opportunity went south when he got bashed. If he stayed alive, I could've got the deal done and made a load of cash." She kept walking around the table, sipping her brew, and then continued, "But he got himself killed. And that ruined my deal. Poof." Passing in front of Busch, she stuck her middle finger in his beer, pulled it out, sucked the foaming brew off her digit, and smacked her lips as her nail popped out of her mouth.

"Was your deal legitimate?" Busch asked.

"A lady never tells who she's kissed," Margarita replied, wagging a finger at him.

"You have an alibi, I suppose."

Margarita tossed back her hair. "Buschie. Buschie. I was in a high stakes straight pool tournament over at The Eight Ball the night Danny bought it. Just check out your facts."

Busch looked down at his violated mug, and said, "You have tons of friends over at The Eight Ball. They'd all lie for you, so that alibi is worth crap."

"Not so," came a voice from the far-left side of the bar. "I've got proof Ms. Gose was there."

"Who the hell are you?" Busch asked, regretting he left the door open and someone overheard them.

"My name's Duke Bruski. I'm the proud proprietor of the pool hall over at The Eight Ball. I know Ms. Gose very well, and I'll vouch for her being there that night. She beat everyone in the joint with that pink cue of hers. On top of that, I have a time-stamped picture of her cute little backside leaning over one of our pool tables, making a side-pocket bank shot." Bruski held up his phone showing Busch the photo.

Busch took his phone and stared at the screenshot of a woman with a pink pool cue, in black leather pants bent over a table, and said, "How do we know that's Mags?"

After the laughter died, Busch said, "Shit. She's gotta be clean." He handed the phone back to Duke and asked, grinning meekly, "Can you send me a copy of that?" He added, "It's evidence." Why was everyone laughing?

Margarita walked over and stuck her middle finger in Busch's beer again. She slipped it between her red lips. "Buschie, you taste real good." She flipped him the bird and sashayed to the pool hall; half the bar followed her.

Busch thought of following, too. Maybe watching Margarita beat the balls off other players would distract him.

"Have some pizza," Tony offered, returning from the men's room. "It's a hell of a lot better than humble pie."

Busch stared at Tony. *I haven't knocked this one off my list yet. A good a time as any to get to know Mr. Bellome better.*

Chapter 47

Tony and Busch had barely begun their feast on Tony's extravagant pizza when the rest of the Beer Buddies showed up. Suspicion oozed around Busch's brain. *It's almost as if they gathered in the parking lot before coming in.* Nathan, Sam, and Bud headed straight for the table, while Amber made a pit stop into the ladies' room. By the time she joined them, the entire group was chowing down and waiting for Honey to deliver something to wash down the pizza.

Busch spoke first. "What a motley crew. Gorging our pie holes like none of us ever had a meal before. We have Tony, here, to thank for all this."

"I didn't have much choice. Buschie wanted to meet me earlier this afternoon so we could talk, but he dragged it out so long, I got hungry. And I wasn't gonna order up for just me this time — not after what happened last time." He lopped off a more than bite-sized chunk and chewed as if he hadn't eaten all week.

"So, what's the big secret? What did you guys talk about?" Sam asked.

"My guess is, if they tell ya, they're going to have to kill you. Right, guys?" Bud snickered. As was often the case, Bud seemed to think he was funnier than he was, especially under the circumstances.

Busch felt sorry Schweitzer was no longer a suspect.

Nathan spoke up, "Poor choice of words, my friend. Besides, you know damn well what they were talking about. Busch has his work cut out for him. We are all just persons of interest here. But no culprit yet. Am I right, Busch?"

Busch rested both forearms against the edge of the table, head down. Nathan nailed it. Repeatedly, Busch zeroed in on a possible killer, only to come up empty-handed. His attempts at fingering Danny's killer proved as slippery as trying to pin a bead of mercury under his thumb. A difficult task, at best. His pose was one of defeat, and 'don't mess with me.' After all, there was still a killer on the loose.

Nathan said, "Yes, my friends, we're all persons of interest. That's why this investigation has taken so much damn time. Right, Busch?"

Sam said softly, "No murderer just walks up and confesses. They do all they can to secrete their handiwork."

Wiping his gaping, open mouth, Tony said. "They what? Did I hear you say 'secrete?' Is that even a word?"

Nathan answered, "Look it up in your *Funk & Wagnalls*, if you need to."

Busch said, "It means to hide or conceal."

Nathan shot a meaningful look at Sam.

Amber raised her glass. "I think we don't give Buschie enough credit for all the hard work he's doing on this investigation. Nobody here's been much help to him. And I, for one, think he knows more words from the dictionary than all the rest of us combined. Don't you?" she asked.

Busch was about to respond when his cell phone vibrated in his jeans pocket. He shifted in his chair to retrieve it, touched the green button, and lifted the phone to his ear. "Busch here."

The Beer Buddies continued talking among themselves until the brief call ended.

Busch announced, "Hey guys, I gotta head out for a couple of minutes, but I'll be back. Tony, save me a small corner of one slice, please? And make sure there's still some pepperoni on it when I return."

Tony nodded.

Busch, clad in his uniform, strode away toward the door. Had he turned, he would have noticed Margarita's admiring glance at his backside.

Busch was gone fewer than fifteen minutes. He had made up his mind that it was not any of their business who called him. They did not need to know that the caller gave him an invitation he could not refuse. In the parking lot, Busch met with Supervising Chief Inspector Detective Oskar Blue of the FBI.

Their encounter, professionally courteous, lasted less than ten minutes, with the Supervising Chief Inspector Detective doing the talking. Near the end of his discourse, the FBI detective reached into his black Cadillac Escalade and retrieved a manila envelope, which he handed to Busch.

Before stepping into his vehicle, the Supervising Chief Inspector Detective placed his hand on Busch's shoulder and offered the detective his hand.

Busch shook hands, and then watched silently as the Escalade left the parking lot, pulled into traffic, and recklessly edged out a golf cart proudly flying Old Glory from the golf bag rack. The cart's driver saluted the Supervising Chief Inspector Detective with a single-digit gesture of contempt.

Busch agreed with the cart driver. He walked to the shade of a clump of palm trees set evenly along the parking lot perimeter. Satisfied nobody was watching, he opened the envelope and examined the contents. Then, tucking the envelope under his arm, he walked over to his pick-up. Opening the door, he grabbed a set of handcuffs from behind the driver seat, notched them onto his belt, and headed back inside World of Beer.

Busch re-entered the bar and walked straight back to his place at the Beer Buddies table.

Mags, who smiled when she first saw him return, frowned when she noticed the handcuffs.

Busch stood by the table.

"You look like a statue," Sam remarked.

"Is everything alright?" Nathan asked.

"Mostly, it is, yeah." Busch nodded his head. "Hey, Tony, did you get to save me that small slice I asked for?"

Tony stopped dead in his tracks, no longer chewing. "Damn, I forgot, Buschie. I'm eating the last piece now. Sorry."

Not a hint of disappointment appeared on Busch's face. "Tony, I'm not sure you and I have finished our conversation."

"Because I ate your slice?" Tony asked.

Busch shook his head.

"What do you mean? I thought we finished up. What else is there?" Tony looked worried.

"Well, my friend, something's come up since we had our brief chat a while ago."

Tony tossed his linen napkin onto the table. "Not this, again? Busch, are we really gonna have to sit through another 'gotcha' scene?"

Amber said, "Busch, honey, it didn't work out so well for you last time, did it?"

Margarita added, "And poor Bud, here. You hurt her feelings. Well, whatever, *she's* still a jolly good fella." She appeared pleased with herself, leering at Bud.

Schweitzer frowned at the potshot, but seemed more concerned with what Busch was up to next.

Nathan weighed in. "Come on, Busch, you've done this drill before, and it got you nowhere. Why persist? Can't we just eat, drink, and be merry? And Bud, here," he gestured with his thumb, "he can be *Mary*."

"That's right," Bud shouted. "Make me the butt of your jokes. You're all nothing but a bunch of closet heterosexuals! That's all."

A few burst into laughter.

Busch blew his whistle. "Hold on. Hold on, folks."

"You blew your whistle in my ear," Sam complained. "Now, my hearing aid is kaput." He tapped it on the table.

Busch ignored him. "Guys, I've got just a question or two for Tony here. So, everybody relax." He looked straight at Tony and said, "On second thought, just drink your suds and enjoy this."

Several of the Beer Buddies looked at each other, shaking their heads and mumbling in disbelief that Deputy Busch was at it again.

Busch focused on Tony. "Mr. Bellome, do you know a guy named Juanito?"

Tony stared at Busch. There was a hardness in his face that had not been evident before. Busch had struck a nerve. "I know a bunch of Juanitos, Busch. I'm from Brooklyn, remember? So what if I know guys named Juanito?"

Busch had been a detective long enough to spot a deflection. "Well, I ain't talking about any Juanitos from Brooklyn, Mr. Bellome. I'm talking about a guy named Juanito from Miami. A short Hispanic, maybe five-six or five-seven, not heavy but solid. A pretty scary-looking dude. A truck driver." He looked at Tony. "Does that Juanito sound familiar?"

A blanket of sweat beads sprouted on Tony's forehead. His eyes darted around the table, checking the reactions of the Beer Buddies to Busch's questions. "Nope. Never heard of him."

Busch placed the envelope on the table. "Well, that's odd. Because the Juanito picked up on a drug bust a week ago, and now in the custody of Supervising Chief Inspector Detective Oskar Blue of the FBI — well, he says he knows you. He's ratted on you, my friend."

"Impossible," Tony said, and wiped his brow with his linen pizza napkin, a move he immediately regretted.

"You got sauce on your glasses," Amber told him.

Tony removed his eyeglasses, and with a handkerchief pulled from his right hip pocket, scrubbed the marinara-covered lens.

"In fact," Busch continued, sensing he was finally in for the kill, "this Juanito has given a sworn statement implicating you in the murder of Danny Barfright."

A gasp rose from the shocked bystanders.

Tony shifted nervously in his seat.

Busch aimed his harpoon. "Admit it, Tony. Don Gaspo invited you to his home back in New York, not long ago."

"Gaspo?" Margarita muttered.

Busch pushed harder, "Gaspo pulled you out of retirement, didn't he?"

Tony raised his voice, "I don't know a damn thing about any of that, Busch. You got a lot of nerve trying to put the squeeze on me here, in front of our friends." He looked around the table, nervous, anxiety written all over his face, eyeglasses sitting crookedly near the end of his nose. "Nobody here believes any of your bullshit anymore. Do you guys?"

Everyone sat stone-faced.

Not allowing for a lull, Busch added, "And during your little social visit with the Don, he put a mark on Danny, and appointed you to carry it out. Isn't that right?"

Tony Bellome jumped up and pointed his index finger at Busch. "You don't know what you're talking about."

Busch charged ahead, "Your sole reason for moving to The Villages from New York was to search for and kill Danny Barfright. That's the truth, and you know it. Admit it! ADMIT IT!"

"Yes, yes, yes," Tony shouted.

Every head at the table — indeed, every pair of eyes in the bar — stared at Tony. The Beer Buddies, to a person, sat in stunned disbelief.

Amber pushed her chair back from the table, away from Tony. Sam, who sat on Tony's left, stared silently, a bewildered look on his face.

Tony spoke again, almost in a whisper, "I was hired to rub Danny out, but I didn't do it."

Busch shook his head. "Are you crazy? Everyone in this bar just heard you admit that you were hired as a hitman to kill Danny. Denying it now is a bit late. Don't you think?"

"I admitted I was hired, but I never admitted to killing Danny," Tony insisted.

Busch did not buy Tony's story. Bellome had admitted he was a hitman. Case closed. He reached for his handcuffs. "Hands behind your back, Tony. Don't try anything."

Bellome looked around the table, hesitated, then raised both arms. "I admit that the Don sent me here to take Danny out. But I admit nothing else." He looked at his friends. "I'm telling you it wasn't me. Buschie, once again, you got the wrong man."

Busch looked at the others gathered around him. "So, now, Tony, your only defense is that you didn't do it? Do I have that right, Mr. Mafia hitman?"

Tony nodded. "Yes, you do. You see, I wasn't in town the night Danny died."

Busch shouted, "Danny didn't die. You killed him."

"I didn't. I wasn't in town, I told you."

"You never mentioned this out-of-town thing before. I wonder why that is? Are you going to tell us you were in a drag queen contest, too?" Busch laughed.

Bud did not.

Tony shook his head. "Let me tell you why I didn't say something before, Busch. You see, I had nothing to do with Danny's murder. About that, I have nothing — NOTHING — to hide. So, when you come snooping around with a bunch of questions, I figure whatever I did that night was none of your business. I mean, folks have private lives. Maybe I got something *personal* to hide, something that's nothing to do with Danny's murder."

"Hear him out, Busch," Amber pleaded.

"What have you got to lose?" Sam asked.

"You got it wrong before," Nathan reminded him.

Busch sighed. "Okay. I'm ready for the hitman's story. You're saying that you were out of town the night Danny got 'rubbed out,' as you put it?"

Tony looked at the door. "Yeah, I was in Key West. If you recall, I missed our regular Tuesday afternoon that day."

"That's right, he did," Nathan confirmed.

Busch felt a headache drumming up. "Anybody else happen to recall if Tony was missing that day?"

Several hands went up.

Sam said, "I don't remember what I had for breakfast this morning."

Busch felt frustration building. *Please, don't tell me I got it wrong again.* "You missing the meeting doesn't mean a damn thing. You could have arranged that, so you had time to plan the murder."

Everyone gasped. Someone said, "That's true."

Tony looked sheepish. "I didn't want to tell anyone, but you leave me no choice. I went to meet up with an old friend. I left early Monday morning. It's a long drive to Key West, you know. We stayed there until Sunday, left around noon."

"You're making this all up, aren't you, Bellome," Busch said, ready to leave with the hand-cuffed hitman. "So, who was the old friend?" he asked.

Tony looked nervous. "I can't say."

"That's it! He can't say." Busch raised his hands to the others. "You heard the hitman. He can't say who he was with. What a crock..."

"Tell Busch who you were with, for god's sake," Margarita implored.

"Who are you protecting?" Nathan asked.

Bracing himself on the table, Tony slowly turned his eyes to his right and looked forlornly at Amber. His voice was almost inaudible. "I'm sorry. I tried." He looked back at Busch, and said, "I was in Key West with Sara, Sara Nevada."

Amber jumped to her feet. "You were there with my mother? The hell you were!"

As if on cue, with the most impeccable timing, Sara Nevada entered the bar, waved to her daughter, and made a beeline for the Beer Buddies' table. Appearing unaware of Amber's angry pose, hands perched on her nicely rounded hips, Sara said, "I'm sorry I was late for our appointment, dear. I went back to the new Lowe's on 466-A, and they let me exchange your fixed spray head sprinkler nozzle with a gear-driven rotor sprinkler head, which the salesman said will cover more territory. They didn't give me any trouble about it, either." She smiled apologetically and suddenly noticed Tony in handcuffs. "What's going on?"

Tony raised his hands in a hand-cuffed wave.

Amber stormed over to her mother. "We have to talk. Okay, Busch?"

"I want to talk to Tony," Sara insisted, staring at the handcuffs.

Busch nodded reluctantly, still digesting what Tony divulged and praying Amber's mother would not knock out another of his suspects. He watched silently as the three moved a short distance from the crowded table. Their conversation was animated, but they spoke only briefly. He waited expectantly as they returned.

Sara looked at Tony, and then spoke in a calm voice, "I'm not sure what all this is about, but there's some question about where Tony was the night someone murdered Danny. Poor Danny. That should never have happened to him. As for Tony, he was with me in Key West the night of the murder."

Busch was boiling mad. "Did Tony ask you to say that? Is that what you three were just talking about over there? Getting your story straight."

Sara looked coldly at Busch. "I do not lie for anybody. No, that is not what we were talking about." She looked at Amber, then back to Busch. "Tony and I had to explain some things to Amber, and that's all we talked about." Sara held Amber's hand. The younger woman looked ready to burst into tears.

Busch glared at Sara. "And I suppose you have someone, or something, to corroborate your story. Do you have some proof of your alleged 'liaison' in Key West the night someone butchered Danny?" His head was pounding. He felt every eye on him.

"I think I just might." Sara set her large purse on the table, between Sam and Bud, and rooted through whatever filled the thing. She sorted through cash register receipts, and then stuffed all but one back into the massive bag as the Buddies watched in fascination. When she spoke again, she held up a slip of paper. "You all know Tony loves to eat."

Everyone nodded their heads.

"Well, on the night of Danny's murder, we ate at Sloppy Joe's Bar at 201 Duval Street. That's at the intersection with Green Street. I had the taco salad, sour cream, and salsa. Tony had the ten-inch Chicken Alfredo Personal Pan Pizza. And yeah, he had one extra topping, pepperoni. He also had two Sloppy Joe's."

Tony swelled with pride at his digestive prowess.

Sara smiled at him. "Of course, we had a pitcher of beer with our dinner. By the way, the beer was *Sloppy Joe's Island Ale*, and I recommend it highly. It's rather crisp and clean with a hint of fruity overtones."

Busch tapped his foot. "Please? If you don't mind?"

Sara held the receipt in front of Busch's eyes. "Oh, yeah, the date on this receipt is the day someone else killed Danny. The timestamp says 7:07 p.m. Our bill was for fifty-five dollars and ninety-seven cents, which included a ten-dollar tip. We paid for it with Tony's credit card." Sara showed the receipt to Tony.

Tony said. "Yep, that's my credit card number." He then burped loudly.

Most of the group burst into laughter.

Busch wasn't laughing. He pulled out the key to the handcuffs, released Tony, and stormed out of the bar. The sound of laughter echoed in his ears.

As he pulled out of the parking lot, Busch mumbled, "I suppose things aren't as bad as they would be if they were worse." *I just don't know how they could get any worse.*

That night, after downing six caffeine-free Diet Coke's and a frozen pepperoni pizza, Busch was bleary-eyed and ready to toss in the towel. His thoughts turned to Honey and why she had lied to him about Barfright leaving big tips. The more he thought, tired as he was, the messier this mess of an investigation seemed. Though he had every good reason to reassess his investigation thus far, top to bottom, he could no longer fight off exhaustion. He collapsed on his bed and enjoyed one of the best night's sleep he had had in a long time. His last fleeting thought before drifting off was that tomorrow would have to be a better day.

Chapter 48

A few days later, the bar's conversation trended in the usual direction. They danced around the police investigation into Danny Barfright's murder. Busch had warned them not to discuss their interviews. They were all suspects.

Sam leaned back in his chair, his eyes on Honey. He had a feeling she was Busch's prime suspect, even if Busch appeared to believe her story. Sam sensed there was something in her past she hid from all of them.

Tony ordered a *Foster's*, but without his usual joke. He added the word "please," something he rarely did with Honey or any other server. He turned to Nathan. "What are you having? My treat."

Nathan looked stunned. "You're buying?"

Tony nodded. "This could be the last time…"

"You aren't killing yourself, are you?" Nathan said, with a half-joking grin. "Next, you'll be giving away all the shit you own…"

Tony snarled, "I'm just buying my Beer Buddies a drink. What the hell ya makin' a big deal out of?"

Nathan replied, "You never buy drinks for us. I just thought with all that's going on…"

Tony looked at Sam. "Do you believe this guy? I'm in a good mood, so I offer to buy him a drink, and he makes a big 'mazzula' out of it?"

"Mazzula?" Sam asked, his eyes squinted in puzzlement.

"You know what you Jews call a big deal. You know what I mean."

Sam chuckled. "Megillah. A big deal is a Megillah."

"Like Magilla Gorilla? Remember him?" Bud asked.

Sam looked puzzled. "The megillah I know was the story of Esther for Purim. Megillah means a big story."

Tony laughed. "Magilla Gorilla. Every kid knew about him. He was a cartoon character like Huckleberry Hound and Yogi Bear. 'I'm smarter than the average bear,' he always said when the ranger couldn't catch him."

Nathan looked at Sam. "You know about Magilla Gorilla, don't you, Sam?"

"The gorilla? We were too poor to have a TV when I was a boy." Sam winked at Bud. "You're supposed to ask, 'How poor were you?'"

"How poor were you?" Bud dutifully asked.

Sam was about to answer when Honey interrupted. "I just heard a rumor, guys. They say the cops found the murder weapon." She leaned over the table.

Sam stared down her top. *God, she's inviting. If only I could reveal my true self to her.* "I'm sorry. What did you say?" He had to stop letting himself be distracted.

Nathan looked attentive, but remained silent.

Tony jumped in. "She said they think they know what the moider weapon was."

Honey nodded. "Busch said he's going to get forensics over to the crime scene at the crack of dawn."

"I gotta leave," Tony said, slapping a twenty-dollar bill on the table.

"You were buying us drinks," Nathan said. "What's your hurry?"

"I have to leave, too," Sam said. "Thank you, Honey. As always, you sweeten my day."

Honey looked surprised. "Thank you, Sam. That was nice of you to say."

Sam stopped walking. If only he could take five minutes. If he could only tell her the truth.

Nathan handed Honey his bill and some cash. "Keep the change, Honey. I have to go too." He took a deep swig of his beer and rushed away from the table.

---  ---

Honey stared at the empty chairs. *Wow. They all rushed out after I delivered Busch's bombshell about finding the weapon.*

Did that mean she was in the clear? Was Busch trying to trap her? *OMG! The others! He used me to trap the others.* She was the Judas.

Honey ran to catch them. They were gone. If this really was a trap, she hoped Busch hit another foul ball.

Chapter 49

The killer looked up into the still night sky. Like the diaphanous veil worn by an Algerian belly dancer, a filmy cloud masked the moon, casting deep purple and black shadows along the path. This place was strange in the middle of the night. No cars. No police. Nothing moving. As still and quiet as a graveyard. Only short stakes and yellow tape marked the crime scene. The killer had to move fast. The veil might slip away at any moment.

The murderer stood beside the car parked under a moss-draped oak. The moon shadow of the tree offered a place to observe the site from a safe distance. Did Busch really find the weapon? Was this a trap? Everything in the tree-shaded, secluded lane appeared the same as it had that night. The bulb from the pole lamp, the only source of light other than the moon, remained missing. Danny's killer had unscrewed the bulb from the socket and later, in the back of a strip mall, crushed it underfoot and tossed the broken pieces into a dumpster. That was why Barfright hadn't seen his attacker until it was too late. *Why didn't the cops replace the bulb?*

The veil drifted off the moon. The killer scanned both ends of the lane. No police anywhere. *Still, I must be careful.*

The veil lifted entirely off the moon. The killer's eyes grew accustomed to the dim moonlight and picked out the birdhouse from a short distance. *It's still there. I should drive away now, but I need to check.*

Alert for an ambush, the killer walked up the cart path. The birdhouse stood on its pole as before. *If the police knew the post was the murder weapon, would they leave it here? Of course not. Honey said Busch let out that he'd taken the suspected weapon to the lab. Poor old Busch must have got the wrong weapon. The bat? Did Busch still think the baseball bat was the murder weapon?*

Visions of the night Danny died swirled through the killer's mind — that pole slammed into Danny's face. *Yes, I planned it perfectly, picked the location, loosened the dirt around the post, undid the screws that held the birdhouse, and removed the lightbulb. A birdhouse post? Ingenious. Nobody would look for that. Who would suspect a lowly post holding up a birdhouse could be a lethal weapon?* Perfect plan. Or was it? Was a mistake made?

Danny's murderer stepped into the cart path and walked silently among the shadows to the birdhouse. No signs indicated that anyone had touched it or dug around the area. A quick glance around confirmed no one was nearby. *I could pull the steel post from the ground and inspect it closer. No, too risky. Better to leave it alone. Get out of here. Busch has the wrong weapon.*

Heading toward his car, the killer relaxed. *I sweated for nothing. No police. No trap.*

A vehicle slowly turned into the lane and illuminated the area with its headlights. It was bright enough to see the light-bar atop the car.

Run? No. I can't escape. I'm sure I can talk my way out of this.

The car pulled up next to him. The window rolled down. A smiling face lit up by dash lights peered out. "You all right?"

Relieved to see the car belonged to the Community Watch, a citizen unit, the killer answered cheerily. "Yes, yes. I'm fine. Thank you. I just like to take my walk while it's cool."

"No problem. Quite a few people in this neighborhood walk early. I thought you might be the person who reported the lost tabby."

"No, that wasn't me."

"If you see a gray tabby, please report it to the Community Watch? The cat's owner is quite distraught." The driver handed over a Community Watch card.

"I'll be sure to do that," the assassin said, taking the card.

"I saw him last night. I caught him on my dashcam, but by the time I got out of my rig, he was long gone into the shrubbery."

"I'll keep an eye out."

"You be safe now." The driver rolled the window up, and then down again. "Do you know someone was killed near here?"

"You don't say?"

When the Community Watch finally drove away, the killer doubled-back to the car. "That was close." Starting the motor, suspicion crept in. *It could still be an ambush.* But nobody prevented the car from driving away. *I'm paranoid. Busch isn't smart enough to plan something like that. And Honey would never do it.* The killer drove home, confident of committing the perfect crime.

Chapter 50

I was a typical Tuesday afternoon at World of Beer. Even with the specter of Danny Barfright's death still hanging over the bar, everyone was having a good time, talking, and laughing as usual.

Nathan said to Amber, "Who do you suppose will be next on the grill for the insightful questioning of the village sleuth?"

Amber laughed.

Tony munching on his pizza, raised a bushy eyebrow.

Margarita stopped at the bar, eyeing the new young bartender.

Honey was setting up orders for another table.

Sam joked around with Bud.

Busch was just returning from the john when Tony jumped to his feet, staring at one of the two giant TVs hanging over the bar. He shouted to the bartender, "Hey, turn up the sound. Ain't that Honey?"

Everyone acted as if Tony was intoxicated and seeing things. They grew silent when Honey's face appeared on the screen.

A female news anchor stood in front of an enlarged photograph of Honey. "KALE-TV reporter Keryn Ichiban has the story."

"Thank you, Mickey. KALE has confirmed that best-selling author, Gloria St. Pauli, has been working undercover in a local watering hole. She has been writing a book exposing sexual exploitation in the bar scene here in Florida."

"Turn it up," Tony shouted. "What the hell?"

The reporter continued, "St. Pauli, a radical feminist, recently gained notoriety when her tell-all exposé, *The Power of Pink,* was reviewed by The Times."

"That can't be Honey," Tony said. "That gal's name is St. Paul or something. Honey ain't even Catholic. Is she?"

"Shhh," Margarita hissed. "I always knew there was something fishy about Miss Sweetness."

The reporter stood before a photo of World of Beer. "World of Beer, where St. Pauli has been working undercover, is the same bar frequented by Danny Barfright, a Villages retiree recently murdered." She smiled sensuously. "An unknown assailant brutally attacked him. The killer smashed in his face, leaving gore everywhere."

Busch trembled. The damn case that wouldn't die was all over the news.

The reporter continued, "We contacted Ms. St. Pauli's editor, Stella R. Troy, by Skype about any connection Ms. St. Pauli might have to the unsolved murder. Here's what she had to say."

A smartly dressed older woman wearing an expensive-looking white suit and pearls appeared on the screen.

Ichiban turned to her guest. "Thank you for joining us, Ms. Troy. Do you know if Ms. St. Pauli was acquainted with the dead man, Mr. Danny Barfright?" She turned to the camera and repeated while smiling, "Mr. Barfright's face was smashed to smithereens. The murderer remains at large."

Busch groaned. This was bad, really, really, bad.

Stella frowned. "Well, yes, Ms. St. Pauli was acquainted with the victim. But I am certain she would not murder him."

"It is true, isn't it, that Barfright was not only an acquaintance, but the primary subject of Ms. St. Pauli's exposé?" The reporter smiled like a barracuda. "Barfright was said to be not only an exploiter of women, but the focus of Ms. St. Pauli's upcoming book. Isn't that correct?"

Stella looked uneasy. "Well, Mr. Barfright was to have been the main character in her book. But I assure you Gloria would never murder anyone."

"But Ms. St. Pauli has a long history of making public hate statements about powerful men. Isn't that true?"

"My dear, hate is far too strong a word. I'm sure when this is all over, the facts will show that Gloria St. Pauli is completely innocent."

"Bullshit," Margarita spat. "That bitch ain't no damn virgin."

"Shhh," Sam hissed. "I have enough trouble hearing without your noise."

"Screw you," Margarita replied. "If you still can?"

Sam shot her a murderous glance, and then aimed his eyeglasses at the screen.

Stella held Gloria's first book up below her cleavage. "Anyone who reads her wonderful book, *The Power of Pink,* can see that Gloria St. Pauli is not likely to commit murder. I'm confident that when St. Pauli's new book, *Pink in the Bar Room,* comes out later this year, it will confirm her innocence." She held up the cover of the new book, again, just below her bosom.

"Like hell, it will," Margarita said. "The lying bitch."

"She looks like Honey," Tony said, not even biting the pizza in his hand.

"It is Honey," Sam said. He called over to Honey. "It is you. Isn't it?"

Honey watched the report silently.

Nathan stared at Honey. "You lied to us."

"She used us. She only pretended to like us for her goddamn book," Margarita spat.

Busch slumped in his chair. Honey's secret was out.

Amber pointed her finger at Honey. "You lied about everything. You did use us."

Bud shook his head. "I gave you good tips."

Amber appeared to be on the verge of tears. "How could you do this to us?"

Honey bit her lip and stared at their angry faces. Tears formed in her eyes. Unable to speak, she walked back to the bar, took off her apron, picked up her jacket, and headed for the door.

Margarita, always claiming the last word, spoke through her clenched jaw, "I'll bet that lying bitch killed Danny."

Chapter 51

As Honey headed for the door of World of Beer with her jacket over her arm, Busch barked at her, "Wait a minute Ms. Gloria St. Pauli, there is an on-going murder investigation, and you have some explaining to do. You told me in our earlier discussion that you were writing a book, but you didn't mention that you hated Danny Barfright. You didn't say anything about your history as a militant feminist."

Tony said, "Busch, take it easy."

The shock showed on Honey's face. Her shoulders drooped as she went to the table where Busch and the other Beer Buddies sat. "What in the name of God are you talking about?"

Busch was merciless. "You know exactly what I mean. For whatever reason, I don't know, and it doesn't matter, you hate men — all men. And you sure as hell hated Danny. When I talked to you at Starbucks — remember that day? — you put on a big tear-jerker show, all just for me. You lied to me, Honey Lovejoy. You lied!" He was yelling now.

"Why would I lie to you?"

"How about you tell us? Fess up, little lady. You told me that Danny had been slipping you big bucks for tips every time he came to the bar. You remember his goody-two-shoes effort to help a single Mom who was waitressing to support her two sons? But Danny never left you big tips. Did he, Honey?"

Everybody's favorite waitress looked skittish, and moved her eyes in a staccato fashion to each of the Beer Buddies's faces.

Busch ramped-up the pressure. "Shall I add false reporting to law enforcement to the list of charges? Murder and false reporting? That will add another ninety days to a life sentence. Is that what you want, Honey?"

221

Honey held up her hand as a stop sign. "Okay. Alright, already." She sighed. "You're right. I didn't tell you the truth at Starbucks. I should have, but I wanted to protect my boys. I was trying to protect their lives, their privacy." She looked at the others. "No, Danny didn't leave me hundred-dollar tips. I should have known you would figure that out. I should have told you the truth. I'm sorry."

Busch lowered his voice. "The truth at last. I see." He looked intently at her. "Well, now that you're here with all the Beer Buddies, care to acquaint us with it? The truth, that is."

Honey pulled out a chair and sat down. Hanging her jacket over the arm of her chair, she wiped her hands on her apron. Her eyes roamed again from one Beer Buddy to the next. None of their eyes showed much in the way of sympathy. Tony's came closest as he picked up and studied yet another slice of pepperoni pizza with double cheese.

Honey turned back to Busch. "Everything I told you at Starbucks was true except for the hundred-dollar tip story. I made that up."

"And why would you do that?" Busch asked, lowering the pressure.

Honey trembled. "Because there was just some stuff I thought I could keep to myself. Stuff I didn't want to have to tell anybody. Stuff that I still think is nobody's business." She looked at Busch with sorrowful eyes. "But I guess I have no choice now."

"You need to come clean," Busch said.

Honey nodded sadly. "The night I went over to Danny's place — you know, the night he was about to become my final chapter — he did something unbelievable. I expected him to attack me. That was to be the big finish for my book." She stopped and swallowed hard. Her voice cracked. "But it didn't play out at all as I expected." She sniffled and dabbed at her nose with a Kleenex. "Danny told me he set up two trust funds, one for Justin and one for Jason, as seed money for them to go to college." Tears welled up in Honey's eyes.

"What? You expect us to believe that?" Busch asked, dangling handcuffs.

Honey sobbed. "It's true. Danny gave my boys forty thousand dollars each, Buschie. FORTY THOUSAND DOLLARS!

I still find it hard to believe. He said he'd known women who had to sacrifice everything for their children. Why he would do such a thing for me — well, it's beyond me. But I'm telling you, it's the honest-to-god truth. It was like manna from heaven."

All eyes were on Honey, and all mouths hung open. Except for Tony's. He was chewing. Amber shook her head in disbelief.

Bud whispered something to Nathan.

Margarita removed a piece of gum from her mouth, wadded it into a napkin, tossed it into a beer mug, and folded her arms. A look of disdain crossed her face.

Busch glared at Honey. He could barely control his anger. "I see," he finally said through taut lips. "I didn't believe your lie about a bunch of crazy hundred-dollar tips. Now you want me to believe that poor Danny boy dumped eighty-grand into your lap?" He stared at the others, and then turned back to Honey. "What do you take me for, Miss Lovejoy? Are you nuts?"

He figured he had her now. This whole thing seemed too unreal. Until Amber disclosed her inheritance from him, there was no hint of generosity in Danny's nature. More importantly, he knew of no reason for Barfright's largesse. So far, Honey had not offered any explanation either. "So," he continued, fiddling with the handcuffs, "do you have anything other than your unbelievable story for me to go on? How can I be sure you haven't made this all up like you made up your first story?" He clicked the handcuffs open, closed, open, closed.

Honey's eyes took on the appearance of moist headlights. "You have to believe me. Please. I'm telling the truth." And then, almost as an afterthought, she said, "I can prove it." Her face lit up. "Yeah, I can prove it. I have the trust papers back at the house. I'll show them to you. They're dated a while back. Danny must have set things up months ago. You'll see."

Busch sighed. He wished he could believe her, but she had lied so many times. "Yes, I'd like to see the trusts if you don't mind. And while we're at it, would you care to tell us what bank is holding the funds?" He looked at the others and shook his head.

Honey raised her eyes to the ceiling. "I can't remember the bank."

Busch grunted. "I thought so."

"Wait! Florida something. Florida Padlock Financial! The Oxford Branch! I have the bank statements, too." Honey dabbed at her eyes, looking a lot more cheerful.

Busch's head was awash with these new revelations. *She wouldn't lie about this. If she has the trust papers, any motive goes bust. She must be telling the truth.* He threw his hands over his head.

The Beer Buddies could have been watching a soap opera. Busch's murder investigation collapsed in front of their eyes. This could be a murder mystery party, except they were at World of Beer, just like every other Tuesday. But Danny's murder was real.

Schweitzer blurted out, "Well, Busch, your batting average sure ain't much to brag about now, is it? How long you gonna keep us here while your little investigation implodes?"

Margarita stood up and adjusted her boobs. "Are we gonna have to miss *Wheel of Fortune* tonight?"

Sam said, "God, how I love to watch Vanna White! I would have loved to make a bra for her."

Bud murmured, "I love her gowns and that figure."

Honey glared at them. "Shut up! All of you. I ain't taking any more heat on this." She looked toward Busch. "I'm not done. Buschie, the night I was at Danny's drinking wine with him on his lanai — remember I told you I misjudged him, that I thought he was going to try to score with me?"

"That's our Danny," Sam said. "What a guy."

Honey shook her head. "No. You have it wrong. He didn't try anything."

Amber nodded. "I believe her."

Busch replied, "Well, I don't believe her. I knew Danny too well."

Honey sighed. "Buschie, I recorded our conversation. Remember, I'm writing a book. I needed documentation. I had a recorder running in my purse, which was right there on the coffee table in front of us."

Honey was writing a book. Busch had promised not to reveal Honey's secret to the others. He believed she had a hidden recorder.

Honey continued, "I got every word from that evening. It's on my iMac, at home, and I have a copy on my iPhone here. She took her phone from her jacket pocket.

Busch said, "Why didn't you tell me about this tape earlier? Why didn't you play it for me? If what you're saying is true, all of this could have been avoided."

"I'm sorry."

She straightened up. "I suppose you want to listen to the tape. It will back-up everything I just told you."

"Yeah, I wanna hear it," said Tony.

The other Beer Buddies agreed.

Honey pushed the play button, and the scene in Barfright's apartment unfolded.

Busch fell into a chair looking forlorn. He heard the others chattering and laughing behind him. *What a mess I made of this. None of the suspects are panning out. Maybe the FBI was right. It was the Cereal Killer. Snap, crackle, pop.* He let out a deep sigh and stood up. He didn't belong with the Beer Buddies, not after believing one of them was a brutal murderer. He felt sad about losing his friends. It was his fault.

"Here, Buschie," Honey placed a mug of *BrewDog Wake Up Call* in front of him. "No hard feelings. You're just doing your job."

Busch was in no mood to drink. Besides, he hoped it wasn't poisoned. He made his way to the head.

Chapter 52

As the recording of Honey's conversation played, the sense of malevolence dissipated in the room.

Several of the Beer Buddies breathed sighs of relief when the recording ended. The recording exonerated Honey; it was clear that she had no motive for murder. Still, she was writing a book about them.

"You know, Honey, I'm still pissed that you felt a need to report us as monsters," said Tony.

"I know, Tony, I'm so sorry. My father was abusive to women he met in bars. I grew up hating him and thinking that all men in bars were like that. Working here has been a real education for me. I would have abandoned this book a month ago, but I'm writing to support my two boys and myself."

Nathan asserted, "Well, we're not monsters!"

"I know Nathan. I found that out while working here. Please forgive me."

Nathan began, in softer tones, "Well . . ."

Mags interrupted, "Don't get your arm out of joint patting yourself on the back. It's not all choir boys who come to bars like this."

Nathan tried again, "Yeah, but . . ."

"I don't want to hear any 'yeah buts.' There isn't a woman alive who hasn't walked into a place like this with thirty men and realized sixty eye-balls were aimed at her boobs."

Everyone present, even Honey, laughed.

Mags continued, "Now cut the girl some slack. She's a working woman with two kids trying to make a living. I'm glad that Danny wasn't a total sleaze ball, but he could have been. You know, there are plenty of them around. As far as I am concerned, she's to be complemented for all the work she's doing to raise her kids alone."

"Here, here," said Tony.

Just getting back from the head, Busch raised his bottle of *Bravus Brewing Oatmeal Stout* and offered a toast. "That's right. Here's to World of Beer's favorite server."

Everyone raised their drink and toasted Honey

"Thank you all, so much," said Honey. "You're a great bunch."

Good-natured banter returned. Even with the specter of murder hanging in the air, life resumed for the Beer Buddies at World of Beer. No one seemed inclined to allow the week's happiest hours to sink under the thought that one of them could be a vicious killer. Danny Barfright was dead. The Beer Buddies had been proven innocent. They accepted that Supervising Detective FBI — whatever his title was — Blue, was right: the murder must have been the act of the Cereal Killer. It was time for things to get back to normal. Normal, for all except poor, dead, Danny Barfright. Even Busch reluctantly accepted the FBI conclusion.

Busch still had threads of the investigation to tie up, fragments of evidence lying about, but those details were no longer a significant concern. The remnants of the murder investigation were now the problem of Blue and the FBI. For Busch, Danny Barfright's demise and the investigation were, mercifully, receding into the past. It was a minor chapter of local history where he had screwed up royally, but his friends forgave him.

At that afternoon's beer-drinking session, everyone laughed with Nathan. He was the last person someone might expect of being a fount of humor. "As a lark, I had a bidet toilet seat installed in my bathroom," he said to everyone's amazement. "It's amazing on my tushy."

The others didn't know Nathan hoped to collect a referral fee if one of the Buddies purchased one. They laughed uproariously at the visual of the great soldier, seated on a bidet. The jokes seemed unending.

With everyone in such a cheerful mood, Busch hatched a plan. With a wave in her direction, he summoned Honey Lovejoy.

When Honey answered Busch's call, he stood up and took her aside for a private consultation. At first, she was nervous, but he allayed her fears, "Honey, I know World of Beer has a bourbon barrel special going on. Do you still have a selection?"

Relief spread across Honey's face. "As a matter of fact, we just got a delivery yesterday."

"Great! I've been kind of an asshole about this murder case, and I want to make a peace offering. Why don't you bring a selection to the table? I'd like to buy a round of something special for my old Beer Buddies."

Honey smiled, "You're not an asshole, Buschie. You were just doing your job."

"Thanks, but I feel like one, and I want to make it up to them."

"You know, bourbon barrels are not cheap."

"I know, but I want to say I'm sorry for ever doubting them."

"Okay. If you're sure." Honey went back behind the bar.

About ten minutes later, Honey returned with a big platter — a great selection of bottles of bourbon-barrel beers.

Unbeknownst to Busch, Honey did not include the *Founders Canadian Breakfast Stout,* at twenty-three dollars a bottle, or the *Goose Island Bourbon County Mon Cheri Stout*, at twenty-seven dollars. Still, Busch's 'peace offering' set him back over a hundred bucks. Buying a round of the rare beers was worth it to put the whole Danny Barfright debacle behind him.

Honey set the platter with the selection of beers on the table and announced, "Detective Busch is buying for his friends, the Beer Buddies. Enjoy!"

The Beer Buddies greeted the announcement with cries of delight. There were shouts of "Well, done, Buschie," and, "Thanks, Busch." Margarita gave him a solid slap on the shoulder, and then a moist kiss on the lips.

Tony picked up the dark bottle of *Innis & Gunn Bourbon Barrel Scotch Ale.* "I've heard about this stuff. I'll try it." He looked at Busch and said, "Thanks, Busch. I forgive you for all the shit you caused me." He smiled and waved the cold bottle for the others to admire. The big guy fumbled with the cap.

Honey took the bottle from Tony and promptly popped the cap. She poured the beer to a foamy head. "It takes a woman to do a man's job," she laughed at Tony's puzzled face.

Bud examined the now empty Innis & Gunn bottle and passed it on. He selected the *New Holland Brewing Dragon's Milk Bourbon Barrel-aged Stout*.

Amber selected *Founders KBS 2019 Release Kentucky Breakfast Stout*. She leaned close to Honey, "I'm only half-done with this *Deschutes Black Butte Porter*. Can you bring the *Founders* to me when I finish this?"

"Sure," Honey said, happy everyone was enjoying Busch's treat.

Margarita, who sat next to Busch, said, "This is so nice of you, Busch. But I'm about done for the day." She put her arm around Busch's shoulder and kissed him on the cheek. "You can fuck up a case again any time."

Busch blushed. That he had fucked up still stung. He walked over to Sam. "What will you have, old friend?" He sat down and whispered, "You know, I feel I have to apologize to you. All along, I thought you were mixed-up in Danny's murder."

Sam looked startled. "An old man like me? I'm flattered. Apology accepted. I'll take the beer." He examined the various labels and tried to choose between *Kentucky Vanilla Barrel Cream Ale* and *Gigantic Brewing's MASSIVE! 2019 Bourbon Barrel-aged Barleywine*. "None of these are kosher," he said. "I like a good *Manischewitz*."

Busch laughed.

At that moment, the World of Beer door flew open.

Supervising Chief Inspector Detective Oskar Blue and Assistant Detective Guinness marched in. When they approached the table, it was as if a black raincloud abruptly descended on the room.

Busch's mood deflated. He thought he was making some headway against the flood of bad memories from his futile investigation. He stared in disbelief at the agents of his humiliation. *What else can go wrong?*

The FBI detective took his large gold shield from inside his suit pocket and held it up for everyone in the bar to see. He said, "Supervising Chief Inspector Detec..."

"Yeah, yeah, yeah," Busch waved him off. "What do you want, Blue?"

Nonplussed by Busch's impertinence, the agent asked, "Is Sam Adams present?"

Sam looked up through his thick lenses. "I am Sam Adams. What can I do for you?"

Giggles circled the table. What did the stuffy FBI Inspector . . . whatever his title was . . . want with the old man?

Busch shook his head.

Blue approached Sam. "Samuel Adams, I am placing you under arrest for the destruction of habitat critical to migrating wildlife."

"What?" Busch demanded.

Sam laughed. "What? Are you *meshuga*?"

"He must be *meshuga*," Nathan said. "That means crazy," he informed Blue.

Blue frowned. "Stand up, Adams. You have destroyed the nest of an endangered bird of international significance."

"I didn't destroy any wildlife habitat. I don't even know what that means." Sam shrugged his shoulders at the others.

Blue leaned lower. "I'm afraid, sir, I have to take you into custody."

Busch burst into laughter. *This guy is crazy.*

Sam asserted, "I'm not going anywhere."

Blue said, "I am afraid you are, sir. The evidence against you is irrefutable."

"What evidence? I didn't do anything to hurt no wildlife," Sam whined in a feeble, old man voice.

"Sir, I beg to differ. We have a videotape of you tampering with a rare bird habitat. Irrefutable." Blue pulled handcuffs from his pocket.

Sam's face darkened. "A video? You're nuts. I want a lawyer."

Blue replied, "You'll be able to contact your attorney as soon as we get you to the station in Orlando. You will be able to present your case at your arraignment tomorrow."

Busch rocked with stifled laughter. *Blue, the 'big-shot FBI Inspector' is arresting a feeble, deaf, old man for doing something to a bird habitat? This is a joke.*

Blue ordered, "Assistant Supervising Chief Inspector Detective Guinness, take Mr. Adams into custody."

"This is *meshuga*," Sam repeated, eyes darting to the door.

Guinness snapped one of Sam's wrists in the manacles and attempted to put his arm behind his back to attach the other.

Sam let out a howl about the arthritis pain in his wrists and shoulders. "At least, you should shackle me in front. My arthritis is killing me."

Assistant Detective Guinness looked questioningly at Blue.

Blue nodded. "I think it will be all right."

Guinness gently placed the remaining cuff on Sam's wrist. "Does that hurt too much?" she asked.

Sam smiled sadly. "No. Thank you. You are very kind. I am fine." He looked at the shocked faces of the Beer Buddies and said, "Thank you and shalom."

"You'll be back soon," Margarita assured him. She stared defiantly at Blue. "You dumb schmucks, arresting an old man for nothing."

"I love you, Sam," Amber said and threw him a kiss.

"I love you all," Sam said and waved his chained hands at them.

"Take him away," Blue commanded.

Busch let out a deep sigh. *What a crock of bull this is. He'll be back in no time, and Blue will have bird shit on his badge.*

No sooner were Guinness and Adams out the door than Blue pulled a chair out from the table and sat down. The Beer Buddies gawked at him, mouths agape. He'd just arrested one of them and now thought he could join them?

Busch was curious as to what Blue wanted.

Blue picked up several of the bottles and inspected the labels. "Bourbon barrel stouts?" He looked at the other Beer Buddies. "Are you guys drinking bourbon barrel stouts?"

"Yes," said Busch. "What about it?"

"Is that a crime too?" Margarita hissed.

"Fantastic." Blue looked at the tray again, "I don't suppose you have *Evil Twin Even More Jesus Imperial Stout*, do you?"

Honey answered, "No, but we have *Evil Twin Harlan's Even More Jesus Barrel-aged Imperial Stout*."

"Wonderful. Bring me one."

Busch's mind buzzed with questions about the arrest of Sam Adams, but he remained silent, wary of the agent now trying to be everybody's pal.

"Amber looked at Blue. "I didn't think you guys could drink on duty."

With what appeared to be a mixture of amazement and disappointment, Blue said, "Of course not! My shift ended an hour ago."

Everyone sighed in unison. "Oh."

Busch eyed him suspiciously. *Oh, shit.*

Margarita flashed her eyelids at the tall, dark, and handsome inspector.

"How's the food here?" Blue asked.

"The Chicago-style pizza is terrific. The calzone — not so much," Tony told him.

"How about the burgers?" Blue asked the group. "I could go for a good cheese…"

Busch cut him off, "Wait a minute! Wait one dang minute! What about Sam Adams?"

Blue stared at Busch. "Oh, yes, Sam Adams. A grave matter, I'm afraid." He looked at the others. "Mr. Adams destroyed the nest of a *Pipilo saccharomyces cerevisiae* or chartreuse-crested Towhee. The crested Towhee is a close relative of the *Pipilo erythrophthalmus* or common Towhee."

"What the hell?" Tony asked. "It's a damn bird. Why the Federal case?"

"Wait a minute. Is that enough to take an old man away in handcuffs?" Busch demanded.

Blue seemed surprised that anyone would ask such a silly question. "Of course, it is. The chartreuse-crested Towhee is an endangered bird. Only nineteen pairs of them are known to exist. It is the U.S. Virgin Islands' territorial bird, even though none are known to have returned to the islands in recent years. It is sacred to the local variant of Santeria. The feathers of the chartreuse crest are an aphrodisiac. It is said, a single feather can cause an erection lasting several days. The extended chartreuse erection may have something to do with the bird's near demise. It was hunted to extinction on the islands so men could experience extended erections. Some anthropologists argue that the *Pipilo saccharomyces cerevisiae* bears partial responsibility for the abnormally high birth rate among the, perhaps misnamed, Virgin Islanders."

Margarita cooed, "An aphrodisiac?" She sounded as though she had just stumbled on a gold mine.

Busch persisted, "Yeah, but still, taking him away in handcuffs seems extreme."

Blue ignored Busch. His beer had arrived.

Everyone looked expectantly at Blue, especially Margarita.

Blue took a long swig of his *Evil Twin Harlan's Even More Jesus Barrel-aged Imperial Stout*. "Aaah, the bourbon flavor really comes through. Aged in black walnut instead of the common white oak whiskey barrels. Yes, excellent."

When Blue wiped the foam from his lips, Busch asked him again, "Did you *have to* take our friend away in handcuffs?"

Ignoring Busch, Blue smiled, "This is delicious." Finally, he turned to Busch. "Yes. I'm afraid so. The video showed the destruction was not accidental."

"I don't understand. It's just a bird," Nathan protested.

Blue shook his head. "The chartreuse-crested is a strange bird. The male does all the nest-making, and he works only at night. And, being such a rare specimen, birdwatchers are always on the lookout for him. A local birdwatcher observed the destruction. She made a somewhat blurry movie, but it shows the destruction of its nest on her phone in the moonlight."

"But it's just a bird," Busch repeated, exasperated.

Blue smiled. "This is an excellent beer." He then burst into laughter. "The irony is that your Mr. Adams pulled a birdhouse from the ground, thus disturbing the nest and scattering the rare breeding pair." He sipped at his beer. "The birdwatcher was so upset, she contacted the local Audubon Society, and they notified our Bureau."

"The FBI got involved in a bird case?" Nathan asked, with his brow furrowed in disbelief.

"What a waste of taxpayer money," Amber remarked, with the indignance of someone who now had to be concerned about taxes on her gigantic inheritance.

"I thought so too," Blue said. "It was quite a letdown from the Barfright murder. But orders are orders." He let out a loud belch. "Pardon me," he muttered and smiled at Margarita. "We studied the video, but weren't sure of the identity of the bird disrupter, not until our forensics lab examined the evidence. That's when we found fingerprints on the shaft supporting the birdhouse."

Busch shook his head. "I don't believe this."

Blue added, "And DNA from Barfright's skull."

"WHAT?" Busch shouted, slopping his *2019 "GRAVITAS by Bravus" Bourbon Barrel-Aged Stout* on his shirt. "You're claiming Sam Adams murdered Danny Barfright?"

"Why, yes. When our forensics lab found Sam Adams' fingerprints in the victim's blood, and the blurry video, it was clear that Sam Adams murdered Danny Barfright.

"We compared the blurry images from the night photography with the clearer dashboard cam of the Community Watch vehicle, which confirmed our suspicion. Indeed, Sam Adams destroyed the birdhouse."

The Beer Buddies fixed all on eyes on Blue.

"Well," said Blue, "We couldn't find a match for the prints in our domestic database, but yes, it looks like your 'old man' used the pole bearing the birdhouse to bludgeon and brutally bash in Barfright's brains."

Busch couldn't believe it. *A tongue-twister?*

Blue continued, "We won't know if Adams is guilty until after some more tests. 'Innocent until proven guilty.' We take that seriously in the Bureau. But there is evidence to support a strong case."

"But you didn't arrest him for murder," Busch said, struggling to understand.

"Out of my jurisdiction," the detective replied. "I'd like another beer," he raised his glass.

"What do you mean out of your jurisdiction? You lead the task force investigating the murder."

"Well, yes and no. I am the lead investigator, but only for the Cereal Killer murders. Sam Adams has alibis for the Cereal Killer murders. Whatever Adams did here, in Florida, he did not cross state lines. So, the Barfright murder is a state, not federal, matter."

"But, you said he killed Danny," Busch protested. "Is he getting away with that?"

Blue chuckled. "Oh, I don't think convicting Adams will be a problem. We have a video of him pulling out the birdhouse pole. We have Barfright's DNA and bone fragments on the pole. And we have fingerprints. We've sent those to Interpol and other international agencies."

"Interpol?" Busch was stunned. "Our Sam Adams?"

Blue nodded. "We can't find a match for the prints domestically. So, yes, we may have an international hitman in our custody. I'll be surprised if something doesn't turn up."

Busch couldn't believe it. "But what if Adams posts bail? If he's a foreigner, he can flee."

Blue looked up from his beer. "Excellent point, Busch. Perhaps you should put in a call to your office. Have someone get in touch with the Bureau in Orlando to make sure they hold him until you can send someone down to charge him." He smiled. "I have to say this is an excellent stout. It is expensive, but you really should give it a try."

"But, but, but . . ." Busch stammered, thrown for a loop by the possibility of Sam being some sort of international murderer.

Blue loosened his tie and turned his attention to Nathan. "Lambic, is it? I understand you spent time in the south of Africa. Have you ever had *Chibuku*?"

"Of course," Nathan replied.

Thus, began a lengthy discourse on the unique merits of fermented sorghum and maize for making beer.

Busch couldn't get over it. *Sweet old Sam was the murderer. The murder weapon was a birdhouse post? At last, it was over. Or was it?* He hurried out of the bar to the station house.

THE

AFTERMATH

Chapter 53

Amber put a small vase of cut flowers on a table that looked out to a beautifully manicured garden and, in the distance, the new Chitty Chatty Bridge spanning Florida 44 near what until recently had been the southernmost part of The Villages. She wanted everything to be perfect for tonight's grand opening. "Maggie," she called to her associate. "You've done a beautiful job with the table settings."

Maggie, a petite, attractive woman in her mid-fifties, tucked an errant strand of silver hair behind her ear. "Amber, dear, this is all you." Amber had met — and stolen — Maggie from her favorite restaurant in New York. A restaurant manager with decades of experience, Maggie was the perfect partner for Amber's new venture.

After Danny's death, Amber followed his advice and went back to school. She enrolled in the Culinary Institute of America in New York. While a fine cook, she soon realized she couldn't hold a candle to the class's top students. Instead, at graduation, she hired the class valedictorian, Suzanne DuBois, to be the chef in her new restaurant. She moved Suzanne and Maggie to Florida, and the three planned out every detail of the restaurant together. Amber fronted the money. Maggie brought expertise. Suzanne provided the talent. Voila! Amber knew *Chez Amber* would be an outstanding success.

Maggie squeezed Amber's shoulder. "Amber, your concept for the restaurant, cuisines of the Mediterranean, gives us so much flexibility we can't miss. Twenty-one countries —from French Haute Couture to Middle-Eastern exotic to Italian comfort foods — we've got it covered."

"Thanks, Maggie. I couldn't do this without you and Suzanne."

"What time do your friends arrive?" Maggie asked.

"At four. I wanted us to have some time to catch up before officially opening the doors to the public. I haven't seen them in a year."

"We'll be ready."

"Hey, Amber," Bud Schweitzer yelled from the doorway. He had a music case slung over his back and a laptop case in his hand. In ass-hugging jeans and a tight black tee-shirt, he looked tanned and hunky.

"Bud!" Amber hurried over and hugged him. "It's great to see you."

"I came early to check out the sound equipment."

"Of course, honey. Let me introduce you to Maggie."

Maggie smiled and held out her hand.

Bud kissed it. "Mademoiselle," he said.

Maggie blushed.

Bud winked at Amber.

"Watch out, Maggie. He's quite the ladies' man."

"Who is?" Nathan asked as he, Busch, Tony, and Honey (Gloria, actually, but they all still called her Honey out of habit) strolled together into the restaurant. None of them had seen Amber since she left for New York over a year ago.

Amber ran up to them. "Welcome! Welcome! I'm so glad you all came."

"I wouldn't miss it, Amber," Busch smiled and kissed her on the cheek. "How's that Mercedes holding up?"

"With you now as my mechanic, I'll probably get two hundred-thousand miles out of her."

Bud hopped off the stage and joined the group. "Hi Buds," he said.

Busch slapped him on the back, and Honey kissed him on the cheek.

Tony looked stockier than ever. "How ya doin', Amber?" He gave her a bear hug, and then slapped Bud so hard on the back he almost knocked him over.

Honey carried a large bag, which she set on the floor. She hugged Amber and told her, "I'm proud of you, dear. When we sit down, I'll tell you all about my news."

Amber pressed her lips together and didn't respond. She still harbored some misgivings toward Honey for deceiving them.

Nathan, ever the gentleman, took Amber's hand. "We've missed you on our Tuesday afternoons." He looked around her beautiful restaurant. "Perhaps we should change venues."

Amber smiled. "Well, that would be nice, but I'm not getting my hopes up just yet." Amber led them to a long table next to open French doors that looked out on the lush garden. "And Tony, I've stocked up kegs from every microbrew in the state just for you guys."

Busch's phone rang, and he pulled it out of his pocket. When he punched the Facetime app, a familiar voice made his face light up. "Hello, you dirty old geezers," Margarita called out. "I'm calling from an undisclosed location somewhere in this goddamn universe." Busch held up his phone, so they could all see her. Margarita, in a hot pink bikini, raised a cocktail glass filled with an electric-blue Curaçao concoction with a pineapple slice and tiny umbrella, and toasted, "Here's to the Beer Buddies. I don't miss you shits one bit."

"Mags, how the hell are you, girl?" Nathan asked.

"How the hell do you think I am?" Margarita turned the phone so that they could see the white sand beach and turquoise sea behind her. As she panned the scene, a gorgeous black woman appeared in the frame, stretched out on a blanket beside her. Black reflective sunglasses hid her eyes, but small, pistol-shaped stud earrings gave her away. A subtle grin creased Busch's face. They all recognized the lithe temptress.

Amber said, "I'm sorry you can't be here. Are you okay?"

Margarita waved her cocktail. "I'm doing pretty damn good. Sorry, I can't be there in person, Amber. I just wanted to let you know I'm rooting for you." She laughed. "Just watch out for these dirty old bastards. You know what they're like."

"I wish you could be here with us, Mags," Amber repeated.

"Me too, Hon. Listen, I have to keep this call untraceable. I can't buy you a drink, so kisses all around. Be good, Buschie. No more screw-ups."

Busch's phone went dark, and he tucked it back in his pocket, still smiling.

"Wherever that undisclosed location is, it looks pretty damn great," Tony said. "Maybe I should turn state's evidence too."

Amber shook her head. "Mom will never forgive you if she has to go into the witness protection program."

Honey, who had been quiet, pulled her bag up onto their table. "I have a surprise for all of you."

"Not another one," Tony grumbled. "I still ain't over your last one."

Amber shot him a wary look.

Honey pulled a stack of books out of the bag. She handed each of them a signed copy of her new book, *Murder of a Beer Buddy*. "Don't be surprised if you recognize yourselves in the characters."

"Oh, no," Busch groaned.

Honey smiled. "Don't worry. I've fictionalized it big time. No one else will guess I based it on us. You're my friends."

They examined the books, flipping through to find themselves.

"Congratulations, Honey," Amber hugged her. "This is wonderful. No doubt, another best-seller."

Tony grunted. "Nice book. You done good."

Nathan smiled. "You make me sound bloody heroic."

Busch let out a breath of relief. "Thank you, Honey."

Honey smiled at them. "My publisher says it's going to be another best-seller. I'm crossing my fingers." She looked sad all of a sudden. "Thanks to Danny, I can write what I want without worrying about how I'm going to provide for my kids' future. It's been liberating to know that." Tears glistened in her eyes.

"I had that guy all wrong," Tony mumbled.

"Not all wrong," Busch said.

Nathan muttered to himself, "The Mossad agent got revenge for his wife's death. I should of have killed the bastard."

"What was that?" asked Busch.

"Oh, nothing. I was just thinking out loud."

Amber held up her glass. "To Danny," she toasted, and then added, "Hell of a way to meet your dad."

Everyone repeated the toast and drank to their departed friend, except Nathan and Bud. Nathan looked around at the group, his face stony. Bud cringed and whispered in Nathan's ear, "I hated that bastard for what he done to me."

Amber slapped her head. "I'm so sorry, Nathan. I know you can't forgive him for the loss of your friends. And dear, Bud."

Nathan nodded, and then picked up his glass. "Allow me to make a toast? Here's to Amber, Honey, and Bud. You've all found a way to move beyond tragedy and pain to create wonderful new lives."

Busch and Tony held up their glasses. "Here, here."

Amber excused herself to greet the first guests. "I'll be back to watch Bud's performance with you. Dinner's on me. Please enjoy yourself. But no groping the wait staff." She wagged a finger at the guys, and then turned to Honey. "You either."

Soon after, Bud left to get ready for his set.

"Break a leg," Amber called to him.

Bud replied, "Amber, I can't thank you enough for giving me a chance to perform. It means a lot to me. And thanks for the wardrobe and makeup tips. You're the hottest chick I know, so I appreciate the expertise."

A half-hour later, Bud signaled to Amber that he was ready to make his entrance.

Amber walked onto the small stage and introduced him. "Ladies and gentlemen, I'd like to welcome to the *Chez Amber* stage the amazing Lavender Schweitzer. Put your hands together in a big round of applause."

The loudest applause came from the Beer Buddies.

Bud walked out in a pale blue chiffon gown, three-quarter length sleeves concealing his massive biceps. Flawless makeup and a long dark wig transformed him into a beautiful, feminine presence. When he smiled, a glint of the mischievous Bud the Beer Buddies all knew showed through.

Busch poked Tony, "He's the bravest one of us all."

Tony nodded between bites of pizza.

Bud played a portable keyboard linked to a laptop, making it sound like a whole band kicked into action. He launched into a rousing rendition of "Bill Bailey Won't You Please Come Home." By the last note, everyone was on their feet, cheering.

Nathan whistled loudly through his fingers, and Tony cranked his arm and hooted.

"This one's for Amber and my Beer Buddies." Bud smiled over at their table. They sat silently through his bluesy, "Lush Life."

A tear rolled down Honey's cheek.

Nathan quickly swiped at his eye before anyone saw.

Maggie sidled over to Amber. "Boy, did I peg your old friend wrong."

Amber laughed. "Bud's straight as an arrow. I promise. He just happens to look better in a dress than half the women around here."

"He's straight?" Maggie gave Bud a warm smile.

It was an evening full of colorful memories for the Beer Buddies. And from that night on, any Beer Buddy, at any time, was assured of a reservation at *Chez Amber*, and a firm and unyielding claim to the table by the French doors, in perpetuity.

Chapter 54

When Nathan Lambic reached the baggage claim area designated for his flight, the conveyer belt sat silent and unmoving. His slower, senior-citizen pace was still faster than the speed at which Logan Airport's ground crew could unload a plane. He hated flying and being herded with the rest of the "cattle" by the penny-pinching airlines. But it was worth the effort.

He looked forward to spending time with Honey and the twins again. Even though she finally revealed her real name to him, he continued to call her Honey. That's how Nathan knew her when he let her into his life and began babysitting the boys. To him, she would always be "Honey."

From the beginning, Gloria sensed Nathan's fondness for her had no sexual overtones, *no quid pro quo* motivation. She appreciated that her feminism and self-confidence did not bother him. He told her that he liked her 'don't-take-any-shit' attitude. He respected her strength and independence. She had qualities he would have liked to have seen in a daughter.

When Honey's call came, Nathan was pleased. She asked if he would come to Boston and look after the twins during their spring break. "I have to work and spend time on a book tour around New England." She hesitated. "I know it's a lot to ask of a friend."

Nathan did not hesitate before saying yes. He had been formulating a plan to take the boys to Zimbabwe during the next summer. The old soldier wanted to teach them how to fish for tiger, show them animals in the wild, let them hear the roar of lions during the night. There was so much he could offer them about the wonders of Africa before it was all gone. With some convincing, he hoped Honey would agree to let them go with him. Even better, maybe she would come along. He imagined her in a camp chair under a fever tree along the Zambezi, enjoying "sundowners" with Duncan, his wife, Fiona, and himself. He decided to try to convince her to join this African Op.

A bell rang. With a jolt, the conveyer belt began moving.

Nathan's bag was the third one out. Perhaps the baggage-handling gods were smiling on him. He grabbed the bag and headed toward the taxi stand outside. He fished out his cell phone and pulled up the address Honey had given him.

The ride from Logan gave Nathan time to think about what he was doing. As tall buildings of the city raced by, he felt out of his depth. By the time the car stopped, he wondered if seeing Honey again was a mistake. Was he making a fool of himself?

After handing the bag to Nathan, the uber driver closed the trunk and got back in the car. As the vehicle pulled away, the front door of the brick townhouse swung open.

Honey waved, and the twins ran out, shouting, "Uncle Nathan!"

That was all Nathan needed.

Honey smiled warmly. "Welcome, Nathan. I'm so glad you're here."

"It's my pleasure. You know I enjoy spending time with the boys."

Honey took his hand. "Come in. The guest room is at the end of the hall."

Nathan headed in the indicated direction, then turned back toward Honey. "I've got a plan I want to talk with you about later."

Honey looked curious.

"And I'm warning you." Nathan wagged a finger at her. "I won't take no for an answer."

"Well, we'll see about that, Mister Lambic. But for now, I've got some ground rules for you." She showed him the bar. "If you want a drink while you're here, you'll have to get it yourself. The barmaid is no longer working."

Chapter 55

Murder on the Zambezi

By

Gloria St. Pauli

The American beauty, Honey Lovejoy, sat snugly in the dhow's prow with a pink parasol raised over her platinum tresses protecting her from the relentless African sun. The heat did not bother her much, since she had spent the last nine years in Las Vegas before Sir Nevil Smithwick picked her out of the chorus line at Caesar's Palace. She handled the humidity of the day as she handled most of the problems of being Nevil's wife, sucking discretely from a flask of Beefeater gin she kept in her handbag.

The handbag and parasol were made of pink satin decorated with red rosebuds and pearls. Honey thought them quite lovely, a perfect match for her milk-pale skin, blond hair, and watery blue eyes. What did it matter if they were shockingly expensive? Her husband could afford them. She gazed at her watch. It was only eleven o'clock, so she was not yet drunk. By teatime, at the rate she drank, Nevil would be tolerable.

"How many fish do you expect to catch?"
Honey asked.

"The number is not that important. It's the
size," answered Nevil.

Wiser words her husband never spoke,
Honey thought with a silent laugh.

"Tell me, Wolfgang, what is the world record
for Tiger Fish?" Nevil asked.

"Zat is quite hard to say, Sir Smithwick.
Eighteen kilograms would be very large."

"Did you hear that, my dear? Eighteen
kilograms or about. Let's see, forty of your
American pounds, if my math is correct. We shall
fish until I catch an eighteen-kilo tiger, unless night
closes in. I aim to take a giraffe and a buffalo
tomorrow."

"I thought you had a buffalo." Honey
commented.

"Of course, I do, but it is rather puny, and
the mounting is not quite right. Wolfgang will put
me onto a trophy. Won't you, old sport?"

"Of course, Sir Smithwick."

Honey visualized her husband stuffed and
mounted as a trophy in her mansion.

"Good man, Kölsch. What ho! What's
that?" Nevil pointed toward a disturbance along the
muddy bank of the river.

Wolfgang Kölsch, the German ex-pat, poled
the dhow around a tree-shrouded bend in the
Zambezi and stopped. They were facing a herd of
hippos roiling the shallows, not fifty meters from the
dhow.

"Hippos," said Kölsch. "Hippos are the deadliest animal in the bush, but not dangerous if you stay away from a cow and her calf."

Nevil pointed his hand, a diamond-studded watch on his chubby wrist. "Not the hippos, you imbecile, the alligators on the bank."

Kölsch bristled at being called an imbecile. He said nothing for a moment, then replied, "Zambezi alligators. Rather large ones."

Honey said, "Aren't they spectacular. I'm told they don't attack boats, but will eat a man in the water."

"What a stupid woman you are," Nevil upbraided. "You and this Kraut guide are a perfect match, all body and vast empty spaces between the ears."

Nevil hauled his bulk onto the casting platform of the boat. He waved his fly rod as if he intended to conduct an orchestra of alligators and hippos. He had just put his fly on the river when Honey Lovejoy folded up her pink umbrella, daintily planted its gold tip on Nevil's back, and pushed him over the side.

The alligators and hippos immediately swam toward the floundering man.

Sir Nevil babbled and blustered as he doggy-paddled furiously toward the boat. "You stupid bitch. What an asinine thing to do."

"Row faster, dear Wolfy," Honey coaxed the guide.

Red-faced and sputtering, Sir Nevil flung a hand over the edge of the dhow. "Made it," he exclaimed, glaring triumphantly at his soon-to-be punished wife. He poised to pull himself up when

Kölsch came down hard on Sir Nevil's diamond-studded watch hand.

"Bloody hell!" bellowed Sir Nevil as he splashed back into the Zambezi.

"Yes," said Kölsch, planting his pole in the center of Nevil's chest. "Bloody hell." The German guide pushed Sir Nevil Smithwick the Third toward the swarming animals.

---  ---

Nathan set the manuscript aside and gazed at his guest, Gloria St. Pauli, sitting comfortably on his veranda in Zimbabwe.

"What do you think?" asked Gloria.

"Well, it certainly starts with a bang. I have to say that. It was a successful formula for *Murder of a Beer Buddy*. Not much question about who the killer is this time."

"I know. I'm going to have to work on the plot."

"You're good with murders. You'll come up with something."

"I have to. The boys' college is paid for, thanks to Danny, but we still have to eat."

"You used your alias from the World of Beer days, 'Honey Lovejoy.' I hope this will not be autographical. I'm taking you tiger fishing tomorrow, you know, and I would rather not have to out-swim a crocodile. By the way, they are crocodiles, not alligators."

Gloria's jaw dropped. "You're right. I'll change it."

Nathan said, "And a dhow is an ocean-going sailboat. There are none on the Zambezi."

"What are they called on the Zambezi?"

"Sampans," said Nathan with a deadpan expression.

Gloria stuck her tongue out at Nathan.

"What about me, Nathan Lambic? Do I get a role in your book?"

"Could be. I see a lot of Nathan Lambic in Sir Nevil Smithwick.

Nathan frowned.

"But I can also see you as a hunky German hunting guide."

"Thank you." Nathan smiled at her.

Just then, Gloria's two sons joined them on the shaded verandah.

"Hi guys," said Gloria. "Nathan and I were just talking about tiger fishing on the Zambezi tomorrow. You guys up for it?"

"With your mom along, it's sure to be an adventure," Nathan said with a wink at Honey.

And so began *Murder on the Zambezi*.

Chapter 56

It was exactly one year since Tony last stood in front of this desk at the B&B in Key West. Eleven months ago, he reluctantly dropped her off in front of the Southwest terminal at the Orlando International Airport. In that time, over dozens of phone and Skype calls, he tried to cajole her into returning to the place they both agreed was the site of the four happiest days of their lives.

"Mr. Bellome?"

"What? Oh, sorry. My mind was a thousand miles away."

"Key West has that effect on people. I was saying, our records show you were here a year ago. Would you like two rooms again?"

Tony wondered. "No. I think just one with two doubles if possible."

"Of course," said the woman, returning his credit card.

Am I hoping for too much, Tony wondered?

Two hours later, Tony paced impatiently in the baggage claim area of Key West International Airport. He kept checking his watch.

When Sara finally came into view, it was all he could do not to run to her like a lovesick boy. Was she as excited?

Sara beamed at him, wrapped her arms around his neck, and gave him a warm kiss.

When they unfolded from the embrace, Tony looked into Sara's eyes and said, "I've missed you."

"I've missed you, too," Sara replied.

Holding her hand, Tony urged, "Let's take your bags to the B&B. We can have a nice lunch and plan the rest of our vacation."

Sara squeezed Tony's hand. "Let the adventure begin. Hey, where's your golf cart?"

Tony laughed.

A short time later, they sat at an outdoor table overlooking the water in Louie's Backyard restaurant. They talked about what had happened during the year they were apart. They laughed, made small talk, and lunched on conch chowder and Rock Shrimp with Mango escabeche.

Lunch nearly done, Sara said, "Tony, before we go any further, I have to ask you something. We need to clear this up."

Tony looked uneasy. "Shoot." Terrible choice of words, he thought.

Sara aimed her eyes at his face. "Did you have anything to do with Danny's murder? Are you still part of the Mafia?"

"Is someone telling you stories?" Tony looked upset.

"Amber gets it from your Beer Buddies. They say Salvador Gaspo sent you to take out Danny. Detective Busch also said that. He said a young guy named Juanito was your henchman. He said Don Gaspo paid you to rub out Danny."

Tony took Sara's hand and assured her, "Whatever was once true, no longer so." He knew he might lose her, but it would be worse if she found out later. He couldn't bear to see her hurt if she caught him in a lie. "Sara, Don Gaspo did send me to Florida to kill Danny. But even before you came back into my life, I was looking hard for a way out. I didn't want to whack nobody. I even got to like Danny. And when you showed up, and I learned that Amber was your daughter — and his daughter — I swore to myself that I'd do nothin' to hurt either of you."

Sara sighed and pulled her hand away.

Tony knew he was about to lose her. "Sara, I swear, my life in the Gaspo family was over before I saw you again. I retired from gang life in New York. I even thought about moving away for my retirement. I hadn't considered settling in Florida, but the order from Gaspo gave me the opening I didn't even know I was looking for." He smiled sadly, "Gaspo made me an 'offer I couldn't refuse.' Fortunately for us, Danny died before I had to make my move and go into hiding. That's the truth. I swear." He reached for her hand again. "I'd never lie to you."

Sara's words came slowly. "Okay, Tony. That's good to hear. I worried about your answer to that question all the way from L.A." She smiled. "Now you wanted to say something. Please, go ahead." She settled back in the chair, her hand still in his.

"Only this . . . Sara Nevada, will you marry me?"

Sara nearly choked on her wine. "Tony, after forty years?"

"I didn't see you for forty years. I didn't have the chance..."

"I have Amber. I have responsibilities. Tony, I don't know. We're not young..."

"Sara, Amber's on her own. You'll be even closer to her if we marry and live in The Villages. I don't want to take you away from her. I just want to marry you and make you, us, happy."

Sara didn't answer.

Tony placed his other hand over hers. "Sara, we lost out on a lot of years. We gotta grab what we got left. I always loved you. I always will."

Sara's eyes met his. "I love you, too. Yes, Tony. I would love to start life again with you."

After another drink on the pier, they went back to their room with the light fading into evening. After changing clothes, they strolled down to Mallory Square to sip margaritas and dance as if making up for all those lost years.

The next day, it was shopping and sightseeing. They stopped at Mel Fisher's Maritime Museum, where Tony bought a wedding ring fashioned from recovered treasure. He lowered himself to one knee and slipped the ring around Sara's finger. The proprietor snapped their photo as they shared a kiss.

Later, they visited Hemingway's house, Truman's vacation home, and were back on Mallory Square dancing away the evening.

Despite the tiring day, Tony could not get to sleep. When Sara came from the bathroom, he watched her with bated breath.

Sara tiptoed across the room and slid into his bed.

Forty years of remembering, of longing, of regretting, swelled up in him. He snuggled Sara's body against his chest.

Soon, Sara moved on top of him.

The next morning, they woke in the same bed.

"I guess this is what our life will be after we're married," Tony said, hugging her close.

"Yes, it is. But we have to be married by a Catholic priest. I want it legal in the eyes of God," Sara demanded.

"No problem. On the way into town, I passed Our Lady Queen of the Sea Church. Jocamo Passatuni is the pastor. We went to elementary school together. He'll make it legal in the eyes of God." He laughed. "I'll make him an offer he can't refuse."

Sara gave him a big kiss and hug.

Tony didn't even want a calzone, let alone a pizza.

He extended their stay for five days. They enjoyed being with each other on the beach, fishing, snorkeling, and, best of all, dancing under the stars.

A few days later, Sara and Tony arrived at the church.

"Hi, Mom."

"Amber? What are you doing here?" Sara's face lighted up in surprise.

Amber handed Sara a bouquet of white roses. "I'm here to escort you down the aisle."

As she entered the small church with Amber, Sara looked at Tony up ahead. Then she saw the Beer Buddies.

Busch, who Tony made his Best Man, waited at the altar. The rest of the Beer Buddies stood in the pews. Even Honey and Nathan made the trip from Africa to be with their friends.

"You did this, you sneaky character," Sara exclaimed when she reached the front of the chapel.

"I wanted our friends with us," Tony said. "I wanted Amber to share the happiest moment in our lives."

After the newlyweds closed the ceremony with a kiss, the Beer Buddies formed a guard of honor as Sara and Tony walked hand-in-hand down the center aisle out of the church.

They held the wedding reception at Sloppy Joe's on Duval Street, guzzling the best beer in town and sharing each other's company as they had for so many years.

The next day, the wedding guests flew back to The Villages while Tony and Sara spent four more days on Mallory Square before driving back to Sara's new home.

Tony loved his new life, but always kept an eye on the door. He finally let down his guard when he read that Don Gaspo was stabbed to death by a young Hispanic recently freed from prison.

Chapter 57

"Your Flamingo Martini is up, Luuk."

The young Dutch waiter leaned over the bar. "Thanks, Kat. It looks perfect." Flashing his best smile back at the bartender, Luuk La Trappe balanced the icy cocktail on his small round tray. "This is number three for her, and she hasn't wavered a bit."

"Well, the lady certainly is drawing a lot of attention from the men around the pool," Kat said, looking over at the slim, busty blonde lounging in the sun in a scandalously tiny bikini.

"She's well preserved," Luuk replied. He walked back to the pool and handed her the glass, accompanied by a winning smile.

"Thanks, Luuk." The woman reached up, taking hold of the martini glass by its stem. "This looks perfect. No more. Okay?"

"As you wish," he replied.

"If I have another, you'll have to carry me up to my room." She shot him a naughty look.

The thought of being alone with Ms. De Vries stirred the hormones of the young waiter. She reminded him of the actress who played a Borg in the *Star Trek* series. He used to whack off over her as a kid.

Luuk had decided to forget about college girls that visited the island. Instead, he would seek the attention of more experienced women. The Natalee Holloway affair almost destroyed this island paradise, and he wanted nothing like that to threaten him. To date, young Luuk had charmed the panties off three women, all of some wealth. Some would classify these 'mature' females as 'cougars,' but he liked his strategy. They were good tippers, for sure. He smiled and flashed his most wicked look at Mrs. DeVries. "You need not worry about that. I would be happy to be the one to get you back to your room."

The woman now using the name Ms. De Vries smiled up at the young stud waiter and said, "Well, I'd be happy to be the one gotten back to my room. Bring me one more of these in about ten minutes."

Ninety minutes later, Ms. De Vries opened the door to her suite in the Renaissance Hotel. Luuk followed her into the room, plotting his next move. He did not want to have this 'Act One' end too soon, erasing any chance for an 'Act Two,' 'Three,' or more. He followed her shapely rear through the spacious foyer into the executive suite.

The woman stopped and turned toward him, her hand reaching for his shirt. She was so drunk she had trouble with his buttons.

Luuk's hand reached around her back.

"Time out, junior," a voice said from the balcony.

Luuk dropped his hand.

The bleary-eyed woman could not see the stranger's face.

A man dressed in a white linen suit stepped through the sliding glass doors. His dark glasses hid his eyes, but the nine-millimeter Ruger he held in his left hand was in plain sight.

The boy trembled in fear.

"Get out," the stranger ordered, pointing at the door with the weapon.

Luuk shot through the door, raced down the stairs, and didn't stop running until he locked his door.

"How've you been, Mags? We missed you up north," the man said, sizing up the scantily-clad woman.

Margarita Gose stared at the man in silence.

"Come on, babe, I need you to give me the whole story. Why don't you do that while we take a ride?" The man flicked his wrist gesturing with the pistol toward the door. "Move it, Mags. And by the way, we want the money. All of it."

---  ---

The distress call came into the Korps Politie Aruba two days later.

The officer in charge of the desk relayed the information up-line: "A guide found the body of a middle-aged female near the exit of The Tunnel of Love, one of the many caves at Ariko National Park, east-southeast of Oranjestad." He added, "Be prepared. It is not a pretty sight."

A detective team from the KPA raced to the site.

The chief investigator gazed down at the unclothed corpse.

The killer had sliced off all the skin from the woman's face. He had removed her teeth and fingertips. Only the bright blond hair remained attached to the head, gleaming in the equatorial sunlight.

The detective in charge looked down at the mutilated body and said, "Shit."

Chapter 58

After what seemed like an interminable delay, the shipping carton arrived in an afternoon delivery from FedEx.

Excited as a ten-year-old on Christmas eve, Bud carried the package to his kitchen table and tore open the box. It was just as pictured on the website, a crystal-clear football helmet display case. Carefully, he peeled off the protective plastic and inspected the case for scratches. It was perfect. He moved it to his living room and held it up to the wall beside the already mounted bracket where Stan Musial's bat was on display. The trophy baseball bat and NFL helmet, side-by-side, would be as impressive as he imagined.

Bud took the display case back to the kitchen table and removed the clear acrylic end cap. He wiped Joe Namath's helmet with a clean towel, and then placed it inside the case. Adjusting the helmet, the coach made sure Joe Namath's signature would be visible at eye level. He lifted the display case into the brackets he had mounted on the wall in anticipation of this moment.

Bud stood back and admired his trophy wall: Stan Musial's bat beside Joe Namath's helmet. This moment was the most satisfying of his forty-plus years of collecting sports memorabilia. He snapped the toggle on the bracket, clamping the display in place, and took another look. It was fantastic. Perfect.

To celebrate his trophy wall's completion, Bud went to his fridge and returned with his last bottle of *Goose Island Bourbon County Double Barrel Stout* and his best crystal beer glass. After pouring the stout, he took a chair facing his trophies, raised the black beer, and said, "Here's to you Stan and Joe, real men in a real man's world." He took a long, full-flavored slug. Then he turned his gaze to the floor-standing trophy case. At its top stood a silver trophy with a marabou boa hanging from it. Emblazoned on the statue of a Greek Goddess were the words: "Lavender Schweitzer — Second Prize, Best in Show, Drag Queen Beauty Pageant, Miami, 2019."

Bud raised his glass again. "Here's to me, once a sacked football coach, but *forever* a man unafraid to be himself in a real man's world." His second swallow of the dark beer was even more satisfying than the first.

Chapter 59

"How much longer for the potatoes, dear? I want time to do the steaks just right," Busch called from the lanai. He got up out of his chaise lounge like a limber teen, surprising his guests.

"Man, you did that fast. How about a little help here?" Adam reached up with his right hand. "Wait a second. I don't want to spill my beer." He placed his can of *Holy Grail* on the glass table next to the chair.

Busch took his neighbor's hand and reached around to grip his back. "My old man passed-on a bunch of problems to me. Thankfully, arthritis isn't one of them."

"Thanks for the lift," Adam said and reached for his *Grail*.

"Anne says I've got about twenty minutes left to scorch the steaks, so I better get going." Busch stepped into the kitchen.

While Anne continued to slice and dice whatever it was she was slicing and dicing, Busch reached into the refrigerator. "Where's Hilda?"

"She stepped into the little girl's room." Anne lowered her voice. "I think she's going to be a great neighbor. She sure knows her way around a kitchen."

Busch set the platter of steaks on the counter and snuggled up behind his wife. "Well, I can tell you," he whispered, "Adam's a hoot. I think we lucked out in the new neighbor department." He found it difficult to keep his hands away from Anne. Her slim waist and more than ample breasts turned many an eye. Always tastefully dressed, today she wore loose white denim shorts along with a revealing turquoise top that worked hard to contain her charms. Standing close behind, he reached under her arm and teasingly swirled his fingers across the front of her breast.

She shooed him away playfully. "Go, git," Anne teased, "we want those steaks done on time."

Busch relented, winked at his wife, and reluctantly walked back to the lanai with the steaks.

Twenty minutes later, the two couples were on the lanai, admiring a delightful spread.

Busch, still at the grill, stared out at the view. The lanai overlooked the green on the third hole at the Gray Fox course — a perfect site for a Fourth of July barbeque. Every so often, a celebration erupted on the green, a good thirty yards away — no doubt the result of some spectacular putt. The noise wasn't enough to disturb the picnickers, but just enough to remind them to take in everything the view had to offer. They all took their seats.

Anne spoke first. "Hilda, you and Adam have been married how long?"

Hilda, armed with her fork and knife, replied, "Fifty-five years, last month. Can you believe I've had to put up with this guy all those years?"

"Yeah. Adam says he's had some problems with you, too." Busch chimed in, a big grin on his face. "He confided, though, that he wouldn't change a thing about you, loves you just the way you are."

Hilda waved the steak knife. "He better say that."

Busch laughed and added, "He just doesn't want you to get any worse."

"I'll bet you never heard that one before, Hilda," Anne chimed in. "Buschie and I just celebrated our second last month."

Hilda raised her glass of Merlot. "Well, Happy Anniversary to the newlyweds!"

Everyone raised their drinks, clinked, and drank to the toast.

Hilda put down her glass. "Tell us about how you two lovebirds met? A Villages romance?"

"It's quite a story," Anne said. "This is my second marriage. Buschie's first."

"How did you stay single all those years, you lucky son of a gun?" Adam asked, with a sideways glance at Hilda.

"Just lucky, I guess," Busch joked. But he quickly adopted a more serious tone. "The truth is, I am the luckiest guy on the planet."

Anne gently and almost inconspicuously lowered her head toward her left shoulder, allowing her gaze to rest on her husband. "We both are," she said. "Are you going to be able to get through this?"

Busch shook his head and reached for his *Heineken Zero*.

"My first husband, the father of my two children, was a great guy. We were high school sweethearts. We married young, and the kids came along pretty soon after. My son within a year, and my daughter fifteen months later." Anne set down her fork leaning it on the edge of her plate and dabbed at her lips with her napkin. "Just after Debbie finished high school, my husband was killed — a farming accident." She paused. "He was my everything. I was devastated. I don't know what I would have done without our kids. My son Jeremy — he's named after his father — quit college to come back to the farm to help. He's still there, raising his own family."

Imperceptibly, Busch sniffled and added, "He's a great kid."

Anne smiled at him. "When Jeremy died, I had to go to work. I worked in an attorney's office. He was a fine man, and I loved my job. I was his receptionist and office manager and worked there for almost 20 years. When my parents passed away, I inherited a little money, so I decided to retire. Seven years ago, I moved here. Among other things, I took up golf." She looked at Busch. "Would you believe that's where we met? On the golf course."

Busch had collected himself enough to pick things up. "You ought to see this little lady play golf. For someone who didn't touch a club for her first sixty years, she's amazing. She beats me most days," he said without the slightest hint of embarrassment. He smiled at his wife.

"Let me tell them," he continued. "Anne and I were singles playing weekly with the couples group up in Pine Ridge, the Pine Ridge Aces. One day, they paired us together. We both played well, and we hit it off. So, we decided we'd become a 'golf couple' when we played with the Aces. From then on, every week, the two of us played together. Not long after that, all hell broke loose."

Busch glanced at Anne and choked up. Adam and Hilda looked enthralled, waiting for him to continue. Busch gazed in Anne's direction and shook his head, almost imperceptibly. "Sorry, hon, you better take it."

Anne shot him a knowing look and continued, "We were playing one day at Bogart. There was a backup ahead of us. We had time to talk. Buschie brought up his time in the Navy. That was the first, I'm sure, I knew that he was former Navy. I remarked that my husband, Jeremy, also served in the Navy during the Vietnam War."

Busch placed his right elbow on the table in front of him, propping up his head, hand under his chin, looking toward his wife. Tears welled up in his eyes. Ann placed her hand on his arm. "It turns out that Buschie and Jeremy served together during the war. They were the best of friends. How about that for coincidence?"

Hilda spoke. "How . . .? You didn't . . . neither of you knew?"

Anne shook her head, her voice cracking. "No. When Jeremy died, I didn't know how I was going to get along. If it hadn't been for my kids, I don't think I could have gotten through his death. Foolishly, I started using my maiden name again, thinking it would help me get a fresh start, to get beyond. I wasn't thinking real straight." She paused. "To make a long story short, when Buschie and I met, I was going by my maiden name, not Chance, Jeremy's last name. So, neither of us saw the connection."

Busch cleared his throat and smiled. "If she had introduced herself as Anne Chance, everything would have added up right away. But it took her to mention Slim's — Jeremy's — stint in the Navy for me to put two and two together. We all called him 'Slim.'" He choked up. "He was my best friend. He saved my life."

Anne picked up the story. "Truth be told, Jeremy often spoke of his best Navy buddy, too. But he always referred to him by a nickname. For years, I couldn't remember his real name. Jeremy was so disappointed that he couldn't reach Buschie before our wedding. He wanted Buschie to be his Best Man. But they had lost touch."

Adam asked, "So, what was your nickname, if you don't mind my asking? What did your shipmates call you in the Navy?"

"Well, I've had a lot of nicknames over the years, but that's not one I've used in a long, long time," Busch said. He caught Anne's eye as she looked at her husband, smiled, winked, and blushed. "No offense, my new friend, but a guy couldn't ask for a better friend than Slim. Honest to God, they would have buried me at sea if it hadn't been for Slim."

"Buschie, that's a story for another day," Anne said as she patted his arm.

Busch saw Slim smiling in agreement.

That evening, their neighbors having left to return home, Busch and Anne watched TV on the lanai. They enjoyed the patriotic music and fireworks display on the National Mall. It was a fitting way to wind down Independence Day, on their chaises, holding hands.

"Do you have any idea, hon, how lucky I feel to be here, at this moment, holding your hand?" Busch said.

Anne replied, "I'd say the odds were against us, but here we are. I still have to pinch myself sometimes."

"Me too."

Anne's voice was soft. "And the fact that my two kids adore you. Well, that just tells me things are as they're supposed to be." She turned her head toward him. "I love you."

"And I, you," Busch replied as they squeezed each other's hands. "What say we call it a day and turn in? Don't we have some unfinished business, Mrs. Busch?"

Anne smiled seductively at her Buschie. "Lead the way, Pony."

Chapter 60

Sam Adams could not risk being revealed as a Mossad agent. He skillfully used the key hidden in his watch to unlock the handcuffs in the squad car transporting him to the police station. He coughed to conceal the click of the locks.

"You okay, old man?" An officer in the front seat asked.

Sam coughed again. "Frog in my throat. But I'm not croaked yet." He faked a raspy laugh and another bout of coughing.

The cop laughed. "That's funny. Frog and croaking." He turned to the front.

Sam was ready when the police car got blocked by a traffic accident one block from the station. He broke from the unlocked door and leaped onto the back of a passing motorcycle, knocking the driver in front of the police car.

"Hey, that old guy is getting away," the cop shouted, jumping from the passenger seat.

"What do you want me to do? Get that kid out of my way," the driver screamed.

The motorcyclist came first. Several minutes later the cop car freed itself from the jam.

Sam heard the horns blaring behind him fade into the distance. A glance in the mirror, and he slowed down and veered into an alley. He pressed the button on his pen to notify that his contact that he was headed for the extraction point, and then sped up again.

Five miles from where he escaped, Sam hid the motorcycle and stopped at a Kosher deli. He ordered a pastrami on rye sandwich, Russian dressing, and coleslaw. The waitress was cute but not Honey, he thought with regret.

Armed with the messy sandwich, Sam strolled to the curb. He tapped the button again. He was ready, and the coast was clear.

When a cop car drove by, he waved the sandwich and smiled. Who would suspect an old man 'noshing' on a gooey sandwich was one of the world's deadliest agents?

A black Mercedes with blacked-tinted windows pulled up beside the curb.

Sam slid into the back of the car. Not knowing the driver, nor trusting Mossad not to eliminate him now that he had blown his cover, he readied the wire in his watch. Just in case.

The driver took Sam to a safe house where he stayed overnight. Exhausted, the agent fell asleep and didn't awake even with the sound of sirens searching for an escaped killer.

The following morning, a woman driving a beat-up Chevy pickup drove him to Fort Pierce's marina. From there, a speedboat took him from the harbor to a designated point beyond the three-mile limit.

Sam thought this would be an optimal opportunity for the spy agency to get rid of an operative who had been caught by the Americans. He suspected his capture might be regarded as an embarrassment to the Mossad. One gunshot, a toss into the ocean, and no more Sam Adams. Nobody would be the wiser. I'm not ready to die yet, he thought, and clutched a key between his knuckles as the boat hit the waves farther from shore.

When the boat stopped in the middle of the Gulf, Sam was ready to defend himself. But nobody attacked.

The skipper pointed.

Sam smiled as an Israeli atomic submarine appeared. It picked him up and left the territorial waters of the United States.

Only after he boarded the submarine did Sam relax enough to think about his stay in Florida and the Beer Buddies who had thought of him as their friend. He knew he could never really be their friend, anyone's friend. It was strange; he felt he'd left something he cared about behind. Would Sam Adams ever return? Not likely, he thought.

When Sam arrived in Tel Aviv, a black SUV awaited him. The driver, a burly man, obviously concealing a large pistol under his jacket, gave him a nod. "The Director is waiting," he said.

Sam knew secret agents could not get a hero's welcome for ridding the world of a bad guy. No parade, reporters, television interviews. He did not want that, but something about the driver made him uneasy. He had completed his mission. But was something wrong?

The car drove through the familiar streets and stopped at the guard station.

Sam pushed open the car door.

"You know where to go?" The driver asked and pulled away.

Sam stared up at the office of Manny Shevitz, his superior. Why didn't the Chief come down to greet him?

A short elevator ride and Sam saw Burgundy Gallo, the dark-haired secretary with the prune face.

"You're home," Gallo said without emotion. "He's expecting you."

Sam thought she sounded nothing like James Bond's seductive secretaries. She would have hit him with a chair if he tried flirting. He nodded politely and walked to the bullet-proof door. He looked back at Gallo, who had already turned away.

Sam knocked twice on the door. It clicked open, and Sam entered Manny's office.

Shevitz, staring out the window, said, "You're back." He turned to Sam. "Sit down. Please."

Sam dropped into a chair, unexpectedly tired.

Shevitz glanced down at Sam. "You could have caused an international incident with our friends in America."

Sam tensed. "He was getting suspicious. It was unavoidable."

"With you, it always is." Shevitz let out a deep sigh. "A glass of wine?" He pulled out a bottle of *Manischewitz Concord Grape*.

"That's for Passover," Sam said, accepting the glass.

Shevitz nodded. "Precisely." He bit his lip. "Because of your actions, I've been passed over as the next head of Mossad."

Sam stopped drinking.

Shevitz put down his glass and handed Sam a 12x18 gray envelope.

"What is this?" Sam asked.

"Open it. See your reward for years of service."

Sam tore open the envelope with his fingernail. He saw the word 'RETIRED' in bold black letters. He shoved the papers back into the darkness. "I accomplished my mission," he said.

Shevitz nodded. "You were caught. That is all they see. Mossad agents do not get arrested...certainly, not for destroying a birdhouse?"

Sam stood. "They're just politicians, worried about foreign relations. I stopped a terrorist..."

Shevitz stared coldly at Sam. "We both know why you beat the crap out of him." He extended his hand. "Shalom, Shmuel. Enjoy your pension in peace, my friend."

Sam left Manny's hand hanging and walked out of the office.

Gallo hardly looked up as Sam walked past her desk.

Back at his apartment, Sam had time to reflect on all the violence he had witnessed during his long career. Some he caused. At night, the former agent sometimes had nightmares, reliving the death and destruction that were such a significant part of his life. Often, he dreamt of the last time he held Hannah. Barfright had paid for that. Sam was dismayed that killing Danny did not make him feel better.

The apartment was a lonely prison cell. Every day, Sam thought Shevitz would call him with another 'emergency.' He was one of their top agents. Irreplaceable. When the call didn't come, he became sad, bored with this life as a well-off, but restless retired secret agent. Even Florida and the Beer Buddies were tempting. He wondered what Honey, aka Gloria, was doing. A worthy woman, he thought, staring at her face on the cover of her book.

Sam returned gradually to his exercise routine. One morning, while he jogged, he heard a woman speaking to a small group by a run-down building near the park. She sounded so sincere, so passionate, that he stopped to listen.

For several weeks, Sam paused and listened to this woman and found himself drawn to, not a religious conversion, but a conversion to the path of peace.

It took time, but Sam's anger, which had been such a quintessential part of his life, began to melt away. Inspired by his new friends, he established an organization called Pax: Pickles-for-Peace. Using his mother's recipe, discovered on the inside of one of her old bra cups, he made pickles. He sold them all over the world, with all profits donated to promote peace between Palestinians and Israelis. After all, what is better to solve one of the world's prickliest political 'pickles' than a jar of piquant pickles?

When the call from Manny Shevitz finally came, Sam had no problem hanging up.

With his new mission of peace firmly in his heart, Shmuel celebrated by sitting on the lanai of his modest home on a hill overlooking Tel Aviv, drinking a precious imported bottle of *Sam Adams* beer.

THE END

ABOUT HONEY LOVEJOY

Honey Lovejoy is the pseudonym for a group of seven authors in The Villages, Florida. These talented writers wanted to have fun and challenge themselves by contributing chapters to a serial anthology initiated by Millard Johnson. Little did we know when we hopped aboard this careening train, it would eventually reach its destination. Not only did it offer our writers a fun project, but after being edited by Millard, Dick Walsh, Clay Gish, and Mark H. Newhouse, it surpassed their expectations and became a teasingly funny murder mystery with surprises at every turn. The biggest surprise was that it worked!

The authors can't thank Millard enough for starting the ball rolling and introducing such memorable characters in a film noir-type mystery with comedic touches. The individual characters were brought to life by our team of authors:

Honey Lovejoy/Gloria St. Pauli	-	Millard Johnson
Bud Schweitzer	-	Millard Johnson
Oskar Blue	-	Millard Johnson
Sara Nevada	-	Millard Johnson
Stella R. Troy	-	Millard Johnson
Danny Barfright/Peroni Azzurro	-	Millard Johnson
Sam Adams	-	Mark Newhouse
Nathan Lambic	-	Bill Jansen
Bumphrey Pillsbusch Frapp, II	-	Dick Walsh
Margarita "Mags" Gose	-	Dick Domann
Amber Bock	-	Clay Gish
Tony Bellome	-	Larry Chizak
Juanito	-	Larry Chizak

The peculiar but lovable characters in "Beer Buddy" were all individually brought to life, and then weaved together in a remarkably cohesive plot. Even Honey would be surprised by how well her novel ties all these disparate characters and storylines together.

It was quite a challenge integrating the highly creative work of these authors, but well worth the effort. Honey Lovejoy hopes you enjoyed her novel as much as she enjoyed putting it together.

Thank you for supporting this hard-working author as she schemes to expose male dominance and murder in a retirement community in Central Florida. If any of the characters bear any resemblance to real-life people, that is your misfortune in knowing such disreputable figments of our collective imaginations. All of our characters are one hundred percent fictional; names changed to protect the authors from specious lawsuits and angry slaps on the face. All our friends are kind and generous people who buy our books and offer kind reviews. (Get the hint?)

Anyway, we hope you had fun in our senior community, and thank Honey Lovejoy for keeping us out of her next book.

Sincerely,
The Authors

Oh, and one more thing. Anyone wanting an autographed copy of *Murder of a Beer Buddy* might want to bring it to World of Beer in Brownwood Paddock Square any Tuesday between 2:00 and 4:00 p.m. after the pandemic is over. Look for the overweight and balding men wearing blue Beer Buddies of Brownwood bowling shirts. Clay Gish is neither overweight nor balding, however she is fond of beer and bowling shirts.

THE AUTHORS

Larry Chizak

Larry Chizak was born in New York City, received a BA in Philosophy from St. Mary's University, Baltimore, MD, and a MA in History from Fordham University. He was a high school principal for twenty years before his retirement. Now, he is a writer of short stories. Those accepted and published are: "There Are No Dahlias In Detroit" in *The Foliate Oak Literary Magazine* from the University of Arkansas-Monticello, winning second place in magazine fiction writing from the Arkansas College Media Association, also published in *Journey's VIII – An Anthology of Award-Winning Stories* by Court Jester

Publications; "My House," in *Stirring: A Literary Collection*; "The Canteen" in *SN Review*; "Fire in the Windows," in *Still Crazy;* "Ralph The Rat: An Urban Fairy Tale," in *Critter Capers – For Animal Lovers (2015),* "My Devil and Me," in *Takahe 93 –* Takahe Magazine, Christchurch, New Zealand and "The Lone Wolf" in *Down in the Dirt,* October 2020.

Richard John Domann

"Dick" enjoys writing, golf, and drinking a variety of beers with his friends, ***"The Beer Buddies of Brownwood."*** He and his wife of forty plus years, Cindy, (*also a Beer Buddies member*) spend their time between a home in The Villages, Florida, and an apartment in Asheville, North Carolina. He received his B.S. in

Psychology from the University of Wisconsin-LaCrosse. After graduate work in counseling psychology at UW Milwaukee, he began a professional career in the pharmaceutical industry spanning over forty years. Active on several charitable boards, he served as President of the Rotary Club of Morrisville, NC, twice. He has published one novel, "The Ghost on Number 2," and is currently working

on a thriller focused on the pharmaceutical industry. He is also working on a collection of short stories based in Asheville, North Carolina.

Clay Gish

For over 25 years, Clay Gish worked as an exhibit designer, developing the vision, educational goals, and scripts for museums

around the world. As a historian and adjunct professor, she taught American history and government and published several scholarly articles on child labor during the industrial revolution. Since retirement, Clay has written the award-winning travel blog, *This Thursday's Child* (www.thisthursdayschild.com). Recently, she turned her hand to fiction with an emphasis on historical

narrative. Her first short story, "Boots, Bonnets & Bayonets" was recently published in the *Copperfield Review Quarterly*. *Murder of a Beer Buddy* has been a fun detour, made more enjoyable by working with a great group of guys.

William (Bill) Jansen

Having authored many professional articles and book chapters, Bill is delving into creative writing and fiction. An anthropologist and retired Foreign Service Officer, he lives in Florida but, after living decades abroad, still maintains a home in Africa. He created

Nathan Lambic for the book and wrote sections from the point of view of this character. In doing so, Bill drew inspiration for Nathan from a variety of his international experiences. He explains: "The more beers I consumed, the better the idea of writing something for *Murder of a Beer Buddy* sounded."

Millard Johnson

A retired librarian, Millard has been writing for more than forty years. He is the author of three books: *Country Songs: living and dying in the heart of America* (an eBook collection of short stories), *Blazing Star* (a murder mystery intended for women who love horses), and *The Heart Doctor* (the best romance novel ever written.) A longtime member of The Beer Buddies of Brownwood, he can be found most

Tuesday afternoons at The World of Beer in Brownwood.

Mark H. Newhouse

Mark, a former Long Island teacher and adjunct professor is the author of more than twenty books. *The Devil's Bookkeepers*, a story of love and survival in the Holocaust was honored with The Grand Prize for a Fiction Series and the Hemingway First Prize for a Wartime Series in the Chanticleer International Book Awards (#CIBA); First Place Historical Fiction in the Eric Hoffer Awards; and The Book of the Year and Gold Medal Historical Fiction from the Florida Writers Association. He enjoyed the challenge

of creating Sam Adams and helping edit this fun mystery with the Beer Buddies.

Dick Walsh

Dick, a former attorney and trial judge, is the author of more judicial opinions than he can count but has written nothing else of note. This is his first foray into serious writing. He, and his wife, Peg, split their retirement time between homes in The Villages and in southcentral Pennsylvania near their two children. "Peg is a gem, having effectively been widowed while I was consumed with fleshing out my character in *Murder of a Beer Buddy*. Bumphrey Pillsbusch Frapp, II has been a mere figment of my imagination since junior high, and I treasured bringing him to life."

Made in the USA
Columbia, SC
03 October 2021